His stance was commanding yet relaxed. His broad shoulders seemed to stretch from one wall to the other. Strong, well-muscled legs were obvious through his evening attire as was his narrow waist. Eve tried to admire him as inconspicuously as possible. When he turned her way, she inhaled sharply. His eyes were matchless in color: a vibrant, sapphire adorned with long, dark lashes. His hair was a rich brown with lighter streaks framing his face, and when he smiled, Eve noticed a single dimple to the left of his full lips. Taking the whole of him in, she felt her stomach tremble.

Introductions were made around the room; Eve tried to stay relaxed and in control of her composure until Donald escorted *him* to her side.

"Lord Beaumont, may I introduce you to Elizabeth's dear friend, Miss Eve Purity. Eve is visiting us from Paris."

Lord Beaumont bowed slowly. When he straightened, he gently picked up Eve's hand. "A pleasure to meet you, *Mademoiselle*." His eyes flashed with brilliance.

Eve felt tiny jolts of pleasure beginning where his hand touched hers, traveling down her arm and spreading over her body. He didn't recognize her—her secret was still safe. As she relaxed in that small victory, she was assaulted again with the realization that he was a spectacular specimen of a man.

"A pleasure to meet you as well, *Monsieur*." She smiled up into his intense eyes. There she witnessed a combination of warmth and savvy. A man to reckon with, of that she was certain.

Loving Purity

by

Lisa Hill

Frances,
Thank
you for your
love & friendship
over the years.
much
love,
Lisa

This is a work of fiction. Names, characters, places, and incidents either are the product of the author's imagination or are used fictitiously, and any resemblance to actual persons living or dead, business establishments, events, or locales, is entirely coincidental.

Loving Purity

Cover Art by *Nicola Martinez*

The Wild Rose Press
PO Box 708
Adams Basin, NY 14410-0706
Visit us at www.thewildrosepress.com

Publishing History
First English Tea Rose Edition, 2010
Print ISBN 1-60154-654-8

Published in the United States of America

Dedication

First to my husband, Terry, for his many months of support, giving up much of his free time so I could write and re-write. To my children who also sacrificed time with me so that I could pursue my dream. I thank you all for the many months of encouragement and love you generously bestowed.

To my best friends, Dawn Comfort, Beverly Matern, and Terry Parent, for cheering me on, offering encouragement and laughs along the way. With you in my corner, I count myself blessed.

To my parents, Domenic and Jean Asenato, who instilled in me a love of reading at a young age. I am thankful to have grown up in a home where people read books! How wonderful for me to have parents who think I can accomplish anything.

And to my critique groups composed of: Elaine Miller, Gene Mage, Martha Manikas-Foster, Anne Siegrist, Laura Rizkallah, Tara Osburn, Elouise Hults, Virginia Cole, Gerda Shank, Doreen Alsen, Don Pizzaro, Felicia Ansty, Diane Martineau, Eric Griffith, and Bob White. I cannot express my appreciation for your patience with me as a writer and your gentle teaching methods. I have learned so much from all of you!

To the Southern Tier Authors of Romance (STAR) our local chapter of Romance Writer's of America for their support, friendship and leading.

And finally to Amanda Barnett, the greatest editor to have ever lived! Thank you for taking a chance on me, and for the time and effort you poured into this book to make it sparkle.

Prologue

Winston Daniel Beaumont, Marquis of Radford and one day Duke of Merdine was a savvy investor, a shrewd businessman, and a bulls-eye shot—every time. He was more stubborn than not, considered broody, and had twice acted as a spy for the crown. Children adored him, women swallowed when he walked by, and men respected him. He had the ways of a rake, a sometimes scoundrel, or so most considered, but beneath his cool exterior, he concealed a secret. Winston Daniel Beaumont was a virgin.

Chapter One

England 1820

*Bath—A place for healing in England's warm
and soothing waters...*

Chills crept over his body. It was happening
again—this walk of horror he re-lived nightly.
Instinct was all he had to follow, leading him again
down a dark corridor. Alone.

The surroundings of his location were unknown
to him. His only point of reference—the stricken
pain in her familiar pale grey eyes. He tried to back
away, fear gripping every inch of his body, but it was
too late.

He watched her falling, gracefully, as if from
some great height. Barely having time to consider
her flight, too soon her head snapped back. A thick
rope encircled her slender neck, jerking her body as
the last moment of life was wrenched from her
slender frame.

"No!" he cried as he came awake, his body
drenched in sweat. He swallowed, surrounded by the
darkness of the chamber, trying to catch his
breath—suffocating from the summer's stifling heat.
For a moment, he was unsure of his surroundings.
He thrust the damp sheet from his body, reached
over, and lit the bedside lamp.

The unfamiliar room became at once familiar.
Beckinbrook Manor, the home of his oldest and most

trustworthy friend, Donald, the Earl of Livingston and his new wife Katherine. Beau found his handkerchief and wiped the perspiration from his face. His burning body prompted him to the window, but there was no breeze. He needed air, needed to walk for a while. He donned his trousers and shirt and let himself into the corridor.

"My Lord?" His valet's voice called from behind, "May I assist you?"

"No, James. I'm going for a walk."

"Would you care for a drink?" James moved closer, a small lantern illuminating his dark hair and complexion.

He knows Beau thought. *He somehow knows I had the dream again.*

"No, I'm going."

"Very good, sir." James retreated to his room.

Beau moved through the quiet house. He encountered no one before letting himself out the side-door. Swift strides pushed him through Donald's manicured gardens, as he attempted again to out run the burdens he had carried for far too long. The choking guilt he swallowed—for to think on that would drive him mad. When a man caused the death of a young woman, he deserved to suffer the consequences of his actions.

And consequences seemed to be invading his life. *The notes...* He received one several weeks ago addressed to the Marquis of Radford. When he opened it, scrawled in a very feminine hand were the words, *"From the grave, I cry out to you."* He dismissed it as some mad joke—delivered to him in error, but then just last week another one arrived. In the same scrolling handwriting were the words, *"Justice will be mine."*

Not one to be fearful, even in the face of war and death, Beau began to feel uneasy. He did not want to alarm his family, and yet he wished there was someone with whom he could share this new burden. He had long wished for a partner of the female variety. No—not just a partner—a soul mate. One who would love him in spite of his title, as if he had none at all.

His well-ordered life was beginning to spin out of his control. His needs were those of any man, yet he could not avail himself to join with the many debutantes and even married woman who threw their bodies at his feet. Not only was it against his principles, but he was all too familiar with the consequences of becoming trapped in a loveless marriage as his father oft reminded him.

"Watch yourself, my son, or you'll end up like me, married to a woman whose love of riches surpasses all else." His father spoke the truth, for Sylvie Beaumont had used her considerable beauty and more considerable charms into securing for herself a position of Marchioness. The result, a stormy marriage where seldom a civil word was spoken unless, of course, others were present—in which case, they presented a display of perfection.

As a result, of his volatile home life, Beau spent every possible moment with his Uncle Nathan, a vicar in the small village of Fenton. "If your father had remained pure until marriage as the Lord teaches, he could have avoided all this unpleasantness."

Beau realized at a young age, the wisdom in heeding his Uncle's words but physical temptations were abundant—he had come close several times to compromising his commitment to abstain from sensual pleasures. He was determined to wed for love, to a woman of his own choosing. He bore his frustration uneasily and those who knew him thought him to be a moody fellow.

The night air began its healing effect. A soft sound called to him, beckoning him on through the moonless night. It sounded like laughter... at nearly two in the morning? *How odd.* Beau listened for a moment and moved quietly toward the sound. Roses in full bloom surrounded him, their bold fragrance drawing him deeper into the night. At the end of the row, a trio of fountains formed a triangle. Several benches and well-shaped topiary trees adorned the elegant sitting area. He ventured forth, just one more curve and—his breath caught.

In the shadows of the night, he beheld a vision. Some elusive goddess perched delicately along the side of the farthest fountain. A lantern sitting upon a nearby bench allowed her silhouette to glow like some sea nymph or garden fairy. She wore only her shift. Now in its wet and transparent state, it clung to her every curve and offered no protection from his hungry eyes. He swallowed and felt the temperature of the night reach new and unimaginable heights.

She kicked her legs and giggled as a puppy swam up beside her. "Refreshing, is it not my little prince?"

The puppy swam off again and she smiled. She then begin to take the pins from her hair. Piece by piece her silky tresses fell down her back like a diamond encrusted veil. Golden highlights shone in the lantern's soft glow.

Dry mouthed, Beau turned away from the scene. He couldn't compromise his honor and didn't want to compromise hers. Although his intentions were pure, his body began to tingle, awash with a wave of craving unlike anything he'd experienced before.

He should go back to the house but leaving her, here alone, gave him cause for concern. What if someone else were to happen by? Donald's gardeners were obviously devoted to their tasks. Instinctively, he reached up to loosen his cravat—only to find he had not worn one.

He stayed, his back to the bathing woman—

affording her privacy. He listened to the gentle sounds she made as she moved through the cool water. Then all grew quiet. Turning back, he almost wished he hadn't. She was sitting at the side of the fountain, gazing up into the starless sky and providing him a tantalizing silhouette of her breasts in the clinging fabric.

Beau let out an almost inaudible groan. Sweat trickled down his back, his skin burned with a consuming fire, while innocently before him stood a lush oasis. It was time to return to the manor; in fact, it was several minutes past time.

He walked toward the house but slowed at the sound of her voice.

"It's too warm not to stay right here." She laughed, a sound of music drifting to him and hanging low beneath the night's thick air.

He heard her moving towards him and turned back to find her stopped at a nearby bench. The lantern's glow revealed her form to him as she slowly peeled the wet shift from her slick body, leisurely as if no urgency existed in the world.

Bathed in nothing but the flickering flame was the most exquisite woman ever to grace the earth. She embodied all that was feminine and sensual. His gaze caressed her swollen breasts and then traveled down to a small, delicate waist. Before he could stop himself, he admired the curve of her middle, where his hand would rest perfectly, then the gentle widening of her hips, and finally her shapely legs. He must go—now. He turned for the third time and began to walk towards the mansion. Every inch of him alert and craving another glance. A full arousal made it difficult to move, but years of denying himself had set precedence, and so he painfully continued.

A low growl sounded. Beau felt a tug on his right trouser leg.

He shook his leg trying to free himself from the tiny jaws and moved closer to the estate. As if he hadn't sweated enough, now in torrents, perspiration washed down the sides of his face.

Prince, as his mistress called him, seemed quite proud of himself. He let a louder, fiercer growl from deep within his little terrier heart and kept the trouser material tight between his sharp puppy teeth.

"Who's there?" His goddess' voice trembled slightly.

Beau couldn't hide from her. "Pardon me, miss…I was just out for a walk…"

She clutched her gown to her dripping body, using it as a shield. "Oh Lord…"

"Please, don't be frightened…when I noticed you were bathing, I turned away. I only remained to keep you safe in case some stranger should happen by."

"Oh Lord…oh Lord…." She pulled the gown over her dripping body. "Who would happen by at this time of night?" Incredulity rang in her voice.

"Well, I did, and you…well…you obviously did…I mean you must have come out a while ago, but nevertheless, we're both here now."

Soaked and her previous pale skin, now tinted a delightful rose, she stood intently—watching the bushes that hid him. Her chin lifted in whereas her small hands trembled. Admiring her false bravado, he longed to both laugh and take her into his arms. His hands itched to touch her, to caress her damp, silky skin.

"Please miss, have no fear of me. Let me properly introduce myself—"

"I believe the situation has lost all vestiges of propriety." She raised her eyebrows haughtily. Beau smiled at her show of dignity.

He moved through the bushes to reveal himself.

Up close, she was exceptionally lovely; her face angelic with large expressive eyes and thick lashes. Her lips were formed to be kissed—and frequently. But seeing the fear she could not quite hide, he halted.

"Good evening…" He caught her fragrance, inhaled, and closed his eyes for a moment. It was something rich and…vanilla…yes, vanilla. "I am Lord Beaumont, Winston Beaumont, but my friends call me Beau. I am here visiting the Earl." *He loved vanilla.* "He and I have been friends since childhood." His eyes drank in her disheveled hair, wet and dripping over her gown. It clung to her like his gaze. In spite of himself, he smiled wider.

"My lord," she nodded her head. "Forgive me for not introducing myself; I'd rather not at the moment." Her tone did not convey a desire to be forgiven; instead, it reeked of annoyance at being discovered. This he found amusing.

Prince upon hearing his mistress' voice, released his prey and trotted over to her side.

"No need." he said, "I realize this is all a bit awkward. Please, let me escort you back to the house. Perhaps we can become better acquainted tomorrow." He held his arm.

"Thank you, my lord but if you'll indulge me, I would rather follow you inside."

"Of course," he turned and began to walk to the manor. He heard her gather her belongings. "May I see you tomorrow?" the smile had not left his lips, she was beyond fetching.

"I ummm…not certain."

He turned slightly, stealing a glimpse as she followed along several yards behind. Prince brought up the rear, ready to capture any other nighttime invaders. "I am dreadfully sorry for frightening you."

Following a long and heavy pause, she spoke, "I do pray, Lord Beaumont, that we can keep this meeting between only the two of us." Her voice edged in panic.

"It's so very late and being so tired, I'm quite certain by morning, I will have forgotten it altogether." He rolled his eyes, knowing the darkness hid his fun. He would never forget what he saw tonight, but he would never betray her by revealing her secret.

"Thank you, my lord."

They walked back the rest of the way in silence.

When Beau reached the manor, he turned to her. "After you, miss."

She hurried by, and as she passed him, she whispered, "Good evening, Lord Beaumont." He knew the velvety night hid his expression from her sight and for that he was grateful.

"Good evening." His words fell into the silence her departure left. *Good evening, indeed.*

He scanned every window at the rear of the estate, hoping for a clue as to which room she might be occupying. He did not see her light, so he made his way back to his stifling chamber. He lay upon the bed, but his *not to be denied arousal* insured there would be no sleep for him this night. The breathtaking woman in the fountain filled his thoughts. Unknowingly seductive, yet innocent in nature, she was just as dangerous to his oath to remain pure, as the much read revered Eve, who brought down more than a man with her beguiling nature.

****

Eve tiptoed up the stairs and made her way to her chamber. The sound of Prince's toenails clicking on the polished floors echoed in the quiet of the night. She had nearly escaped into her room when the door of the Earl's chamber opened, revealing Katherine, Countess of Livingston, with the babe Glennora in her arms.

"Eve?" her voice was little more than a whisper.

Cursing her luck, she turned, "My lady..."

Katherine took in her dripping cousin and began to shake her head. "With so much to be angry about, I scarce can speak—"

"Please don't... be angry, I mean I realize I shouldn't have gone out there. I couldn't sleep, the night is so disagreeable...no one was about..." *All right, that much wasn't true, but it would do for now.*

"What if Gregory were looking for you tonight? Have you considered he could be roaming the grounds under the cover of darkness? What if one of the guests had seen you..." Katherine paused, taking in the very wet appearance of her dearest friend and cousin, "You were in the fountains, weren't you?"

"Yes, I realize it was a mistake." *A huge mistake!*

"Indeed." Katherine shook her head back and forth in amazement, "You asked me to help hide you from Gregory. Donald and I are doing our best to keep you safe. Why would you go out at such a late hour un-chaperoned? Swimming, no less? If not at Gregory's mercy, you might have been ruined, scandalized..." She adjusted the sleeping baby to her shoulder.

"A poor decision," Eve nodded in agreement, "you are correct, and I give you my word, it will not happen again."

"My dear, I just don't want him to get his hands on you. Last time you were lucky enough to escape his clutches, who knows if you will find such luck again?"

"I know. Please, return to bed, I am sorry for disturbing you."

Katherine nodded, then moved inside her chamber and closed the door. Eve entered the chamber assigned to her and closed the door with a sigh. She was grateful to be here at Beckinbrook

Manor. Katherine had taken her in when she had no place to turn. With her stepfather gone, and her mother ill, Eve had been at the mercy of her lecherous stepbrother, Gregory Searsly. She had escaped his attempt to ruin her and had come to her distant cousin and best childhood friend for help.

When Eve arrived at Beckinbrook, her virtue was barely intact and her composure shakened. However, her demeanor was thankful, and her attitude quite determined. She knew she needed a time of refuge—to plot the course of her future, and most importantly—to plan how she would return to Kentwood, her home, to care for her mother and the estate.

Katherine had offered her more than help. She offered her a home, a new identity, and a chance for a future. Eve would be forever in debt to Katherine for this chance at freedom and a new life. She served in her new position as nurse to Glennora with great enthusiasm and genuine love for the adorable, redheaded little girl. Six months had passed without incident, and Eve was more than grateful.

Beckinbrook Manor was a safe and peaceful place, but concerns of home were never far from her heart. Often, as she lay upon her bed at night, her mind wandered back to her mother, Lady Laura Searsly, so very ill at Kentwood.

Three months had passed since her last furtive visit to see her mother, and it was past time for a visit. Working the details through her mind, she begin to form a plan. First a visit back home, then perhaps she could bring her mother here and care for her herself.

Eve removed her ruined gown and donned a light night rail.

And what of tonight? Running into Lord Beaumont in the garden...it had been pure foolishness on her part. Thank goodness, he had been a gentleman or so he claimed.

Thoughts of Lord Beaumont warmed her—there was definitely something about the man. The darkness concealed so much of his countenance from her, but she was left with distinct and deep impressions of him. Despite his large frame, she detected a gentleness about him, and his voice conveyed sincerity. Rich and husky with emotion, could it have been kindness she heard? Confidence? Or something deeper, more mysterious?

Fear washed over her at his sudden arrival, but as he neared her, it changed into a heightened awareness, something she could not name, tempting, and nearly forbidden. Oh, she must stop these senseless musings. Katherine was furious with her, and she *had* behaved recklessly tonight.

No more—that was the last foolish chance she would take. She must be more cautious, and she would be for her sake and the sake of her mother. As she lay near sleep, she remembered the realization of his nearness and the surprising involuntary sensations his presence affected on her—one could almost call them pleasurable. In her darkened chamber, she smiled faintly. Thoughts of the handsome Beau enveloped her as she crossed the bridge to slumber.

****

Beau, naked, lay upon his bed tossing and turning, his mind filled with images of the bathing woman. He was fast losing the battle to forget her, instead, he found himself yearning for her more. His lips ached to kiss her, his fingers itched to touch her damp, silken skin, and his mind sought its own respite in her warm, heady fragrance.

In a half dream state, he could see her lying beside him, her skin still damp from her bath, her eyes reflecting desire in the flickering bedside lamp. He would slowly drink in her essence, touching every inch of her skin. Would she respond to him with the unrestrained passion he believed she was capable of? Or would he have to slowly coax her into finding fulfillment in his embrace? What a wickedly delightful mystery to uncover.

Then he would touch her, discover the secrets hidden in her satiny flesh. He would be gentle, giving her pleasure, slowly joining with her to become one.

When they were satiated, he would hold her and drink in her softness for the remaining nighttime hours. Or he would take her repeatedly.

He could envision her sitting up beside him, bathed in morning's first light, her hair flowing wildly about her. He would caress each silky strand, and bury his head into her neck—inhaling her fragrance. Memorizing her scent, carrying it throughout the day until nightfall, when she would join him once again, for rapturous lovemaking.

As he wrestled with these thoughts, Beau anticipated the dawn. He would ask Donald about other guests staying this weekend. He wanted to know more about his mysterious night-beauty.

Her impetuous nature intrigued him. Her uninhibited innocence enraptured him.

He could scarce recall an unplanned or unscheduled moment in what felt like a lifetime.

What must it be like to share a day with a woman possessing such winsome attributes?

His body stirred again, and he tried to shake off the desire, but then he remembered her soft laughter. It was no use; she had invaded every part of him; his head, his heart, and his desires. If not a dream, she was everything he had been wishing for.

But he must take care. Eligible virgins often flocked to him once they were aware of his title. He was determined to avoid the trap that so easily ensnared his father. He must be cautious of his overwhelming desire. At last, he uttered, "Dear Lord, help me do what's right."

****

Tossing and turning in the master chamber's grand bed, Gregory finally rose and walked to the open window. Six months he had been looking for her. With every passing day, his anger grew stronger, his thirst for revenge greater, and his desire to have her more powerful. Oh, he would find her. He would bring her back to this very room and have his way with her, wiping that proud expression off her pretty face forever. Perhaps he'd delight in choking the life from her wretched neck as she squirmed beneath him. A satisfied smile wormed its way across his face in grand delight as he imagined the pain he would slowly inflict. He would double his efforts to find her, and soon, very soon, enjoy the incomparable taste of sweet revenge.

Chapter Two

Eve woke with a myriad of thoughts fighting inside her head. Although returning to Kentwood was not possible as long as her stepbrother, Gregory, was in residence, her deep love and loyalty to her mother would not allow her to rest in the situation.

She must find a way to care for her mother but without money and a home—it was impossible. Relying on the kindness of Katherine and Donald seemed to be her only option. Perhaps they could be persuaded to help not only herself but her mother as well.

As Eve moved around her chamber, she began to feel breathless, restless. Anger came and slipped inside her soul. She was tired; so very tired of having to depend on others for her welfare and her family's well being.

A strong desire to protect and care for her mother wasn't her only problem. Her feelings had deepened into a longing for her own life, a life in which she could be mistress of her own home and household. A position where she would make decisions based on what she determined to be best. Asking permission to live her life was no longer acceptable. The time had come to stand alone if necessary—but how?

And to complicate matters further, her thoughts returned to Donald's guest. He was a large man, with longish dark hair. Quite tall and well built, handsome even, and seemed genuinely kind. Her body reacted to his memory, and she chided herself again. Could she trust him? Would he reveal their meeting to Donald or some other person? She hoped not but didn't dare to believe the best.

She began to dress in her servant clothing, donning her spectacles, and pulling her hair into a tight bun. She added her muslin cap and tied it below her chin. Katherine would not be overjoyed to see her this morning, but she must get the baby and begin her masquerade as the nurse.

A soft knock interrupted her thoughts. She opened the door to find the Countess still in her nightclothes.

"My lady?" Eve began.

Katherine entered and closed the door. "I just got her back to sleep, I'm going to join her for a nap, and I will bring her to you later."

"As you wish." Eve straightened her apron.

"Before I go, I think we should talk about what happened last night." Katherine did not wait for a yay or nay, but moved right along. "Why would you seek safety here at Beckinbrook, only to foolishly leave yourself vulnerable to that horrible man?"

Eve turned and moved to her sitting area. Katherine followed. They sat as the Countess waited for a logical response.

"Do you not realize that any unseemly behavior occurring at Beckinbrook will reflect upon the Earl?" Katherine exhaled sharply. "How could you risk, not only your reputation, but the Earl's as well?"

"It *was* foolish, and I apologize." She met Katherine's tired green eyes with her own. "Lately, I've been feeling trapped, frustrated by restrictions I am forced to endure because of my step-brother's actions." She looked around the room. Its lavish appointments spoke more of a beloved guest than a servant. "My mother is at his mercy, as am I, even though I am far away."

"I can imagine the frustration you are describing but acting on foolish impulses will do nothing but complicate all of our lives." The Countess stood up and paced the room. "The Earl and I are doing the best we can for you."

Eve nodded her head. "Yes, you are, I do not mean to infer otherwise. Yet, the circumstances make me fear for my mother's safety. Gregory may be hurting her and by staying away from Kentwood, I would never know."

"What would you do? Return to your home and fight him off daily?" Katherine was looking as frustrated as Eve felt.

"No. I know I cannot return right now." She let her words hang in the air.

"What then?" Katherine questioned.

"I believe it would be best if my mother lived here at Beckinbrook. Here where I could care for her and be certain all is being done for her welfare."

The Countess rubbed her head as if it pounded. "Mr. Searsly will never allow that...and if we asked for her, he would surely know your whereabouts."

"I'm not suggesting we *ask* him anything...I'd like to steal her away and bring her here." Eve met Katherine's eyes and saw them flash in surprise.

The Countess began to speak hesitantly, as if choosing each word with great care. "Eve...I understand how desperate you must feel, to even think of trying to steal your mother from Kentwood, but we must be careful for your safety as well."

"I am safe now. The Earl will not let my stepbrother have me back."

Sighing, Katherine argued, "Donald would never give you over *willingly*, but even with all of his influence, he is still bound by the law."

"Bound by the law to return me to a man whose only interest in me is to ruin me, to humiliate me?" Eve watched as her friend struggled to answer.

"No, bound by the law to return you to your step-brother, who happens to now be Lord of Kentwood and your legal guardian."

Anger, desperation, and a vacuum of despair all fought inside Eve's heart. She tried to hide this pain from Katherine.

Pulling her robe tightly around her, The Countess reached out for Eve's hand, "Let me speak to the Earl. He must know your plans, and if he deems it possible, we will help you."

Eve knew the law, and truly, it was not Katherine's fault it did little to protect her. She must be patient. As she struggled with the longing to go to her mother, she knew the best course of action would be to have Donald's support. Resolving herself to wait, she raised her gaze to Katherine.

"Thank you. I will try to be patient." The fire of frustration burned deep within Eve's soul. No matter how she explained her concerns, Katherine simply didn't understand.

"This is not a time for rash decisions; we must put our concerns in God's hands. The Earl always has wisdom in such matters. Between God and Donald, we will find a way."

Both women sat in an uncomfortable silence. Eve felt as if her disappointment drenched the air. "My lady..." she began.

"Yes."

"Have you any word of Lord Farrell?" She spoke casually, trying not to betray the hope in knowing he still might care.

Lord Timothy Farrell had been a constant suitor of Eve's before her flight from Kentwood. The Marquis of Shorewood was charming, handsome, and well received within the ton. When Eve was forced to flee, she had no choice but to also flee his attentions. Although only just beginning to court, her feelings for him were much stronger than feelings of friendship.

Katherine pursed her lips. "No, I have not heard any word of that gentleman." Katherine brushed an invisible thread from her nightclothes, failing to meet Eve's gaze.

"I see." Eve swallowed her disappointment and then changed the subject to her heart's desire. "Thank you for considering my request. You know how I worry over my mother."

The Countess nodded.

"I'll go down to breakfast now." Eve said. Both women walked to the corridor. Eve turned right, while Katherine moved to the left.

"Eve, wait."

"Yes, my lady?"

"Your hair, the blonde, I see it showing through. Wait here just a moment. I have more herbs in my chamber." The Countess entered her chamber and returned quickly with a small packet.

"Thank you. When I rose this morning, it was still quite dark, I forgot to check my hair in the morning sunlight."

"At least you remembered your spectacles. They are not much in the way of a disguise, but they do help to hide those aqua eyes of yours."

Eve thanked the Countess and re-entered her chamber. Although masquerading as a servant, her bedroom, attached to Glennora's nursery, was elegantly appointed. The Earl and Countess allowed the other servants to believe Eve was a poor relation who had lived in Paris most of her life.

Once in her room, Eve removed her spectacles and the pins from her hair, letting it fall down her back. She combed the thick mass, and when it was tangle-free, she mixed the herbs with some water, making a thick, dark brown paste. She then proceeded to comb the herb color throughout her hair, turning her hair brown. She curled the mass into a tight bun, befitting the station of a nurse, and pinned it up again. Once again, she donned the spectacles fitted with only clear glass lenses. Her appearance in the mirror, revealed a new woman. Gone was Evelyn Purittson, blonde, carefree heiress of Kentwood. The mirror reflected Eve Purity, servant, nurse, and poor relation.

She checked her grey muslin day gown and apron, finding crisp creases on both. Some days she longed to dress in her old gowns of sky blue, rose, lavender, and even sunny yellow. But posing as Glennora's nurse did not allow her to dress in such a way. Still, there had been several nights when she attended dinner parties at Beckinbrook Manor. In disguise as *Eve,* she wore her own gowns, their silky texture skimming her body, and for a night or two, she reveled in the feeling of once again being a lady.

The Countess decided it best to introduce her as a distant relation visiting from Paris. Because Eve spent many summer holidays on the continent, she was very familiar with the romantic city and could converse about the country and if necessary in French.

Eve recalled how in disguise, she strolled through the moonlit gardens. It had been just a taste of the life her parents meant for her. But Gregory, her drunken stepbrother, had curtailed every delight. A sharp pang stabbed her heart, as her thoughts drifted again to Lord Farrell and the life they might have shared, would have in fact, had it not been for her stepbrother's evil ways. She was not a woman bent on revenge, but anger rose up within her as she considered yet again all she had lost.

Taking her emotions firmly in hand, she determined to be strong and patient. It would not be easy, nor had it been up to this point, but necessity dictated her need to stay in hiding. One day she would find a way to resolve her problem with

Gregory and pick up the life she once enjoyed and was forced to flee.

Until that day, she would find contentment at Beckinbrook Manor. She loved little Glennora and was grateful for the protection Donald and Katherine provided. She would nip her longings before they could unfold into discontent.

Chapter Three

Lord Beaumont rose from his bed of twisted sheets, yanked the curtains aside, and looked out onto the great lawn of Beckinbrook Manor. His gaze took in the rising sun, brilliant already this mid-summer morning. Well-designed rose gardens, placed to the left and right of the manor, brightly decorated the otherwise green vista. Although the summer had been stifling, rains were frequent and all vegetation thrived and displayed lush and full color.

Running his hand through his tangled hair, he shook his head, dizzy from a fitful night's sleep. Sensual images caressed his mind while reasoning and logic tried to make sense of it all. A powerful urge to know the answer to the question that plagued him all night spurred him on. He would find his answers, and he would find them soon.

Moving to the washbasin, he used the tepid water to begin his ablutions, all the while longing for a respite from the already sticky day. His valet appeared, shaved him, and helped him dress.

"May I be of further service, my lord?" James asked.

"That will be all for now," he replied.

James made his exit, and Beau followed, his destination ever foremost in his mind.

He'd thought of nothing but her since his first wakeful moment this morning, and he felt a gentle pulling deep within his soul—for once moving him toward something—instead of away.

Once outside, he couldn't fight the growing excitement as he strolled through the back gardens. Passing the exotic and brilliantly colored plants, he finally reached the trio of fountains where a strong sensation shot through his veins.

Of course, she wasn't there. He stood for a moment, as the image of her silky body taunted him yet again. What was wrong with him? Why this assault of emotion? Yes, she was real, exquisite, and mysterious. But who was she? His body drove him like never before.

Could she be a servant? Would someone in the earl's employ risk losing her position for a late night bath? *Doubtful.* She must be another guest. She moved with such grace and lightness, as if she floated just above the earth. Her tone and posture indicated her to be a lady but her choice to bathe in the fountain—impulsive, absurd.

He returned to the house and found the dining room sideboard filled with a tempting array of morning fare. He helped himself to eggs, toast, and ham and then joined the Earl and Countess at the table.

"Good morning, my lord," Katherine began.

Nodding to Donald and Katherine, Beau greeted them in return. "Thank you for the invitation to spend this time in the country." He cut a piece of seasoned ham, its honeyed taste melting in his mouth. "The gardens are spectacular with all the rain we have been enjoying this year."

"Hinesdale the gardener takes pride in his labors," the Earl replied. He turned to Katherine, "I'm surprised Lord Beaumont has noticed our gardens, dear. Usually his mind is consumed with business matters and all things dull and serious."

Beau smiled at the gentle barb. "Well, my lord, had I a lovely wife such as you do, perhaps my mind would be otherwise occupied."

"See here," Katherine joined in, "the gentleman is knowledgeable as well as handsome."

Beau raised his teacup in a lighthearted salute. "Speaking of gentlemen, are there any other guests spending the weekend here at Beckinbrook?"

The Countess replied, "No gentlemen, but Lady Foster is visiting here with her two lovely daughters, Violet and Lillian."

Beau tried to seem unaffected by the news but secretly felt elated. He had heard of the beautiful Foster daughters, both well-bred and demure young ladies of the ton. Forgetting his general distrust of women, he raised his brows, wondering which daughter he had beheld in the fountain.

Beau noticed an amused expression cross the Earl's face and realized he must have revealed more than he intended.

"You will meet the ladies this evening at dinner, unless you happen to stumble upon them in the gardens this afternoon," the countess added.

Or last night. Beau thought. "I look forward to meeting them."

"I think Lord Beaumont is interested in more than just meeting our house guests, dear." Donald winked at Katherine.

"It is always good to broaden one's horizons by meeting new and interesting people, don't you agree?" Beau inserted in feigned innocence.

"Good indeed." Katherine responded. "It is also good when those *new and interesting* people are young, beautiful, and female." She raised her brows and teacup in perfect unison. "And there I add, unattached?"

"I see she understands my position." Beau nodded at Donald.

"Oh, she understands *everything.*" Looking at his wife, he added, "Indeed".

They all laughed easily together, chatting comfortably as they finished their morning meal.

****

Katherine joined Eve and Glennora in the gardens, where Eve had spread a blanket beneath a large apple tree. There they enjoyed the filtered shade and freshness of the morning. Glennora, smiling and cooing, played with carved, miniature, animal figurines, while Prince dozed nearby. The temperature began to rise, as the sun brought every color to vibrancy, spreading brightness over the lush countryside.

"I spoke with Donald regarding your mother," Katherine began.

"What are his thoughts?" Eve asked.

"He understands your desire to have your mother here, but there are many risks to consider. He will need to think on it a bit more."

Sighing, Eve accepted her friend's comment. "I cannot tell you how very grateful I am for your kindness to me—how much I appreciate you and Donald even considering yet another request." Eve moved the crawling baby back toward the center of the blanket. "I just want to be certain she is properly cared for."

"Trust Donald. He will not let any harm come to your mother."

"I do trust him."

"I know you do. We will somehow find a way to help your dear mother."

"You are like my own dear guardian angel. Again, I thank you." Eve's eyes filled with tears. As frustrated as she sometimes felt, she knew the love and care of friends.

"Well then, let us speak of other topics." The Countess brushed a stray leaf from her muslin day gown. "Tonight is the first night the Fosters will be with us. You remember Violet and Lillian?"

Eve smiled. "How could I forget?"

"Well, as much as I enjoyed watching you make their delicate faces turn green with nausea many years ago, we must remember to keep our little secret. Tonight, some business associates of Donald's will be arriving, and we will be hosting a small dinner party. I would like you to attend. But remember, if the Fosters realize who you are, knowing the speed in which gossip travels, Gregory may learn of your whereabouts."

"Do not worry. I will be the quiet and demure Eve Purity, even though I detest their haughty bearing. No sharp words will I utter to the spoiled heiresses."

Katherine laughed and Eve was quite sure she was remembering Lillian Foster's surprise as Eve had easily outwitted her. Miss Foster had tried to steal Lord Farrell's attentions and was made to look quite the fool.

"I will be a perfect model of decorum. Don't worry."

"Hmmm...two words, when spoken from you, cause my heart to pound."

Eve picked up the gurgling Glennora and smiled innocently at her friend, then winked wickedly.

****

Beau returned to his chamber after breakfast. He found it somewhat cooler than last night and decided to sit and review several projects of interest.

His chamber possessed a definite masculine air, decorated in shades of blue and silver. The counterpane's navy coloring matched the drapes at the window. Cherry furniture in the room gleamed in the morning sun, warming the cooler colors therein. It was a tranquil place, but tranquility was a state Beau seldom experienced.

His shoulders were tense as he reviewed columns of numbers, investments, and expenditures.

27

He shuffled through the velum papers and found lists of responsibilities that varied in their degree of importance. Being ever conscientious, he determined every item on each list would be tended to with patience and expertise.

He sat lost in calculations and mental debates for some time. Then his mind began to wander. He tried to push all thoughts of the fountain nymph away, but they remained and danced around him. Right now, he imagined her indulging in play, with a zest for life the likes of which he'd never partaken. He shook his head, trying to clear the memories but instead heard her laughter. It was like tinkling chimes, full of joy and clear of malice.

He rose from his chair and went to the window. Looking out at the front lawns, he found no respite. Sitting down again he began to think on the matter.

It had been some time since he had paid a visit to his Uncle Nathan. His Uncle had always been his confidant in matters concerning women. But even with the wise Vicar, Beau held back a piece of himself. How would his uncle respond if he knew the truth and depth of his shame? In his quest to avoid entrapment, he had hurt an innocent girl and caused the unthinkable.

Now he found himself trapped in a heady vice of sensual memories. Although beautiful women had always been a plentiful distraction in his life, never had anyone come close to equaling the one he beheld in the fountain. His body came alive at the thought of touching her, losing himself in her warm and mesmerizing scent. *He had to find her soon.*

He tried to order his thoughts back to work, but at last, he gave in. He decided to stroll through the gardens, perhaps he would *accidentally* come upon the Foster sisters. His eagerness to put a name to the image that tortured him all night and all morning prodded him forth.

He made his way to the rear of the castle. Somehow, he found himself heading toward the fountains and realized there were many other places in the vast gardens the ladies could be.

Listening for voices, he stepped through a section of vibrant pink hydrangeas stretching out in full bloom. He then heard the soft sounds of voices and made his way toward them.

Off to his left, he saw Katherine at a small, white, wrought iron table, chatting with a woman. He couldn't see anything other than her large pale blue hat and her matching gown. As he willed himself to slowly approach, Katherine smiled at him.

"Oh, it's the Marquis of Radford. Lord Beaumont, please come and meet Lady Foster."

A very attractive woman, her brunette hair and dark chocolate eyes nearly matched. Her complexion clear, pink, and gently refined. She held herself with an air of regality, quite common for a woman of her age and social standing. In addition, she seemed open and friendly. A few tiny lines framed her eyes, but in no way were detrimental to her handsomeness.

The woman turned her head and lifted her hand in a subtle greeting. Beau grasped it and in his most charming manner said, "It is a pleasure to meet you, Lady Foster."

Lady Foster smiled briefly and returned the compliment, "The pleasure is all mine, Marquis Radford."

Motioning to the chair beside her, Katherine asked, "Would you care to join us for some tea?"

"Indeed. I can think of nothing I'd rather be doing." Beau sat and smiled at Lady Foster.

Katherine motioned to a nearby servant and Beau was served his tea. He sipped and behaved as the perfect gentleman, nodding and laughing at all the appropriate times while he waited for the Foster sisters to join their gathering.

Finally, after what seemed like hours, but in truth had been mere minutes, two more gentle voices could be heard.

"It's over here, through the hydrangeas," the first voice offered.

"Yes. I see them now," replied the other young lady.

Before the fair sisters neared the table, Beau's expectations were crushed. Although fresh and attractive, neither of the sisters resembled the goddess in the fountain. He noticed their gentle raven curls as they graciously made his acquaintance. They were also much taller and somewhat straighter compared to the softly curved woman who had thoroughly enchanted him.

Doing his best to hide his disappointment, he engaged the girls and their mother in polite conversation.

The young women performed perfectly, displaying their polished manners, practiced lash fluttering, and animated laughter—on cue. Topics of weather, society functions, and the gardens were all discussed with ease and decorum. Beau longed for escape, his mind numb with their senseless chattering.

After a while, he excused himself and made his way back to the mansion. His thoughts churned— who was she? He would speak with Donald without betraying her secret. Certainly there must be someone at the estate who matched the mysterious woman's description.

Chapter Four

Beau knocked on the library door.

"Come in." Donald called.

Stepping into the spacious room, he glanced around to see the book lined walls, heavy mahogany furniture, and deep colored upholstery. It was here; his long-time friend chose to spend his mornings working. Donald rose from his desk and closed the door.

"Am I interrupting?"

"No. I am quite finished and finding everything to be as it aught. You, my friend are just what I was waiting for." Donald winked and moved to the small bar cabinet.

"Oh really... how is that, my lord?" Beau smiled and chose a comfortable chair before the window overlooking the back gardens.

"You, my lord, are my excuse to have a brandy." Donald began to pour but Beau shook his head.

"Thank you, no."

"No brandy? Is it a holy day?" Donald's light eyes twinkled with mischief.

"It might be...somewhere." A small smirk crossed Beau's lips.

"Well, I'm having one. You are looking sharp enough to cut glass, and I can't abide such seriousness so early in the morning." Donald took his drink and sat across from Beau.

"No, not seriousness, my lord...I believe the word you are looking for is gratefulness."

Lisa Hill

"What thing of wonder have I done now? Wait, don't answer...let me guess."

Beau shook his head at Donald's antics. Since his marriage to Katherine, his dry sense of humor had been making an appearance on a regular basis. Some of his calloused edges from time spent in war had been softened, and it might even be said that the young Earl seemed, could the word be, happy?

"I wouldn't go so far as to say you have done anything worthy of wonder. But I do appreciate the invitation to spend the week here at Beckinbrook with you and your family. Hartford has been monotonous and dull of late."

"Perhaps...but I've heard of your exploits in London," Donald winked, "It sounds as if things have been, shall we say, bountiful?"

"Exploits in London? I've been working at Hartford, here in Bath, with my father as we await Paul's return from the continent. I haven't been to London since the season began."

"The gentlemen at the club have been spreading rumors then...to what end, I cannot imagine." Donald said.

This concerned Beau. He had become friendly with beautiful women from time to time, but never had he indulged in the way Donald was implying. Why would anyone concern themselves with his personal affairs?

"At any rate, you are always welcome here...especially when Katherine invites young eligible misses who are seeking a wealthy and titled lord. You are even more welcome at those times." Donald cleared his throat and sipped his brandy. His expression was of amused boredom.

"Is that the why of it then? To leg-shackle me to one of the Foster sisters?"

"My dear boy, you have hit the proverbial nail on the proverbial head."

Beau laughed and shook his head. "While I appreciate Katherine's efforts to end my bachelor days, I am not certain I am ready to court some society chit."

"Are you certain you don't want a brandy? At times like this, it makes life a bit easier with every swallow."

Beau shook his head.

"All right, I'm listening. Why aren't you ready to court some lovely young virgin who trembles at the thought of your...title?"

Where was the Donald, Beau had grown up with? The cautious, young earl, who thought things through carefully, measured every risk before indulging and took life seriously?

"Are you foxed, my lord?"

"No, not yet."

"Very good, then." Beau closed his eyes. Marriage was doing strange things to his best friend. "Is there really a rush to all of that?"

"Absolutely not. You could wait until you are gray or even bald headed, bent over with rheumatism, and half blind. That may be the perfect time to find yourself a woman to wed."

"Your wit slays me, my lord." Beau answered as if bored beyond reason.

"What of the ducal bed? Surely you must find a woman to warm your old, brittle bones before you breathe your last." Donald took another sip of brandy.

"My bones are warm enough, thank you." Donald would never know the heights his temperature had reached of late.

"...and we all know every Duke must produce an heir...the thought of anything less would surely give your father apoplexy."

"That's just it. I have no desire to find myself married for life, to some title-craving, member of the ton—I have impregnated in a moment of lust. Growing up at Hartford has made me wary of women who will use their considerable wiles to become the next Duchess of Merdine." Beau stood and crossed the room. "That is why, I choose my courting carefully."

"Then choose your courting carefully, what does all of this have to do with being grateful to me?" Donald's pale blue eyes cleared of humor.

Beau looked out the window at the gardens. Where was she now?

"I may have chosen someone to possibly court." Beau used his most common tone, although his heart pounded wildly in his chest.

"May have, possibly? Oh such conviction."

When Beau glanced back at Donald, he noticed an intent expression on his face. "What is it?" Beau asked.

"I was about to ask you that very question. What has you so distracted, my friend? Is there something interesting outside in the gardens?"

It's more of a someone than a something.

"Something unusual happened last night..." Beau's voice trailed off. He closed his eyes and was overcome with the images of her...her sleek, wet skin, her generous curves, long lush hair that shimmered like diamonds in the lantern's soft glow. The heat—he felt the heat again. A tiny drop of perspiration ran down the side of his face. When he inhaled to clear his mind, he smelled vanilla.

Donald's eyes focused on him. "What is it?"

Beau chose his words. Donald had served his mother country in the Burmese war as an exemplary espionage agent. His discerning looks had a way of cutting through even the most hardened criminals.

"Last night, quite late, I found myself unable to sleep. I decided a stroll in the gardens would be just the thing to set me right." He paused. How much should he divulge? He promised he would not reveal their meeting, but if he mentioned only that he saw her, perhaps no harm would come to her. If the woman he had seen was a servant, she could lose her position over her late night bath. He needed to know who she was...he needed to talk to her, to be with her.

Before Beau could continue, a gentle knock sounded at the library door.

"Come in." Donald called.

The door opened slowly and Katherine entered.

"Good morning, darling," she then turned, "Lord Beaumont."

Beau and Katherine exchanged greetings.

Beau watched as Donald's eyes danced with life. "Come, sit, and listen with me to our dear friend, he was just relaying an unusual event from last night."

Katherine sat down next to Donald. Beau watched the subtle movements of his friend. He stretched his arm behind Katherine, pulling her closer. They both smiled, small, knowing smiles of people in love. As he observed their tenderness, he wondered if he could ever enjoy the casual intimacy his friends unknowingly displayed.

"Lord Beaumont, please go on with your story, I am sorry to have interrupted." Katherine's voice was gentle as always.

Beau looked down at his empty hands. Perhaps he *should* have asked for a brandy. "Last night, between the stifling heat and my clouded head, I could not sleep." He remembered the vivid nightmare that had tormented him yet again. "Although it was quite late, I left the manor and walked through your gardens."

As Beau relayed his modified tale, he observed the most peculiar thing. Lady Katherine, Countess of Livingston was beginning to turn a very undignified shade of green. Her relaxed posture of only seconds before, became stilted. Her pleasant expression of serenity gave way to a more serious one of nervousness.

"While wandering, I beheld a young woman."

"Alone?" Donald asked.

"No, she was accompanied by a small pup."

"I can't imagine the Foster sisters meandering through the gardens in the middle of the night." Donald offered.

"I am certain it wasn't either of the young ladies, as I met them just this afternoon." Memories of long, drenched golden hair filled his mind. "The woman I saw had golden hair...straight golden hair."

Beau looked at Katherine's face, her eyes were pressed tightly shut, her face flushed. What had he said?

Donald's mouth was now set in a grim line, his voice serious as the grave. "Impossible."

Katherine lowered her gaze, finding something immensely interesting in the plush Aubusson rug that covered the library's floor.

"Darling, isn't that the most unusual thing?" Donald's hand reached out to Katherine and tilted her chin to his. His face conveyed his complete lack of humor.

"Well...yes...quite unusual." Katherine's color changed from green to red. *Fascinating...in a bizarre kind of way,* Beau thought.

"What of it?" Donald asked. He and Katherine seemed to hang in midair waiting for Beau's response.

"I wondered who she might be...I wish to become acquainted with her."

"Why?" Donald whispered. His friend had a pained look on his face. Perhaps he should have kept quiet. What if he had now betrayed the young woman's identity?

"She intrigued me." *She caused me to feel things*

I cannot name, she drew me to herself somehow, so very lovely, so very tempting.

Katherine bolted to her feet. "Excuse me, darling," then turning to Beau, "Lord Beaumont. There is a matter which needs my attention." Katherine stood, nodded, and then departed at once.

What on earth was going on here? Why would his friends act so strangely, and why shouldn't he inquire about another guest?

Donald stood and poured himself another brandy. He took a long sip, then turned to Beau. "I have never seen you show such interest in a woman before."

"I just noticed her, that's all."

Donald walked to the far end of the library, then turned back to Beau. "You of all men, have exhibited a reluctance to marry."

"Seeing a woman and asking about her is not necessarily an offer for marriage."

For the briefest second, grey eyes flashed in his memory. He saw again the rope, the tiny feet swaying limp in the air, and he shook his head as if to clear the image that never would leave.

"I just wondered about the young woman. The thought of marriage is one I have tried to banish from my mind." Beau looked again to the gardens, if only he could escape the horror he had caused.

Donald remained silent.

Beau stood, sensing their conversation had come to an end.

"Why is that, my friend?" Donald asked.

Beau thought of the slender body dangling from the rope. "I've made mistakes in my life...some have changed my future." He smiled and turned from the Earl. "I'd better go. I'll see you at dinner."

Donald walked him to the door and opened it, "Have hope, my friend. The future is for men of hope."

Beau walked through the door and shook his head. If the Earl and Countess had no knowledge of the young woman, why had they adopted such strange behavior?

Chapter Five

Baby Glennora slept peacefully in her crib. The nursery's subdued shades of pink and yellow, a blend of tranquility. The large oval rug, centered in the room, warmed the polished wood flooring, and two door-sized windows, framed with bright white lace curtains, welcomed the gentle mid-day breeze. A sturdy rocking chair sat against the far wall, a pile of small picture books on the floor beside it. Eve straightened the room and arranged the blankets and clean linens in Glennora's wardrobe. She smiled when she spied Katherine's approach.

"She's sleeping like a little angel." Eve began.

Katherine smiled lovingly at her daughter. She looked over to Eve, a frown marred her face. "What is it?" Eve asked.

"I've just spoken to Donald and one of our guests. It seems you were observed last night."

"Oh no..."

"I did not tell Donald of our conversation or of your late-night bath, and now I fear he may discover I have been deceitful." Katherine added.

"Oh dear, I am terribly sorry." Eve frowned.

Katherine crossed to Eve. "Our guest, Lord Beaumont said he saw a woman with *golden hair* walking about the gardens, tiny pup in tow."

Eve's heartbeat slowed, so perhaps he hadn't revealed all to Donald.

Katherine walked to the rocking chair, lowered herself, and began to rock.

Eve paced the oval rug.

"Apparently he found you intriguing. He's wondering who you are, he even went to Donald asking about other guests we have staying for the week."

"I see."

"Take care tonight, Eve. Lord Beaumont will be attending the dinner party. Be certain your hair is darkened and your spectacles in place. I'm certain he will suspect nothing if your hair is hidden.

"You may retire to your chamber now; I will stay here until Glennora wakes. Please, think about your actions." Katherine stood and grasped Eve's hands in her own. "I'd be sick if Gregory every got his hands on you."

Eve nodded solemnly. She made her way from the nursery to her room. Katherine had been worried, and rightfully so, but Eve was growing weary of both Donald's and her over-protectiveness. Still, the memory of a stranger watching her bathe in the fountain did little to placate her restless bent. She must be careful, truly indeed, but she also had a need for some private time—to breathe un-chaperoned and un-encumbered.

She entered her large, lavishly decorated chamber and barely noticed the elegant appointments, fresh roses, and comfortable furniture. It was not the room of a nurse or any servant. The appointments were meant for a well-loved guest.

Katherine spared no expense as she re-decorated the once sparse room into something more feminine and personal. Only shades of mauve and cream would do and only silks and satins would adorn the windows, bed, and furniture. Again, her generosity overflowed, and Eve hated herself for wanting anything more.

But she did want more. She wanted to see her

mother, evaluate her condition. She wanted to one day be the mistress of her own home with her own family. She paced her lavish chamber and wondered how she would journey from hiding as a nurse at Beckinbrook to having a husband, home, and family.

She hadn't thought along those lines in the past. Living out her dream was just supposed to *happen*. But Eve realized, without some plan, it would never just *happen*. If she didn't think this through, the years of her life would come and go. She would survive due only to the kindness of her friends. Caring for their children as she watched them build their lives together.

It was time to make plans and decide how and when to see her mother. In a wave of urgency, she realized she must now chart a course for her future happiness.

She rose and sat at her dressing table and removed her spectacles. Slowly she loosened the tight bun, carefully removing the pins and freeing her heavy tresses. Picking up a brush, she went to work, relaxing beneath the mundane task. Beneath the darkened sections, a brilliant gold slid through her brush.

"I am Evelyn Purittson," she spoke to no one and to herself. "Though I disguise my appearance, I will never disguise my soul, my intentions, and my dreams." She looked around her room as if expecting someone to show themselves, but found herself quite alone. "I will make my plans and with help or without, I will achieve my goals."

Gazing into the mirror, her memory became a play, and she looked on as if seated in the audience.

She entered her chamber and closed the door. Here in her bedroom she felt safe, surrounded with many favorite childhood memories. The shelves on the south wall held her most prized possessions, a tiny porcelain ring box Father had purchased in

Paris, a well loved doll, now dirty from years of companionship, a miniature of mother and grand-mother, three books about current scientific discoveries to name but a few.

In the middle of the room stood her lace draped, canopy bed. Lying upon it, she felt safe and feminine. A small, antique escritoire sat across from the bed, with a delicate overstuffed boudoir chair beside it. To the right, a changing screen and behind that, her wardrobe.

Tonight she would attend the ball of her mother's dear friends, Lord and Lady Mechaine. Excitement bubbled up within her. She had chosen an aqua colored gown with a white satin bow on the side and tiny-ribboned roses along the bottom hem. She felt like a princess when she last tried it on, and soon she would finally be able to wear it and perhaps even dance with a handsome prince. Lord Farrell had been a constant companion of late, perhaps later this very evening he might even kiss her...

She decided to have a look at it, once more before her bath. She rose from the bed and as she neared the screen, a hand reached out from behind it and jerked her by the arm.

Too frightened to scream, she looked up in shock and found herself inhaling the stale smell of whisky and perspiration. She shook her head in disgust as she realized the identity of her unwelcome visitor.

"Gregory—let me go!"

"Hello, princess." He leered at her.

Evelyn noticed his red-rimmed, silver-blue eyes and disheveled appearance. Coupled with his offensive odor, there was no question as to his sobriety.

"What's the matter, love? Surprised to see your favorite brother?"

"I said let me go." Evelyn's senses were alive with fear. Gregory was drunk, and his eyes reflected a violent lust.

"If you make a bloody sound, I'll have to put something inside your mouth, like say, my handkerchief...or my fist." His eyes told the truth of his statement.

Evelyn felt fear slide from her stomach over her trembling body. In its place came rage. She stomped down with every ounce of strength she could muster on the top of Gregory's foot.

"You!" He released her for a precious moment and grabbed his foot with both hands.

Evelyn bolted for the door, but he reached it first and blocked her exit with his thin but wiry body. "You are drunk! Leave my room at once, or I will tell Mama you have hidden in here and threatened me."

He began to walk toward her on unsteady feet, swaying slightly. Evelyn backed up closer to the window.

"She'll not believe you, especially when I tell her how you lured me in here and pressed your body against mine as you tried to remove my clothes." He began to loosen his cravat and then slipped his vest off, letting it fall upon the floor.

"My mother certainly will believe me." She tried to guess how quickly she could open the window and climb through without him getting to her.

Suddenly she swayed, "Oh my, I need air." She released the latch and opened the window. She looked at Gregory who seemed somewhat unsure as to how to proceed. It was only a moment, but she took advantage of it, hoisted herself upon the sill, and scrambled to the outer ledge. She hung from the casing by her fingertips and then wasting no time on thought, let go. She landed with a thud on her feet first, then her behind. She jumped up and ran toward the stables.

Looking back, she saw Gregory attempt to climb out of the window behind her. In doing so, in his state of intoxication, his foot caught upon the sill and he fell head first. He lay there as if dead. Evelyn did not go to him, she continued, heart in mouth, for the stables and the safety Francis, a loyal stable hand, would provide.

****

Eve shuddered as she recalled her narrow escape. Gregory had broken his arm that day, and his hatred for her had escalated. Surely, his physical discomfort and shame contributed, but Eve took no pity on him. He had reaped the consequences of his actions. Her mother had believed her and had severely reprimanded Gregory. She began to make arrangements for him to spend the winter at a distant relative's home.

Not long afterwards, her mother began to forget things. Her health deteriorated slowly. Evelyn tried to help her, but soon it was evident her mind had almost entirely left her. Gregory used this to his advantage and frequently laid in wait for Evelyn. She always managed to escape, but his persistence intensified until finally she was forced to flee her home.

Instead of letting fear grip her heart, she recalled her strength in outwitting him and fighting him off. She had won; she had protected her own virtue and would continue to do so. Looking into the mirror at her own reflection, she willed herself with steely determination to be strong, fearless, and brave. Her mother needed her, and she would not let her down.

****

James chose a navy blazer for Beau. "You look well, your grace."

Beau nodded in response. "Thank you."

James moved around the chamber, returning everything to its proper place. "Good evening, sir."

"Good evening, James." Once James left, Beau

checked his appearance in the mirror. He reached up to straighten his cravat but lowered his hand again. James already knotted it perfectly.

He exited his chamber and made his way to the dining room, a slight smile on his lips. His gait was eager, and he hummed a lively tune. For he hoped after dinner ended, concealed by darkness, forced out by the stifling heat, the lovely fountain bather might emerge once again—under the moonlit sky.

Only tonight, he would be there too.

Chapter Six

Eve began to ready herself for dinner in the small alcove beside her sitting room. Submerged in the tub, scented with her favorite vanilla fragrance, she allowed herself to relax for a moment. Looking toward the armoire filled with her favorite gowns, she smiled. No nanny disguise tonight—tonight she would be a lady.

She rose from the tub and dried off. Once she rubbed her body with her favorite lotion, she begin to dress. Opening the armoire, she chose a new gown. Katherine had given it to her two months ago. It had been tailored for Eve as a gift for her care of Glennora.

Eve hung the gown on the tiny hook beside the armoire and admired it again. So beautifully made, satin and designed in the Grecian style; light weight, in a creamy, champagne color. Two knotted straps held the low neckline in place. A circlet of delicate crystal beads, accented the high empire waist. The gown although simple in design was elegant in its simplicity.

Matching satin slippers had been delivered with the dress. Eve smiled for a moment, *a girl can never have too many pairs of slippers*, she thought.

She turned from the gown and began to dress her hair. First, she combed the herb paste through each strand, until it darkened considerably. As it dried, she began to arrange the mass in a series of curls atop her head. She chose a style she had never worn before, another attempt to avoid recognition by the Foster sisters. As Evelyn, she often wore her hair in a simple chignon, but tonight with that glorious dress, a more elaborate style would be appropriate.

She slipped into the gown, letting the cool satin glide over her already warm body. The dress fit perfectly. Stepping into her slippers, she looked into the mirror again. Her hair had dried completely, and she released a few curls from her coiffure. Soft tendril waves framed her face and fell down her back. She felt more natural and more like Evelyn. She hated to don her spectacles with such a lovely dress, but she knew Donald and Katherine would expect it, so she did.

Time to go. She took a deep breath and reminded herself to be careful. It wasn't a fear of Gregory, only that she might not please her protectors. She wanted them to know how much she appreciated all they had done.

Composure intact, Eve made her way to the sitting room where Katherine would receive her dinner guests. Her gaze quickly found Lady Foster and her daughters, then she quickly looked away. The room décor stated femininity, shades of pale yellow and soft green served as the backdrop for the women as they became reacquainted and visited. The Foster sisters and their mother were dressed elegantly in shades of blue. With their dark hair and haughty demeanor, they appeared wealthy and high titled.

Katherine wore a beautiful salmon colored creation, which was also a Grecian style. The color was dazzling on her. Circling her neck, a large round cut emerald in a liquid gold setting complimented her gown. Katherine looked like a queen and the ladies, her adoring court.

The countess stood and greeted Eve. "Ladies,

please meet my dear friend Miss Purity. She is visiting from Paris."

The ladies one by one stood to greet Eve, seemingly happy to make the acquaintance of a special friend of the Countess. The Foster sisters curtsied gently. Her disguise combined with their apparent adoration, effectively served to conceal the truth of her identity.

Lady Sands approached, smiling widely, "Your gown is exquisite! Do tell, my dear, is it some French creation?"

Eve liked Lady Sands immediately. Her dark brown eyes were large and smiling. Her once dark hair swirled with silvery strands that hinted at her age but did not disclose her years. Her smile could only be described as genuine and warm.

"The gown was a gift from Katherine. I am not certain where it was made."

"Well its loveliness is surpassed only by your own."

"Thank you, my lady. I was just admiring your gown. The color is rare and warm."

Lady Sands winked. "Thank you, my dear. My late husband had the fabric made before his passing. He loved anything that sparkled."

"Then it is plain why he chose a lady such as yourself." Eve truly meant the compliment. Lady Sands' gown was a shimmering caramel color with pleating and tucks in all the right places. Although worn by a woman well into middle age, the gown looked stunning and lacked no allure.

The ladies continued to chatter politely until the gentlemen entered to escort them to the dining room.

Donald entered first, followed by Lord Marvelle Sr. Lord Marvelle Sr. was an imposing gentleman, with snowy white hair and a matching moustache, and he was now surveying every detail of the room.

Lord Stenworth entered next. Handsome and young, he smiled warmly and appreciatively at the younger ladies and greeted the older women with sincere respect. Finally, Lord Marvelle Jr. entered. Lord Marvelle was quiet like his father, but as she observed him, a vague feeling of unease washed over her spine. Distrust and skepticism caused her to stand a bit straighter and to her dismay, the tiny hairs at the nape of her neck prickled a warning. Every thing about the man was thin, his light brown hair, his body, his personality and Eve suspected, his integrity.

However, the man who entered after him was quite the opposite. The room suddenly seemed to fill with his appearance. His stance was commanding yet relaxed. His broad shoulders seemed to stretch from one wall to the other. Strong, well-muscled legs were obvious through his evening attire as was his narrow waist. Eve tried to admire him as inconspicuously as possible. When he turned her way, she inhaled sharply. His eyes were matchless in color; a vibrant, sapphire adorned with long, dark lashes. His hair a rich brown with lighter streaks framing his face, and when he smiled, Eve noticed a single dimple to the left of his full lips. Taking the whole of him in, she felt her stomach tremble.

Introductions were made around the room; Eve tried to stay relaxed and in control of her composure until Donald escorted *him* to her side.

"Lord Beaumont, may I introduce you to Elizabeth's dear friend, Miss Eve Purity. Eve is visiting us from Paris."

Lord Beaumont bowed slowly. When he straightened, he gently picked up Eve's hand. "A pleasure to meet you *Mademoiselle*." His eyes flashed with brilliance.

Eve felt tiny jolts of pleasure beginning where his hand touched hers, traveling down her arm and spreading over her body. He didn't recognize her—her secret was still safe. As she relaxed in that small victory, she was assaulted again with the realization that he was a spectacular specimen of a man.

"A pleasure to meet you as well, *Monsieur*." She smiled up into his intense eyes. There she witnessed a combination of warmth and savvy. A man to reckon with, of that she was certain.

His hand lingered on hers for the briefest of moments and then reluctantly, Beau released his grip. The woman standing before him was exquisite in every way. With a mass of dark hair, aqua eyes, and small, feminine body, he was drawn to her like a bee to a pollen-laden flower. She moved gracefully, as to music playing she alone could hear. His heart accelerated its beat. He watched her bring a delicate hand to her face and brush a soft curl away from her jewel-like eyes, framed in small spectacles. He thought it odd that Donald had not mentioned her presence here.

Ah, at last…Eve Purity…what sweet music… to know your name.

Donald's voice broke into his thoughts. "Percy tells me dinner is ready. Shall we?" He held his arm out to Elizabeth. They began the procession with the Earl and Countess, followed by Lord Marvelle Sr. escorting Lady Sands, Lord Marvelle Jr. escorting Lillian, and Lord Stenworth was eager to offer his arm to Violet. Finally, Lord Beaumont was left with Eve and Lady Foster. In a quandary over whom to escort first, he was relieved when Donald returned and escorted Lady Foster out. Beau turned to Eve.

"May I have the honor?" He offered her his arm.

Softly, like an angel's kiss, she laid her hand upon his sleeve and together they strolled into the candle lit dining room.

Chapter Seven

Everyone took their designated places, while the aroma of the courses to come wafted enticingly through the air. Eve was happy to find herself seated directly across from Lord Beaumont. She stole a glance his way as he passed the honey-glazed carrots to his right. So masculine, so large, and so beautiful.

Could a man be beautiful? She had never pondered the thought; then again, she had never had a gentleman of his caliber sitting mere inches away.

Lady Sands, seated to Lord Beaumont's right, began at once to draw Eve into the conversation. "Please tell us, Miss Purity, where in Paris you lived," she paused and sipped her wine slowly, "it has been many years since I have visited your lovely city, but I may know the area."

Eve smiled, wistfully remembering her last summer in Paris with both her mother and father. "We lived near Eglise de Sacre Cour, which is Sacred Heart Church. As a young girl, I would walk to the church with my mother each morning for prayer. We spent many warm afternoons strolling around the ancient church, visiting the nuns and priests and sometimes even having tea with them."

"How delightful," Lady Sands smiled, "surely you also visited the quaint shops and museums?"

"As often as possible." Eve replied.

As he ate, Beau studied her inconspicuously. Her movements, her grace, they called to him—

teasing with memories of the fountain. A wave of heat, mixed with the heady feeling of anticipation, rolled over him. He raised his eyes to view her fully, finding it difficult to forget the womanly shape hidden by her elegant gown. She nearly glowed with sensuality; every movement she made drew him deeper to her. His mind swam with memories of wet flesh in the lantern's dim light. And now watching her dark lashes closing and opening as if she were being kissed…

"Do you enjoy the work displayed in Paris?" Beau entered the conversation.

"I love art, in its many forms, but my favorite pieces of work are the sculptures."

"What is it about the sculptures that fascinate you so?" Would she also tell him what caused her eyes to glow like live jewels, and her skin to glisten in such a way as to beg his touch? Would she reveal to him the secret her body used to call to his, a call to be held and crushed within his embrace?

"It is the passion the sculptor possesses that draws me to his pieces. The attention to every detail, as if missing one small curve or line would be a terrible sin. The care in which he portrays each expression shows his talent and love." She paused, moistening her lips. Beau felt the effect of her slight movement as if she had moistened his.

"The works I greatly admire speak more to me of the creator than the actual piece."

Beau swallowed, his eyes, now slaves to her full, velvety lips. Hearing her comment, he understood the vast importance of including every comely curve. He wondered what it might be like to take her away to Paris and stroll through a gallery of sculptures with her by his side.

"I have never heard anyone express their love of art quite that way. I admire your perspective and will remember your words the next time I view a masterpiece." *I'm viewing one right now.*

"Thank you, my lord." She replied.

Smiling at Eve, Lady Sands spoke again, "What is it you miss most about Paris, now that you are melting here in England with the rest of us?" She fanned herself with her linen napkin for added emphasis.

"Paris is a beautiful city. But I also love my homeland. I am always happy here or on the continent. But if I had to choose one thing I missed, it would be my parents."

"They remain in Paris?" Lord Beaumont offered. Though he spoke softly, the rich timbre of his voice hummed through the room, drowning out all other sounds.

Eve wished it were so. She wished her father still lived, strolling the streets of Paris with her healthy mother proudly beside him. She could even accept a lesser happiness of her mother and stepfather living quietly at Kentwood, both happy and enjoying each other. But with both her father and stepfather gone, and her mother near death, those happy wishes would remain naught.

Knowing the response, both Donald and Katherine required, she answered, "Yes."

Eve sipped her wine and noticed Lord Beaumont's rather obvious observation. When her gaze met his, instead of looking away, a slow smile stretched out across his handsome face, revealing twinkling eyes, a flash of brilliant white teeth, and *that* dimple.

In response, she offered him a small smile. His gaze held her so intently; she wondered if he could see her heart thudding beneath her Grecian gown. From the look in his eye, she determined he could.

She finally looked to her dinner plate and began to sample the delicious array of foods. Every bite was a tiny taste of heaven; in fact, she did not recall ever enjoying any cuisine as she enjoyed the fare this night.

She heard the soft rumble of Lord Beaumont's husky voice. He was speaking to Lord Marvelle Jr., and then Donald joined in as well. They spoke of investments in different ventures. Lord Marvelle seemed to have one question after another for Lord Beaumont. Each one seemed to border on passive hostility, as if he were trying to find some inconsistency in Lord Beaumont's character or business expertise.

Lord Beaumont was ever patient. He answered each question politely and in respectful tones. He seemed to care little what Marvelle thought or insinuated. Finally, Donald ended the inquisition.

"I tell you this, Marvelle," he began, "I have dabbled here and there, over the years, with many different ventures, sometimes successful and sometimes just the opposite. But whenever I invest with Beaumont, I always turn a profit."

"I've never seen the likes of such behavior. An Earl and a Marquis investing like untitled men from the colonies. It isn't done." Lord Marvelle tilted his aristocratic chin higher and stared snootily at Beaumont.

The Earl responded with a curt smile. "Some gentlemen enjoy a good hunt, some like to ride, and others," he paused looking at Marvelle intently, "frequent houses of baser urges...I see no harm with helping a man launch a well planned business venture."

Lord Marvelle snapped his thin lips together and gave a nod. Lillian who was seated across from Marvelle sought to engage the handsome Lord Beaumont in conversation. She employed her most seductive expression.

"What do you find yourself interested in at the moment?" She lowered her long lashes demurely and then lifted them.

Eve had the strongest urge to accidentally spill her plate upon Lillian's bobbing head. If she was sly enough, she might even be able to kick her soundly. She smiled at her musings and then with a sigh restrained herself.

She glanced across the table and caught Lord Beaumont's eye. For one moment, she feared he had read her thoughts. Quickly, as if a master at illusions, he gave his attention back to Miss Foster.

"Many things interest me at the present, although I do not wish to bore you with my talk of business anymore this evening."

"Oh, I find it terribly intriguing—a man such as yourself, choosing to work when you could be enjoying the simpler pleasures of your station."

Eve could feel his eyes on her again. She raised her head slightly, and he winked at her. Her face seemed to catch fire. She resisted the strong urge to fan herself.

Eve listened and watched as Lillian sought to draw Lord Beaumont's attention to her but though polite, he simply did not seem interested.

Dinner continued and before they finished dessert, a faint rumbling could be heard in the distance. A strong, cool, breeze entered through the open French doors and swirled through the dining room.

"Ahh." Exclaimed Lady Sands.

The others smiled appreciatively. Perhaps the coming rain would finally cool things off. Lady Foster rose and began to say goodnight to the other guests. All the gentlemen stood.

"Cigars and brandy, gentlemen?" Donald inquired.

The rest of the ladies made their way to the sitting room. Eve thought it would be a good time for her to depart as she did not want to chance too much time in the Foster daughters' company.

Beau lifted Eve's hand to his lips, "Sleep well, Miss Purity. I look forward to seeing you again soon." He kissed her hand, and Eve thought she might swoon right there. "Perhaps tomorrow?"

"Well I ...perhaps." She stuttered like an idiot. What had come over her?

The others bid her goodnight, and she slowly climbed the stairs to her chamber. Thoughts of the handsome Lord Beaumont filled her mind, *Beau*, Donald had called him. What an appropriate name for one so beautiful.

She entered her chamber and lit a lamp. A cool breeze from the open window brushed her heated flesh. A swim would be lovely, but no. There were far too many people around and besides, it was about to storm. The thought of a heavy rainstorm gave her an idea. A very wonderful and wicked idea.

Quickly she removed her elegant apparel and in mere seconds donned an old dark-colored gown. Not wanting to take the time to remove her coiffure, she simply set her spectacles on her dressing table and extinguished her lamp. Before the room darkened again, she crossed the long hallway and descended the servants' staircase.

She exited the manor and quickly circled around to the front where she peeked into the dining room. Everyone had departed. Good. She circled back around the manor and found the path that led to the fountain. Again, a gentle rumble could be heard, not far off. She didn't stop to admire the gardens in the moonlight. Without slowing down, she strode across the south lawn to the stables.

Eve reached the stables and to her relief, she found John the stable boy alone. John and Eve had become friends during the last six months. Eve often took Glennora to the stables to show her the beautiful thoroughbreds Donald had acquired, and whenever she had the opportunity, she would have John saddle her a mount for a leisurely exploration of the many trails on the estate.

She never dared to ride without letting Katherine know her plans, but tonight, she was desperate.

The stable, neat and orderly, smelled of fresh hay. The back door was propped open, allowing the fresh night air to flow across and cool the large animals. John sat on a small wooden stool, a lantern's soft glow nearby, polishing a well-worn saddle. He started when he saw her, but then greeted her warmly.

"John, I need a favor. We must keep this between just ourselves."

"What is it?"

"I have a dear friend who is quite ill, and I must ride to see her at once."

"I'll have a carriage brought around immediately." He offered.

"No, I mean, no thank you. I cannot let anyone know I am leaving. I just want to take one of the horses and go by myself. Can you quickly saddle Victor for me?"

"But Miss Eve, it is late and about to storm. The Earl and Countess would have my head if any harm were to come to you." His brows drew together in worry.

"John, no harm will come to me. I need to go *alone*, and the Earl and Countess cannot find out about my leaving."

"Then I shall ride with you. I will be your escort tonight." He turned to begin to ready the horses.

"No. I cannot have you come with me, I must go alone. Please, trust me; I will be back before morning."

"If something happens to you, I would never forgive myself."

"I will take care. Please John; this is something I must do."

"I believe this to be a dangerous idea, but I will saddle Victor. If you are not back by morning, I will go to the Earl myself and tell him."

John led the large black stallion out of his stall. While he saddled him, Eve fed him a carrot and stroked his velvety nose. The second John finished, she leaped upon Victor's back and began to ride away. "Don't worry...I'll be back before morning."

Beau made his way through the stable, leading his saddled, dove grey stallion. He easily discerned worry in the boy's voice, and rightfully so, he thought as the rumbles of thunder grew stronger.

"I heard everything she said. Don't worry, I will follow her and keep her safe. I will not betray your confidence. I hope you will not betray mine."

"Nay, my lord. She is a special one, that Eve."

"Beau nodded. *Special indeed.* He mounted Wind Keeper and off he went on the un-known mission.

Chapter Eight

The wind at his back thrust Beau forward into the deepening darkness. Slivers of moonlight granted him just enough light to follow Eve, and still remain at a comfortable distance. He had only known of her one day and already this was the third time he'd found himself on her trail. The winds quickened, the storm was nearly upon them and still she rode on. He kept up well, his time in the saddle giving him opportunity to re-examine the havoc she had carved on his mind and nerves over the last day and night.

First, he had seen her in the fountain. When he had questioned Donald, he had not revealed Eve. Why hadn't he? Was he trying to conceal her presence at Beckinbrook Manor?

And her hair, that glorious silk he had beheld at the fountain. Tonight it had been wavy, and darker. Well, women had their beauty secrets, and whatever Eve's were, they were certainly

working on him.

Now, a late night summons to visit an ailing friend. Perhaps a servant had given her word, yet why hadn't Donald or Katherine been notified? Why wouldn't Eve take a carriage or a chaperone?

Every thought surrounding her was a mystery. Tonight with a stroke of luck, he might find a clue to this enigma who aroused his every sense to obsession.

Eve kept a cautious eye on the road. The storm was a perfect distraction to allow her this chance to see her mother. The thunder would help mask her entry and exit to her mother's chamber in case Gregory was in residence. The servants at Kentwood were still loyal to her and would aid her in her secrecy. But even with the storm and the servants, Eve knew she would have to be careful. Gregory, always a dangerous man, had allowed his lust and hatred for her to turn him into almost a monster. If he were to catch her, she could scarcely imagine what he might do in revenge.

Finally, the rain started. It did not begin gently and then slowly crescendo into a full-fledged storm. Instead, it rain as if Heaven had opened a long plugged dam, letting torrents of water gush down to earth. In mere seconds, Eve was soaked. For several minutes, she reveled in the relief from the heat, but soon she began to shiver—icy tendrils slashed straight to her spine. There was still at least another half hour of riding before she would reach Kentwood. Thoughts of her beloved mother strengthened her resolve, and she pressed onward to her childhood estate.

A bit later, she turned a corner and saw the structure, a dark form sitting regally on a shallow plateau. She was home. Gregory might keep her away for a time, but not forever, and one day she would return for good.

She rode to the stable and found the elderly Francis sleeping in the barn. She reached down and gently shook him. Groggily he looked up at her.

"Miss Evelyn?"

"Francis, please take Victor and see that he is well rested. I cannot stay long, I will be returning within the hour."

"Aye, missy. We'll be quiet as two mouses, that we will." He led the stallion to the rear of the barn.

Eve entered through the servant's entrance and tiptoed up the stairs—her shoes and gown sodden with rainwater. Several months ago, Gregory moved her mother out of the master's chamber and into the guest wing. The move had been a stroke of luck, as the guest wing was in the left wing and the master's chamber was the farthest chamber on the right.

Eve came to her mother's door and paused. She took several deep breaths before she slowly opened the door.

The room was dark except for one small lantern on the bedside table. It flickered and lent warmth to the darkness. Her mother rested in the center of the large bed, her nightdress buttoned to her neck, a lightweight blanket folded neatly across her chest. Her pale, blonde hair, now threaded with silver strands, was brushed neatly—away from her face.

Eve quietly closed the door, but the sound of the latch catching woke Mary, her mother's maid, from her slumber in an overstuffed wing chair.

Blinking rapidly, she donned her spectacles and looked at Eve. "Evelyn, is it really you, dear?"

Eve went to her at once and whispered, "How is mother?"

"She is the same, my dear."

Eve carefully touched her mother's cheek. It felt cool and lifeless. She looked at the bedside table. It held a glass of water, her mother's Bible, and a small dark colored bottle filled with liquid.

"What is this?" Eve carefully lifted the bottle and removed the cork in its neck.

"Gregory had Dr. Colton look in on your mum; he left this medicine."

Eve held the bottle beneath her nose and inhaled—no scent. She dabbed a tiny bit on her finger and tasted it. It was sour and made her thirsty. She set the bottle down and took a sip from the water glass.

"Does it help her?" Eve motioned to the medicine.

"It's difficult to say. She has been taking it since you left, and her condition has not improved. It has not worsened either." Mary replied.

As her eyes became more adjusted to the darkness, Eve looked around the room. Everything was nicely polished and well organized.

"Is there something I can do for you, my dear, perhaps a fresh gown?"

Eve nodded slowly. A tear slid down her face, but in the semi-darkness, it was invisible to Mary.

Mary went to the wardrobe; she chose a navy blue summer dress. She hung it on the nearby hook and began to smooth the folds of fabric out with her hands.

"Mary, there is no need for that. I must leave soon."

"Yes, my dear." Mary knew of the danger that would befall Eve if she were to be caught. She moved the screen away from the wall.

"Come, change your gown and then we can sit beside your mum and read to her. She enjoys hearing the Psalms."

Another tear fell upon her damp cheek, then another and another. Hanging her head, she moved behind the screen and quickly removed her gown. She slipped the dry one over her head and stepped out so Mary could fasten the buttons in the back.

When they were fastened, Mary turned Eve to face her. "What would you have me do for her?"

Eve tried to control the shaking in her voice. "She looks well cared for. I am sure whatever you are doing for her is the best." Mary had been Laura's maid for over twenty-five years. Her devotion to Eve's mother was not in question, nor had it ever been.

"Come, let's sit here and talk to your mum."

Eve sat on the edge of the bed and picked up one of her mother's tiny, still hands. She gently rubbed the back with her thumb as Mary in a hushed voice, began to read from the Bible, "The Lord is my Shepherd, I shall not want..."

Laura's aqua eyes flickered and opened. She stared straight ahead and then looked into toward Eve. "Evelyn?"

Mary dropped the Bible, it landed with a soft thud.

"Mother!" Eve could barely contain her joy. It had been months since her mother had recognized her.

"Darling, you've come home!" Laura exclaimed.

Thunder shook the castle, followed closely by a streak of lightning.

"I'm here to visit you. I have missed you."

"I've missed you too." Laura looked around the room. "Where am I?"

"You are in the guest wing. You have been ill."

"What is wrong with me?"

"We are not certain." Eve brought her mother's hand to her lips and kissed it.

"Send for Dr. Ford in the morning." Laura said.

"Dr. Colton has been seeing you, mother."

Her mouth formed an "Oh" and her eyes began to glaze over.

"Mother, Mother!" Eve knew she couldn't yell, but she saw her slipping away again. She gently shook her shoulders, and Laura looked into her eyes for one moment more. "I love you, mother."

Laura's face seemed to respond, she looked at peace for just a moment, and then her expression became blank once again.

Eve turned to Mary and sobbed in her arms. Tears of joy mingled with despair and frustration. Mary held her; she understood and cried along with her.

Finally Eve rose. "I must go back, Mary."

"Do they know you're here?"

"No, they would never have let me come during the storm."

"They care for you, my dear."

"I know they do. But Mary, I need to see her more regularly, care for her myself."

"Gregory, although a spawn of Satan himself, has been good to your mum. He sends the doctor over every week and sees to it she has her special teas and broth."

Eve nodded. "I know, but I still don't trust him. I want to take her to Beckinbrook."

Mary's head nodded, causing her gray curls to stir. "Speak to the Earl and Countess; they will give you council as to what should be done."

"I have, and they are thinking on the matter." Eve moved to her mother and kissed her softly on her forehead. "I wish we could arrive on a plan soon. I fear she may slip away at any moment, and I would not be with her." Her shoulders lurched with a sorrowful sob.

"Listen," Mary said, "The storm is letting up. Go now, and if there is any change with your mother, I will send word to Beckinbrook at once."

Eve agreed and told Mary of the trail of water she had left throughout the house. Mary agreed to wipe it up and went to fetch some rags. Eve looked at her mother one last time and made her way back through the servant's quarters and out to the stables.

Sounds echoed throughout Kentwood, waking Gregory from his fitful sleep. He chose to exit his chamber without a lantern, moving secretly through the old manor. Several paces ahead, he watched as Mary, his stepmother's maid scurried to wipe puddles from the thick mahogany floors.

Silently, he approached her. "A bit late for

mopping floors, is it not, Mary?"

He enjoyed watching her startle. "Yes, my lord."

"Do you care to explain your actions, or shall I wait here all night?"

Her lips quivered. The senile wench was nearly as bad as her mistress.

"I was taking a basin to bathe my lady and I spilled a bit."

Gregory moved closer and observed the trail of water leading down the hallway.

"More than a little, I would say." He arched his brow in the most intimidating manner he could fashion.

"Yes, my lord." Mary began to ring her hands. She was lying.

"I will polish the floors at sunrise."

"See that you do." He turned and slowly strutted back to his chamber. "I'm always watching, Mary. Always." He chuckled. She remained quiet, and deep inside; he reveled in the knowledge of her fear.

"Yur stallion is ready, Miss Evelyn." Francis said.

Eve stroked Victor's nose and mounted him. She thanked Francis and made her way outside. The rain was falling more gently now. Crickets and other nighttime creatures could once again be heard. It was as if man and nature alike gave a sigh of contentment. The heat had finally abated and all were greatly relieved.

The sun was just climbing above the horizon when Eve arrived on Donald and Elizabeth's property. She slowed her pace and relaxed. She was tired from her arduous journey and melancholy with worries and concerns. Her hair was a tangled mess—her pins long gone and the dark color mostly rinsed out in the rain. She looked around hoping no one was about and rode up to the stable.

John was sleeping where she had left him last

night.

"John, wake-up."

"Oh, Miss Eve, you've returned."

Eve smiled weakly. "Yes."

"I'll take Victor here, you go get some sleep."

"Thank you, John." She turned and began a slow walk back to the manor.

Minutes later, Beau arrived at the stable, his clothes beginning to dry from the repeated drenching throughout the night. He led Wind Keeper to his stall and met John as he brushed Victor.

"I'm glad ye looked after her."

"As am I." Beau replied.

"All is well, then?" John asked.

"Yes, we rode through the storm for quite a while, but your lady is an adept horseman, she continued on valiantly." Beau saw the genuine concern shining in the lad's dark eyes, and his relief upon seeing her home safe. He was happy to put the fellow at ease.

Beau turned to go back to the house but stopped. He looked at John, "Does she often go about in the middle of the night, alone?"

"Nay, my lord. But Eve has her secrets and I respect them."

"What do you mean, secrets?"

"Pardon, my lord but I'll not betray my friend."

Beau nodded. "I understand—but John, if she leaves in the night again, please inform me at once. I would like to chaperone her, unbeknownst of course, and protect her safety."

"We have an accord, my lord." John extended his hand, something not done between servant and lord, but Beau eagerly shook with the stable boy and was grateful for his trust.

Beau entered the manor and climbed the stairs to his chamber; his mind swimming with questions, ideas, and plans. He summoned James immediately.

"James, I need you to send word to my father and Paul immediately. I will be staying on at Beckinbrook for longer than originally planned. I will need you to bring me my files and investment ledgers from my study at once."

"Yes, my lord. Would you like to sleep now, or shall I have a bath drawn?"

Beau glanced at his reflection and noted the dark shadows beneath his eyes. Sleep sounded heavenly, but he had too many plans to set in motion. Sleep would have to wait. "Draw me a bath then head to Hartford at once. I'll shave and dress myself."

"Very good, my lord. I shall depart post haste."

"James?"

He turned. "Yes?"

"Thank you."

"Yes, my lord."

****

Eve entered her chamber after making a detour through the gardens. She peeled her gown away from her body and sat down at her dressing table and brushed the snarls from her long, tangled mass. She washed the mud from her hands, face and legs, and then headed for her bed.

She welcomed the touch of the comfortable mattress and closed her eyes. Visions of her mother filled her with peace and eagerness. Bringing her mother to Beckinbrook would be so wonderful; perhaps Mary would come along as well.

Last night, she had been the model of decorum, vaguely answering questions and never once giving away her identity to the Foster sisters. She hoped this had helped erase her faux pas of being seen in the garden by Lord Beaumont.

Ah yes, Lord Beaumont. In her half sleep state, she saw him fill the sitting room with his presence and his shoulders. His eyes sparkled warmly and somehow found a way to do strange things to her stomach. When he smiled his dimple called to her, she wished to touch it... His voice whispered over her, deep and harmonious. In fact, every adjective she could think of to describe the young lord was positive, indeed.

She wondered what it might be like to have Lord Beaumont hold her in his strong arms. She could scarcely imagine such delight, yet as she drifted off to sleep, her mind played a dream of his arms encircling her waist, while full lips lowered to meet her waiting mouth.

****

Gregory woke from his tortured slumber. He often found it difficult to enjoy a deep sleep; nightmares often haunted him—his sister's face contorted with pain. He sat up and glared at the sunlight streaming into the chamber. Some men just seemed to prefer the darkness.

He began to pace the room. Something was not right. It was as if that little scene with Mary held a clue to an underhanded plot, yet he could not quite ascertain what that plot may be.

Evelyn's face laughed at him, mockingly. "You'll never catch me."

He was tired of that vision, and it was time to find the insolent wench. He summoned his valet.

"Smyth, I want you to contact some of our people and persuade them through whatever means necessary to find my stepsister. I want her here in a fortnight. I do not want her harmed unless it is absolutely necessary in bringing her back home. Do you understand?"

"Yes, my lord. My people have been unable to locate her at present, but—"

"THEN GET SOME NEW PEOPLE!" Gregory bellowed.

"Ah, very good, my lord." Smyth exited the

chamber.

Once the door closed, Gregory hissed, "I'll find you, very soon, Evelyn. Perhaps when your mother's illness suddenly progresses, you will come home. I'll surprise you with many delights at that time. Many delights."

Gregory summoned the butler. "Send for Dr. Colton, I want to see him immediately!"

Chapter Nine

Refreshed after his bath, shaved, and dressed in clean clothing, Beau embraced the day. His mind, remarkably clear after a sleepless night, although in the far recesses of his memory, something was niggling for his attention.

What was it? It had something to do with Kentwood Manor. He had recognized it, for as a young boy he had once visited the ancient stone castle with his father. The old lord had been a client of Rudolf Beaumont's. Beau remembered sitting in the carriage while his father delivered a document to Lord Simon Purittson, Viscount of Wilmington.

But Lord Simon had died several years ago. Did any of the family still reside at Kentwood? And more importantly, what malady could have prompted Eve to ride for two hours, in the middle of the night, amidst a dangerous storm? Well, mysteries needed to be solved, and Beau was up to the task.

When James returned with his ledgers, he would tend to his business matters. Until then, he would focus on the lovely Eve.

Beau descended the grand staircase and entered the dining room. Even with the early hour, daylight streamed in through the open windows accenting the elegant room. Donald was there, slowly drinking his tea. He nodded as Beau entered and filled his plate with the offered breakfast fare.

Beau sat across from his long time friend while a servant hastened to bring him some tea. A moment later, he picked up his teacup, "That was quite a storm we had last night, but it cooled things off considerably."

"Indeed. This is truly the first cool morning we've enjoyed in over a fortnight."

"Hmm." Beau sipped his tea, considering how best to broach the subject of the lovely Miss Purity.

"Surely you didn't come down to discuss the weather." Donald raised an eyebrow and smiled slightly.

"I came down for breakfast," Beau chose a roll and began to butter it. "Commenting on the weather was merely my attempt at polite conversation."

"Yes." Donald nodded. "Did you sleep well?"

"Surely, you don't wish to discuss my sleep habits."

"No, twas just *my* attempt at polite conversation."

They sat in companionable silence for a moment. "I believe I have discovered the identity of the lady strolling about the gardens the other night."

"Oh?" Donald feigned innocence.

"Yes, I believe it was Katherine's friend, Lady Purity."

"Her hair is not golden, but quite dark." Donald commented.

"Yes," Beau knew he had seen golden streaks in the early morning light, but it didn't matter now. "I must have been mistaken about the color, it was quite dark, you know."

"I see." Donald turned back to his tea.

"Anyhow, I would like to write to her parents and ask permission to court her while she is here at Beckinbrook." Beau watched for Donald's response. Beau could not be certain, but it seemed Donald was making an extraordinary effort to appear unaffected.

"Miss Purity is a lovely girl, but courting is quite a serious step, for a scoundrel like you." Donald sipped his tea.

Beau set his cup down and leaned back in his chair. "Even scoundrels need an heir."

Donald met Beau's eyes across the table. "I find it curious that you would consider something so rash after only just meeting Miss Purity and spending so little time in her company."

Beau leaned forward and lowered his voice, "I am ready to move forward with my life." After an intentional pause, he continued, "Miss Purity seems...different from the other misses of the ton."

Donald leaned back and picked up his cup. "Yes...she does." He chose a roll for himself and began to break it apart. "Go on and write your letter, I will see to its delivery as soon as possible." He put a small piece in his mouth and began to chew it. "Do you think Miss Purity will be agreeable to courting you?"

"I don't know. I was hoping to speak with her this afternoon. I have already sent word to my father. I need to discuss this with him as well." Beau hoped his father would understand, at some point, a man must learn to trust.

"Speak to her then. I hope all goes well for you." Donald smiled.

"Thank you. I sense something special about Lady Purity." Beau stood and nodded to Donald.

"Good day." Donald said.

"I believe it will be." Beau smiled broadly.

With his valet gone, Beau stopped at the kitchen and left instructions for the cook. He made his way back to his chamber, thoughts of *her* filling his mind. His weighty responsibilities were also trying their best to vie for their familiar residence upon Beau's shoulders, but he was having none of them today.

These last few years, he had poured his energies into different business ventures. His goal to amass enough wealth to care for himself, his brother, and their potential offspring. Financial success had come to him by route of careful decisions and dedication to his family.

His brother now attended a well-reputed school, and the family coffers were filled to overflowing.

But somewhere deep inside, Beau still felt a prod to keep going. It was as if he looked for others to care for, as if he had a need to rescue and set right the downcast and the poor. He dared not link his work ethic to that horrible night long ago...

He had begun to reach out to the common man, working beside them in their inventions, lending guidance, and financing when necessary. It was as if a gentle voice commanded him, "Take care of them."

Now for the first time, his attention was diverted somewhere else. He would not ignore the prodding of his heart to attend to the needs of others; it just wasn't the only passion in his life anymore.

He felt the changes wash over him, an unknown territory but one he longed to explore. Now with the same abandon he had shown for investing and hard work, he would turn his focus on trying to find himself a measure of happiness.

First, he sat at his desk and wrote a letter to Lord and Lady Purity, requesting their permission to court Eve. Next, he penned a letter to his father, announcing his desire to visit soon. When he finished, he set both letters upon a silver tray and lay upon his bed for a short rest. Soon he would see her again. He closed his eyes for only a moment as the memory of a gentle touch upon his arm caused a stirring in his heart. He hoped to spend time with her this afternoon, to gaze upon her in the sun's bright light and see the laughter in her eyes...

****

He started as he came awake, he must have dozed off for a moment. A quick glance at his watch fob indicated it had been a long nap. He smiled to no one in particular; it was nearly the noon hour.

He quickly splashed water on his face and combed his hair. Straightening his cravat, Beau descended into the great manor.

He came upon the ladies chatting happily; their voices lilting like excited birds on the first day of spring. They were seated with Elizabeth in the sitting room on lady-sized velvet covered upholstered chairs. The room and ladies alike appeared cool and fresh. Lady Sands spoke first as he entered the feminine company.

"My dear Lord Beaumont, what a pleasure to see you. Isn't the air lovely today?"

Beau scanned the room and found the object of his quest sitting beside Katherine, holding baby Glennora. She was dressed in a pale green, day gown, its gentle ruffles skimmed against her vibrant skin. *Oh, to be a ruffle...*

"Lovely indeed." He responded to the greeting, while his eyes rested on Eve alone.

"I believe the temperature of the room just increased." Lady Sands whispered to Katherine.

"Please, do come join us for tea." The Countess invited.

Beau sat on a creamy yellow colored settee across from Eve, Katherine, and Lady Sands. The Foster sisters were sitting across the room, their eager eyes following his every move.

The group chatted politely, while a servant went to fetch more tea. Beau nodded to the Foster sisters then turned his head and attention back to the reason he had come to the room in the first place.

"My dear Miss Purity, how good to see you looking so well rested this morning."

Eve smiled and nodded, "Thank you, my lord."

Beau took in her clear beautiful eyes, absent of guile yet full of some deep emotion. He began to experience a feeling that was coming to be familiar whenever he was near her. A feeling of intense heat, accompanied by the pulsing of his heartbeat—as well as other parts of his anatomy. How could she affect him with barely a spoken word?

She looked so innocent, yet the stable boy had confirmed she had secrets—riding out last night in the storm confirmed that to be a truth. What mystery was she hiding? He felt a jolt of pleasure; he would enjoy the finding out.

Eve held the baby comfortably on her lap. The baby seemed to delight in the attention she received from all the women in the room. Lady Sands reached her hand out across Katherine and gently rubbed Glennora's chubby cheek. Glennora smiled and gurgled in response.

"Lord Sands and I were never blessed with children, but we were content in our love for one another. Still whenever I see a beautiful baby such as this one, a part of me longs for a little one of my own."

Eve stood and carried Glennora over to her. "Then you must hold her and spoil her for a while. Glennora can always tell when someone wants to shower her with love."

Lady Sands gently took the round little bundle of love and set her upon her lap. Glennora smiled and played with the rings on Lady Sands' fingers.

"I was about to take a walk anyway. It is a beautiful day to linger in the gardens."

Faster than he meant to, Beau rose. "Please, let me escort you. The thorns on the rose bushes can be especially perilous after a storm such as last night's."

The Countess rolled her eyes. The Foster sisters exchanged glances laced with daggers.

Eve raised an eyebrow, "And you will protect me from these treacherous, garden bushes?"

Beau answered her in all seriousness. "Not the bushes, my dear, just the thorns."

Katherine and Lady Sands exchanged knowing glances. The Foster sisters did as well. Beau caught it all and couldn't help smiling to himself. *Women.*

Eve placed her slim hand upon Beau's arm as they stepped out of the room.

"Allow me, if you will. I have a small errand to run on our way out."

"Certainly." The delightful smells greeted them before they entered the room, baking apples, flavored meats, and spices of varying aromas. Several young maids scurried about carrying sacks of flour and pouches tied with string. Another stood in the center of the large room chopping and dicing vegetables and assorted fruits and laying them attractively on a tray. A large, older woman stood at the stove stirring pots and humming a happy unfamiliar tune.

As the two stepped further into the busy kitchen, all heads snapped up at once. The younger girls looked to the woman at the stove who set her spoon down and crossed the room to greet the couple.

She wiped her hands on her apron as she approached. "G'day, mi lord." She then bobbed a curtsy to the couple. Eve smiled.

"I 'ave yur basket 'ere, mi lord."

"Thank you, my dear." Lord Beaumont looked at her with delight. He withdrew several coins from his pocket and handed them to Nigella.

"'Tis not necessary, mi lord. The Earl and Countess pay mi wages."

"I realize that, but this was a special favor for me, and I want you to know I appreciate it greatly."

Nigella's face held a tinge of red. The young maids looked longingly at one another.

"I thank ye, mi lord." Nigella returned to her

place at the stove, a tiny smile at her lips.

Beau led Eve out of the kitchen and back towards the garden door.

"What a kind man you are, Lord Beaumont. First wanting to protect me from the evil thorns and then making a dear old woman blush with happiness."

Beau looked down into the crystal aqua of her eyes. They were teasing and warm. He was feeling that "feeling" again. "I am a man with an abundance of talents; thorn protecting and blush making are only the first two."

"Humility must certainly be the third." She smiled widely.

"Yes, well, when trying to impress a lovely lady such as yourself, one sometimes feels one should display one's best attributes."

"I see. So then, you are trying to impress me?"

"I am."

"I think, perhaps it's working." She looked at him, her cheeks slightly flushed and smiled again.

How many smiles could he win from her today? He would make it his mission to find out.

"I'm glad." He stopped walking and turned to catch her gaze with his.

The emotion shimmering between them was already strong, and they had only begun their walk. "Miss Purity, I hope you do not think me forward, but my intention in visiting Elizabeth's sitting room was to ask you to accompany me on a picnic."

He held up the basket, and a thread of uncertainty crossed his mind. "I hoped you would oblige me, as I found you terribly intriguing last night and desired to spend some time in your company—alone."

"It would give me great pleasure to picnic with you."

He winked and turned to lead her further into

the garden.

They walked together for a while, without speaking, both enjoying the fair day. When they reached the fountains, Beau motioned to one of the ornate stone benches.

"Let's rest here a moment."

Eve sat down. Beau set the basket in the grass and joined her. He turned to her and caught his breath.

The gentle breeze had released a few strands of hair from her coiffure—they swirled around her face. Her cheeks were sun-kissed. Her expression expectant and her eyes pierced his heart, as she looked straight into his soul.

How to begin to know her? He had never before been so aware of another individual. Every fiber of his body responded to her nearness, a delightful anticipation sizzled over him as a welcome stranger. Never before had he strove to make conversation— flawlessly. She was more than exquisite, she was a rare gem, and he calmed himself as he sought to connect with her. He was careful to be gentle in his prodding, so as not to reveal his consuming interest.

But when he finally spoke, all guile flew from his speech; his true feelings were spoken aloud, without warning even to himself.

"How is it I feel as if we have some wonderful connection, when I have only just made your acquaintance?"

"I do not know, my lord."

"Forgive me for being forward, but do you sense this attraction between the two of us, or am I alone in my intuition?"

She raised her eyes to his expectant visage. He was so handsome. She took a breath. The sunlight revealed the intensity of his gaze, and her heart thudded rapidly against her chest. How could God have created such a perfect specimen? His maleness was unsurpassed, and it called to her as she observed him.

"I believe I feel what you are describing."

He looked relieved. "I thought you might feel it too. I again ask you to forgive my forward nature, but I spoke with the Earl about you this morning. I informed him of my decision to write to your parents in Paris, to ask their permission to court you."

Eve wished she were a tiny fly in the room during their conversation. "And the Earl's response?"

"He encouraged me to speak with you first. I thought I might be correct in my impression that you could be agreeable to courting me."

A lone sparrow sang a cheerful song nearby. The fountains' gentle music could also be heard, and Eve's heart pounded on loudly.

"Can you discern my thoughts so easily then?" She offered a tiny smile. She hoped it appeared somewhat aloof.

"Forgive me, no—I would never presume to know your thoughts." He looked at her with some consideration.

"Yet you have already spoken to the Earl?"

"Yes, and I have already written to your parents, although, I wanted to speak with you first before I have the letter delivered."

She looked at him skeptically and then toward the roses, yet inside she was delighted.

"I thought we shared a tendre."

"And what if you were incorrect?" Eve lowered her voice and looked back at him, "Tell me, what I am thinking now?"

He looked first into her eyes, their gazes locked, and then she watched as his gaze dropped to her lips. Slowly he raised his hand and gently caressed her cheek. He moved his fingers beneath her chin and tilted her face up to his. Their eyes met for a brief magical moment as he lowered his head.

The sensation of his lips against hers was more intense than anything Eve had ever experienced. His kiss was gentle, persistent, and filled with promise. He slipped his tongue between her lips. He tasted like exotic wine, intoxicating and debilitating. With every gentle thrust of his tongue, her body tingled wildly. She felt herself soar to a dimension of emotion she never knew existed. Her arms instinctively reached around his neck and pulled him closer. His arms encircled her back, holding her tenderly but firmly. She reveled in his embrace and dared to free her hand, slowly moving it to his face. She lightly brushed her fingers over his chiseled jaw, amazed at its smoothness and warmth. She brushed her finger over his enticing dimple, all the while her fingertips burning with sensations. A soft sigh escaped her. His lips, his arms, his scent were rendering her weak with desire.

Eve knew she should not be kissing him, but she was powerless to stop. He was everything she ever imagined in a man and so much more.

Beau felt his body's desire growing to a height he soon would be powerless against. His kiss had been answered richly—wildly. Holding her tightly, he smelled the sweet scent of vanilla, felt her curvaceous breasts against his chest, her tiny hand skimming his cheek. The pounding of his heart was the only sound he could hear...he gave up trying to think—he had now definitely lost that ability. He could only hold her, taste her, and revel in her succulent mouth. His manhood ached to be freed, to find release, but he would not, could not... Finally, some semblance of reality returned. He knew he had to release the angel in his arms. Slowly he drew away from her moist lips, a sigh of frustration falling from his.

Eve's sighs caressed his neck. He carefully

brushed a dark tendril from her face and met her dreamy eyes with his. He was quite unprepared for her statement.

"Perhaps you do have some intuition, my lord."

Chapter Ten

They sat for several moments in silence, Beau willing his emotions to submit to the rules of propriety and he assumed Eve was doing the same. Finally he spoke, "Would you care to picnic here, or shall we walk out toward the wooded area?"

Eve truly wondered if she could swallow food. She dared not go further from the house with Lord Beaumont. It wasn't that she didn't trust him to behave in a gentlemanly fashion—she was finding it difficult to trust herself at the moment.

"I think this would be a lovely spot for our picnic."

"Very well, then." He smiled and rose from their shared bench.

She watched him bend and open the large basket. After removing a floral cloth, he spread it over the freshly clipped grass. He then began unpacking bowls and serving dishes, some covered with small pieces of fabric. He also removed a bottle of wine, a jug of lemonade, plates, cups, and cutlery.

Eve enjoyed watching the way he set up the picnic. He moved with a rough grace, like a man unaccustomed to delicate surroundings, yet enjoying, becoming familiar with such things.

When he finished, he stood and offered her his hand. Grasping it, she let him guide her up from the bench, all the while enjoying the delightful feelings his touch rekindled.

Once seated, he began to remove the covers of

the various dishes the cook had provided.

"Allow me, my lord." Eve began to place assorted fruits and cheeses on their plates.

Beau watched her carefully. Eve was extremely aware of his gaze and wondered what he might be thinking. If he wanted to court her, he would want to know of her history, her family name. He might find out Purity was a fake. She thought it best to inquire about his ancestry instead.

"Tell me Lord Beaumont, where exactly are you from?"

"Please, Miss Purity, call me Beau. If we are to explore a possible courtship, we can dispense with some formality. Do you not agree?"

Eve began to feel the heat washing over her body, not just from his nearness, but also from his words. "Oh yes, well, Beau...you may call me Eve if you like."

"Eve." He spoke her name as if it were more than a word. As if it was a painting, a sculpture, a delicacy.

"Your name suits you, Miss Purity...uh...Eve."

"How so?"

"Eve was the first woman. You are the first woman who has captured my interest and attention so thoroughly and completely." His smile a slash of white. "Perhaps Adam felt the same way as he looked upon his Eve?"

"That sounds like the sort of flattery one would use on all the young ladies one might meet." She teased.

"It's quite true." He raised his dark brows, "All the young ladies named Eve, that is."

"And have there been many young ladies in your past, Beau?" A direct inquiry would do for her. She had little patience for playing at word games.

A trifle taken back he replied, "Truthfully, there have not been any young ladies in my past." He paused as silver tear-filled eyes begged for a place in his heart—he pushed the thought away. "I do not believe in trifling with the delicate feelings and emotions of young ladies."

"I find that surprising, my lord," she picked up a red grape and popped it into her mouth. "…and refreshing."

Beau knew she would expect him to ask all the usual questions in hopes of gaining insight on her standing in society, her wealth, and that of her family. Knowing her to be a woman full of mystery, he chose a different approach.

"Tell me, Eve, what is it you long for most in life?"

Her eyes filled with some bitter emotion he couldn't name and then she answered him slowly, "I long to have my family with me again."

Her answer somewhat surprised him. He had expected her to tell of dreams of marriage and children. In her answer, she showed again her uniqueness.

"Then you wish to go back to Paris?" He asked.

"I would not mind going back to France but having my family here would be more to my liking."

Beau filled both cups with lemonade and handed her one. "Will your parents travel here to be with you?"

"Oh, they would if it were possible, but my mother is quite ill at the moment." She bit her trembling lip.

"Have you any sisters or brothers?"

"I am an only child."

As an avid student of human nature and comportment, Beau watched Eve's body positioning. He knew she was erecting an unseen wall to protect one of her mysterious secrets. He would not guide her further into conversation that made her uncomfortable. He would be patient and win her trust—on her terms—in her time.

"And what of your wishes, my lord, what is it you most long for in life?"

"Ahh...that is quite the question. I have recently been asking myself that very thing."

"And what do you answer yourself?" Eve smiled playfully.

Beau sipped his lemonade and looked directly into her eyes. "I long for an intelligent friend. One with whom I can discuss some of my business matters with, who may offer insight in areas I may have failed to see. One who can bring me fresh ideas, matters to ponder, puzzles to solve. Perhaps even relieve me of the pressure I sometimes feel—a friend who simply by her presence could help me alleviate the aloneness I often experience."

Simply by her presence... he was looking for a lady friend. Did he think her to be a possibility?

"That is quite a revealing answer, my lord. I am somewhat surprised at your frankness." She looked up into his eyes and found they sparked with intensity. She guessed she might be in the running.

"And if you had such a friend, what would you be willing to offer *her?*" Eve asked half playfully and even more seriously.

"I would offer *said friend* all I am, my honesty, my faithfulness, companionship...everything."

"Protection from thorns and an ability to make cooks blush?"

"Don't forget humility." He added.

They smiled together. A gentle breeze played softly at their hair, birds happily chirped nearby, and one even found its way to the edge of the fountain. He busily washed himself, flitting and moving every which way. Beau eyed the bird, a faraway expression on his face.

He turned back to her. "I would like to stay on at Beckinbrook and spend as much time with you as you feel would be appropriate. I already feel as if we have become friends."

"You know so little about me. I am not certain I am the friend you are seeking."

"I believe I know my own mind. But knowing more of who you are is exactly what I'm proposing. When you wish to reveal any detail of your life to me, I will be happy to listen. I am a patient man; I have no desire to rush you or the situation."

Eve looked around the garden; the mansion rose to the south, glowing as if ablaze by the sun; a fortress, strong, sturdy, and immovable. To the north, she saw the woods. Inside their protective arms, one could find shade, refreshment, and freedom. For so long, her choices had been mostly taken from her hand but now she had a chance to make her own decisions. How much security was she willing to risk to step into the direction of her dreams for the future?

"Let us be friends then."

Beau set his plate down and leaned over toward Eve. His movement surprised her, but as his lips neared her own, she clearly knew his intentions.

Softly he touched his lips to her own, and she felt all care fall away from her heart. Instead, a thudding began to increase and warmly spread out to every nerve in her body. She gasped for a breath as his kiss grew more intense, and he pulled her into his strong embrace. She leaned against him, inhaling the wonderful scent of his masculinity. Her body swam in un-nameable sensations, and Eve dove deeper into these new delights.

He pulled away slowly, sighing. "Yes, I believe our friendship is already off to a roaring start."

They enjoyed the rest of their picnic. The well-packed basket was reduced by only a small amount, as the food and drink were hardly touched in favor of conversation, laughter, and stolen kisses.

****

Eve readied herself for dinner with excited anticipation. Reining in her emotions, she donned her dinner gown and through her open windows observed the sun slowly sinking into the countryside.

Last night's storm had cooled the mansion considerably. The day had been glorious as if rejoicing in relief and dancing gaily because the heat had finally lifted. Eve recalled the way the cool breeze had freshened the air during her picnic with Beau, but an inner furnace raised her temperature higher than all the past weather combined.

She pressed a cool cloth to her brow, trying to calm herself. So much had transpired in such a short time. She didn't want to allow the budding *friendship* with Lord Beaumont to overshadow the wonderful fact that her mother had been lucid for several minutes last night.

In the midst of her illness, the raging storm, and the late hour, she had connected with the woman she loved most in the world and had the opportunity to un-burden her heart.

Optimistic thoughts of her mother recovering filled her mind. She would only accept such impressions; any negative ideas were strictly banished from contemplation.

As beautiful of a diversion as Lord Beaumont presented, nothing would stop her from trying to unite with her mother and nurse her back to complete health.

At last, her face felt cool. She must stop swooning over him as if he were the sun itself. Many men had claimed to be straightforward and honest, desiring friendship or more, yet time often revealed their selfish ways and lax integrity. It would be best to hold back her emotions and observe him for a bit. Time would reveal his true character, and time would help her get her mother here to Beckinbrook.

She began to make her way to the dining room. The Fosters and gentlemen guests had left hours ago, and Lady Sands was visiting a nearby friend—the handsome and distinguished Lord Penchotte. The only ones at dinner tonight would be Donald, Katherine, Beau, and herself.

Eve entered the dining room just as the others came in from the terrace overlooking the garden. The room was subtle with candlelight and fragrant scents of the evening's fare permeated the air. Amidst the delicate and calm atmosphere, *he* stepped into the room, a tower of masculine beauty, his presence filling the space with a rich, warm color. His face, eyes, vibrancy, all bespoke of the aliveness that set the room spinning.

Donald held a chair as Katherine gracefully sat down. The two of them did not seem to notice just how much Lord Beaumont could affect a dinner. Lord Beaumont smiled in greeting and then moved behind her to help with her chair. The scent of him sent her mind reeling. Memories of their afternoon rushed over her with fluttering wings. She closed her eyes and inhaled discreetly.

"Thank you, my lord."

"'Tis my pleasure. Perhaps I should thank you for the honor?"

"There you go again, trying to flatter me with your charming ways."

Beau took his seat across from Eve. She was lovely tonight in a pale mauve gown. The silk barely skimmed her body, and the color set her skin aglow. For a moment, he lost his place in their teasing banter.

Recovering, he spoke, "When one speaks the truth, it can hardly be called flattery."

Donald spoke up, "It seems to me, my dear Katherine, that our guests are so intent upon each other, they have forgotten we too are dining with them this evening." He smiled wickedly, and Beau wondered if his words were meant as playfulness or if he was unhappy about his exchange with Eve.

"Nonsense. How could we forget the two of you, if not for your generous invitation, we never would have met." Beau reached for his napkin and laid it upon his lap. "Katherine you are lovely this evening, as always." Then turning to Donald, "And you, my friend, are dashing and very handsome, if I do say so myself."

"I'm glad my valet's work has met with your approval."

"Always," Beau replied absurdly serious.

A footman stepped forward and began to fill their wine glasses.

"Tell me, Beau, are things progressing well with Mr. Rockwell?"

Beau sipped his wine. He set his glass down, and looked into Eve's eyes for only a second before answering Donald. "Mr. Rockwell is exceedingly well as are his ventures. I plan on visiting him within the week, and you may come along if you so desire."

"I would like that very much. I believe his work is fascinating. His inventions will be very beneficial to many people."

"What kind of inventions is Mr. Rockwell responsible for?" Eve asked.

"Mr. Rockwell is a chemist. After exploring the world for the last fifteen years, he and his wife have returned to England, along with several hundred herbs they have collected in their vast travels." Donald answered.

"Mrs. Rockwell, is an avid botanist, she cares for their garden and growing house with more than an adept eye and green thumb. She knows what herbs can be mixed together to form new varieties and the proper times to plant and harvest these herbs." Beau added.

"When the herbs are harvested, Mr. Rockwell grinds them, or dries them, sometimes adding other ingredients, sometimes cooking them over a flame, and sometimes freezing them for months on end. When the recipe is as he believes it to be, it can be used for medication, and some of his inventions are being tested as liquids that can help identify unknown substances." Donald offered.

"That is fascinating." Katherine said. "How did you come to meet Mr. Rockwell, Donald?"

"Beau introduced me to him the last time we traveled to London. He persuaded me, quite easily I might add, to invest some funds in this highly valuable venture."

"So far, Mr. Rockwell has developed a liquid medication to help reduce fever and relieve the pain of some types of headaches."

"There are so many who suffer from unknown maladies, it sounds like Mr. Rockwell's work might be beneficial for some of these who suffer continuously." Eve said. Thoughts of her mother filling her mind as usual.

Katherine seeming to know Eve's thoughts spoke, "Perhaps with the funding Donald and Lord Beaumont are offering, Mr. Rockwell will have success in treating many of these mystery maladies."

If only she could bring Mr. Rockwell, a man she did not even know, to visit with her mother. Perhaps he might have some insight as to what was causing her illness. She would first have to bring her mother to Beckinbrook. Then perhaps Mr. Rockwell would come...maybe Beau would persuade him...maybe her mother would be well again. She looked across the table into his sapphire eyes. *Oh, Lord Beaumont, you may be so much more to me than a friend.*

He seemed to read her look and answered in kind. Eve did not know what his warm gaze meant, but she knew it was good.

The four were served a delicious meal, featuring an array of exotic seafood, cooked with gentle spices and served in a light butter sauce. The desserts then surpassed the meal in their flavor and appeal. As the meal ended, Beau asked if he could escort Eve for a walk in the gardens.

"I'm sure that would be fine." Donald said. "Perhaps it should be a short walk; it does appear it will storm again soon."

The breeze had increased, but it was still pleasant enough.

"We shall not go far or be gone overly long," Beau replied.

He offered Eve his strong arm, and she rose on trembling legs. She could not let him know just how strongly he affected her. Slowly and gently, with great restraint, she laid her hand upon his arm.

As they stepped outside, they were greeted at once with the cool night air. "I wish it were not so overcast," Beau began, "I should like to observe the stars with you some night."

"That would be lovely." Eve suddenly seemed bereft of thought. Being with him in the garden's darkness was heady stuff indeed. Thoughts of kisses and flutters low in her belly came to the forefront of her mind.

"Tomorrow, early, I plan to visit my father at our home, Hartford Estate. It is only a short ride from here. I should be back after the midday meal, at which time I hope to spend some time with you again."

Beau's words helped to break the tension of her unruly thoughts. "I hope all is well with your father."

"Oh, most assuredly. It's just that I haven't paid a visit in over a fortnight. And I believe my brother Paul has returned from his trip to Italy."

"Do you have any other siblings?"

They walked along, serenaded by cricket songs and gentle whispers from the breeze.

"No, it's just Paul and I. He is five years my junior. My mother died ten years ago, so it's just the three of us men in desperate need of some female influence." He smiled.

"I am terribly sorry for the loss of your mother."

"Thank you."

Eve remained silent for a moment, acknowledging the deep respect she felt for his loss.

"Well then, I wish you a safe trip, and I look forward to seeing you upon your return."

"Thank you," He paused, "Where would you like to walk, my dear?"

"Let's go to the trio of fountains, it is beautiful by day and even lovelier at night."

They walked there in silence; mysterious vibrations surrounded them with a sense of wonder and expectancy.

They turned the last corner to find the fountains and stone benches.

"Would you like to sit here?" Beau motioned to the bench they had shared earlier.

Eve sat down and he moved close beside her. Memories of her in the fountain aroused him as he fought to push them from his mind. Wordlessly he picked up her hand and pressed a kiss upon the underside of her wrist. He heard her sharp intake of breath and knew it affected her nearly as much as it did him. Again, he lifted the slender hand to his lips and allowed them to linger there. He smelled the alluring scent of vanilla and almost in fear, he raised his gaze to her face.

Her eyes swam with passion, inviting him to come and taste her lips. He leaned in closer and held his lips only a sliver of light from hers. He breathed in her breath and then, at once, met her trembling lips with his eager ones.

The kiss was strong and searching. Eve opened to his questing tongue. Their kiss deepened. Beau felt as if he were flying. Faster, harder, he soared into the night. Every nerve alive to the intoxicating sensation of her lips. She tasted sweet and womanly. Her breasts rose and fell against his chest and burned him through his waistcoat and shirt. He imagined lowering her gown, his hands and lips seeking the her curves. Those thoughts threatened to push him off the edge. He should stop while he still could, but he didn't.

The kissing continued and Eve pulled at the hair touching his collar as she arched her body against his. Finally, he could stand no more, he pulled back a tiny bit, and they both gasped for air. Their bodies were crushed together as they held each other out of necessity and desire.

"Eve." It was all he could manage.

She opened her eyes and took in the fire in his gaze. His cheeks were flushed and his breathing labored. She lifted her hand and caressed the side of his face. The friction from his nighttime beard prickled her hand. Before she knew what was happening, his lips were upon hers again.

They moved backward to her jaw, then below her ear. He kissed, sucked, and nipped her ever so gently. Wantonly she arched her neck in invitation, and he began to kiss her more frantically. She felt his tongue against her collarbone, and his hand began to move up her side as if he would meet it with his kisses. Her breasts throbbed and screamed to be caressed but he stopped again.

"I'm so sorry; I am carried away beyond reason." His ragged breathing confirmed it.

"I… um… certainly understand."

"Eve, I must stop now, or I fear I will lose control. You are so beautiful. I have never felt anything like this before, and the strength of it is overwhelming."

His words were like honey over her warm body. She understood the strength he spoke of, for she too felt the overwhelming passion.

"Lord Beaumont, Beau, please know, I have never kissed a gentleman before…like this."

He pulled her to him and held her there. "Nor have I. Thank you for the kiss, for sharing this night with me, for your kind words, your beauty, your scent. It's been quite an evening."

Her legs trembled in response to his words.

He stood to escort her back and she grasped his arm. Her life was changing. Had it only been a day since she'd met him? They walked back towards the manor, both of them thankful for the cool breeze that did it's best to ease the flush from their faces. As they approached the door, a drop of rain fell, then another but before the heavens released their deluge, they were safely inside.

Chapter Eleven

Eve arose early the next morning. She washed quickly, combed the herbal paste through her hair, donned a lavender day gown, and placed her spectacles firmly upon her nose.

She quietly descended the grand staircase in hopes of catching Beau before he left for his home. She made her way to the dining room, its delicious aroma calling to her empty stomach. She entered and found herself quite alone.

Sitting down, she scanned the gardens through the open French doors. All was quiet. A maid brought her tea and soon the sideboard was laden with steaming eggs, muffins, toast, and an assortment of meats. Eve filled her plate absently. She was hungry but so terribly preoccupied with thoughts of him.

In a flurry of activity, Katherine and Donald entered the dining room. They were speaking excitedly.

"I must take Glennora," Katherine began.

"It will be a long, hot journey. It might be better for her to stay here."

"I will not allow some wet nurse to feed our daughter. I wish to keep her with us."

"I have no objections, my dear. My only concern is for your comfort and that of our daughter."

Suddenly they noticed the dining room was not empty. Eve smiled. "Good morning."

Katherine rushed to Eve, pulled out the chair

beside her, and plopped down in a manner more of a ten-year-old boy than a mature Countess.

"Eve, John has sent word, Julia's time is near. Donald and I are going to depart for Scotland early tomorrow morning!"

Eve hugged her friend warmly. "How exciting! I do hope you arrive in time to help."

"So do I." Katherine spoke rapidly, "Eve, as you have probably already guessed, Donald and I are taking Glennora with us. Although, I know you would take wonderful care of her, I cannot bear to be away from her for such an indiscriminate amount of time."

"I understand completely. Let me help you prepare for your journey. I will pack her things, her little animals, picture books, clothes, and such."

"Oh Eve, thank you!" Katherine smiled at Donald, "We may be an aunt and uncle before the week is done."

Katherine and Donald filled their plates. They chattered a bit more about the needed preparations. After several minutes, they turned their attention back to Eve. "How are things with you, this morning?" The Earl asked.

"Very good, my lord." She answered flatly.

"Hmmm...and how are things between you and Lord Beaumont?"

"Donald, that is no concern of yours...I mean ours!" Katherine flashed him a look of indignation.

Eve's head snapped up. She looked from one friend to the other, not certain what to make of Donald's questions and Katherine's manner.

"Lord Beaumont and I are becoming friends. I enjoy his company and he seems to enjoy mine."

"Do you wish me to give him permission to court you?"

Eve's heart raced, she could feel her cheeks warming, yet she replied in as aloof manner as possible, "That would be acceptable."

"Acceptable?" Katherine shot her a knowing glance. "The man is handsome beyond belief, and he nearly swoons whenever he is around you. He is wealthy, titled, and from a good family. All you can say is acceptable?"

"I don't think he swoons," interjected Donald.

"I've seen it, he swoons." Katherine said. Her wry expression conveyed her amusement.

Eve's face felt like a fire had started in her cheeks. "I have only been acquainted with the gentleman for one day. Acceptable is all I can declare with any amount of certainty." She hoped this would be sufficient to end the current discussion.

Katherine offered her a look that said something between *oh sure* and *have you forgotten I can nearly read your mind?*

Eve occupied herself by fidgeting with her napkin and stirring her tea. She even hummed a little tune for good measure.

Seemingly, disgusted, Katherine turned her attention back to Donald, but spoke loudly and clearly enough to alert Eve that the conversation was for her ears as well.

"Lady Sands will be returning from the Penchotte's estate this evening. I would like to ask her to stay on and serve as chaperone for Eve while Lord Beaumont is here *courting* her."

"That sounds like a splendid plan to me. Is that acceptable to you, Eve?"

"Perfectly." She smiled so widely in exaggeration her cheeks ached.

Katherine looked at Eve once more, rolled her eyes, and then smiled at her husband. "I cannot wait to see my sister. Just think of all the fun Glennora will have with her new little cousin..." Her voice trailed off as Eve sat lost in her thoughts of stolen kisses and a future of her very own.

When breakfast was finished and it became obvious Beau had already left to visit his father, Eve decided to spend some time with Glennora as she packed for the trip to Edinburgh.

The nursemaid greeted Eve and then left to wash the baby's linens. Eve packed a small valise with all the baby's favorite toys and picture books. She packed a larger one with blankets, booties, dresses, and sweaters. She would miss the little darling, but she was happy for the family who would enjoy their trip together.

Before Eve left her room, she held Glennora tightly and kissed her auburn curls as she said her goodbyes. The baby snuggled against her chest, peacefully, sighing softly in her sleep.

When she returned to her chamber, an idea began to bloom in her placid mind. With Donald and Katherine gone, it might be the perfect time to bring her mother here. Lady Sands would be serving as her chaperone, but she might be easy to evade. Eve thought through various scenarios, imagining how it might all just work together perfectly.

****

Beau arrived at Hartford Estate early, filled with hopes for the future. His father was quite happy about seeing his son in such high spirits, and Beau was even happier to find his brother Paul back home from his travels.

After a large breakfast, the gentlemen retreated to Rudolf Beaumont's study. It was a deep, rich colored room decorated in shades of brown with splashes of rust and black to accentuate the mahogany furniture. The furniture was upholstered in dark hunter green colors and several paintings of Lord Beaumont's ancestors hung on the tall, cherry covered walls. It was a man's room to be certain, and the three men who tarried there fit the scene perfectly.

Beau looked up into his father's dark brown eyes. Although Beau and Paul both towered over most men they met, there was at least one man they still had to look up to—in more ways than one.

Rudolf was an imposing man, both large and well muscled; he stood several inches above six foot and was a force to be reckoned with—even in his middle age. His snow-white hair softened his otherwise rugged face, dark, ruddy complexion, and black-brown eyes. Although in appearance he was strength personified, in personality, he was a kind and fair gentleman.

Lord Rudolf Beaumont, Duke of Merdine was like Beau, the eldest son of a Duke. He enjoyed his days at the House of Lords so much so, that he chose the education and life of a Barrister. He found the law a fascinating, an almost alive profession, and enjoyed the opportunity his career afforded him to help others.

The three men visited with one another, Beau listening to Paul's tales of the Italian countryside, the beautiful cities of Rome and Venice, and his frequent trips to the museums.

"Are there many sculptures in the museums you frequented?" Beau asked.

"There are many sculptures everywhere in Italy. The fountains themselves are works of art as are the opera houses, the churches, and the carvings on the common buildings."

Beau imagined touring the country of his grandmother's birthplace with Eve, showing her the art she so loved and trying to experience it through her enticing aqua eyes.

"I would like to visit Italy myself. Perhaps in the near future."

Beau felt his father's gaze on him. Was he puzzled by his newfound calm, his preoccupation?

"Paul please give me a moment with father. I have a matter of some importance to discuss with him."

"I look forward to seeing you before you leave, Beau." Paul flashed a bright white smile as he left the study, closing the door soundlessly behind him.

"Let's sit." Rudolf settled into the well-loved leather chair behind his massive pedestal library table then thought better of it and made his way to the sofa.

Beau chose a comfortable chair across from his father.

"You are looking incredibly well, son." Rudolf smiled, "It is good to see you so...could relaxed be the word?"

"Relaxed may be the word, Father."

"Tell me, what is responsible for the talk of travel, the preoccupied look in your eye, and the relaxed state of my very meticulous son?" Rudolf leaned forward as if studying Beau's eyes and expression as he waited for his reply.

"Lately I have been making some decisions about my future, and after much thought and contemplation, I believe I may have arrived upon a solution to a problem I wasn't quite aware I had." Beau paused to see his father's reaction, yet he looked calm enough, "Until just recently."

Beau watched his father smile lazily.

"If I were a betting man, I believe I'd lay down a goodly sum in prediction of where this conversation is heading."

"If I were a betting man, I might not oppose you." Beau replied.

"Sorry to have interrupted... please go on." Rudolf smiled.

"As you are well aware, I have always respected your instruction to me regarding taking cautions to preserve my freedom. I have not dallied with women as the other noblemen do, but have kept myself until I could find a woman I might one day marry." He looked at his father and saw no disappointment or anger. He took a breath and went on. "I have met an intriguing young woman with whom I believe I may have some future."

Rudolf stroked his chin. Beau watched his expression carefully to attempt to understand his father's thoughts.

"Beau, I do assume she is of some standing and not just another title craving shrew? I would not speak ill of the dead, or of your mother, but frankly I've had more than my share of that sort of nightmare." He leaned forward and looked Beau squarely in the eye. "I believe I have raised a son wise enough to know the difference between a selfish seeker of wealth and a woman of virtue." Now he nodded his head slowly, "If I once had reservations as to whether you could distinguish between one type of woman and another, I no longer do."

"I knew you would understand my position." Beau exhaled in relief. Although he fully intended to court Eve, he would have dreaded having to go against his father's wishes.

Rudolf leaned back on the sofa. "Your uncle Nathan has filled your heart with many good things...good things that will help you as you take the title and good things that will help you choose a mate."

"Uncle Nathan was full of wisdom in many matters."

Changing the subject, Rudolf asked, "Her name?"

"Miss Purity, Eve." Just speaking her name aloud brought the warm rushing *feeling* back again. He couldn't wait to get back to Beckinbrook. "My business ventures often leave me tired and agitated, and I had begun to long for a confident, a friend, a person who might be there at the end of the day. I felt like I needed someone whom I could share with, who might listen and offer some comfort and insight."

"How did you meet her?"

"Donald and Katherine invited me to stay at Beckinbrook for a time. It has been ages since I have spent time in their company, and we decided to join together in several business opportunities." Beau leaned forward, excited in at the prospect of talking about Eve.

"While out walking in their gardens quite late one night, I came upon the most beautiful woman I have ever seen. I became acquainted with her and have found her to be quite delightful."

"What do you know of her family? Where is she from?"

"She is English, but has been living in Paris with her parents for quite some time." He exhaled, paused, and continued deliberately. "There is something rare... and wonderful about her."

"But what of her father, who is he?"

"Father, I have not asked her. She seems somewhat private and reluctant to reveal much of her identity or her history. I, having only just met her, would like to give her the opportunity to share her story with me as she feels comfortable."

"It's not that I don't trust your judgment, son, but a beautiful woman can make a man forget things he shouldn't which could lead to unwise decisions. Be careful."

Beau smiled. "Thank you."

Changing to a more relaxed tone, his father said, "Very well then. When can I meet the young lady who has captured my son's heart?"

"I would like you to meet her soon." Beau replied.

"Wonderful! I will look forward to it. Do you

know what else I look forward to, son?"

"I am almost fearful to ask."

"Nonsense! I am looking forward to some grandchildren to bounce on my knee. I have a need to spoil some little ones with sweets, and toys, and stories in the gardens. You and Paul have become far too stodgy for my tastes." He smiled.

"One thing at a time, Father."

"Yes, well remember, I am an old man."

The rest of the morning was spent in conversations pertaining to business, listening to Paul relate the perils and joys of traveling, and father and sons took a leisurely stroll through the well-tended gardens.

As Beau was getting ready to return to Beckinbrook, he remembered the question he wished to ask his father.

"Father, do you remember several years ago taking me with you on an errand to Kentwood Manor?"

"Vaguely, why?"

"I was just wondering if you could tell me anything about the family who lives there."

"As a matter of fact, I can tell you a great deal."

Beau's skin prickled.

"Lord Simon Purittson, the Viscount of Wilmington was the master when we visited. He hired me to draw up a very unusual will for his only daughter, Evelyn." He stopped and thought for a moment, "His health had been failing, and having no sons, he wanted to be sure his daughter would be well cared for in the event of his death. Having no male relatives to trust with this special request, he chose me to be the beneficiary of his will. The fortune he left to his wife was great indeed. In fact, it was so great; she never knew there was still a smaller fortune set aside for their daughter." He stopped as if to recall the events carefully.

"When I learned of his death, only four months ago, I went to the estate in search of the daughter. I was to give the funds directly to her and help her to invest them as she saw fit."

Rudolf moved to his desk and shuffled through the drawers.

"But when I arrived, I found his widow to be quite ill, unable to speak to me, and I learned from the staff, the daughter Evelyn had run away two months prior to my arrival. Something didn't seem quite right to me. The servants told me Lord Purittson had passed on over five years ago. Lady Purittson had remarried only two years ago, and after only several months of marriage to a Baron, Lord Martin Searsly, he then passed on."

Searsly—the name fell upon Beau like a boulder. Again those eyes haunted him, begged him to notice her, but he quickly pushed the unwelcome memory away.

"Something seemed strange to me. I have hired a bow street runner to help locate Evelyn as I fear she may be in some danger."

"Because she abandoned her mother?" Beau asked.

"According to the staff, Evelyn adored her mother and father. When her father passed on and her mother remarried, Evelyn even adored her stepfather. Apparently she is a very accepting young woman." He continued to sift through his files, "the fact that she up and left, while her mother was and is still quite ill, is certainly suspicious, not only to myself, but to every servant residing at Kentwood."

Finding a document, he quickly scanned the paper. "Yes, it is all as I have said." His father handed the will to Beau, "I fear she may be in grave danger. If someone has discovered the validity of this document and the great fortune she stands to inherit, they may wish to take her money and do away with her."

"Does she know she has inherited such funds?" Beau asked.

"That is another mystery. If she knew about her inheritance, why did she not come to me five years ago when her father first passed? Scratching his head, he added, "And if she doesn't know, then why has she fled her home and her dying mother?"

"Well, it certainly is a mystery."

"May I ask why you are inquiring about this?" Rudolf asked.

"For now, let me just say I am trying to solve my own mystery."

"It you learn of anything regarding this matter, will you come to me at once? I am quite concerned about the young lady in question.

"I will come to you." Beau smiled. "But now, I must take my leave." Aqua eyes were calling to him, his body responded promptly, ever their willing slave.

"It has been good seeing you, son."

"I shall return soon and introduce you to my...er...Miss Purity."

His words earned him a warm smile from his father, "Finally, something to look forward to." The men began to walk to the door. "Oh, I nearly forgot. This came for you yesterday." Beau took the note from his father. Seeing the familiar scroll of the writer's hand, he felt sickened. He would wait until later to read the cryptic missive.

Chapter Twelve

Beckinbrook stood proudly before the setting sun. Beau approached the manor, his thoughts full, and his emotions just beneath the thin surface of his once impenetrable will. He was eager to see her again. It was taking all of his inner strength to ride slowly to the stables, leisurely dismount, and first visit his room to bathe and dress for dinner.

He strode to the manor at an appropriate pace. It was nearly dinnertime, the end of the day, yet in his heart, it was the beginning. He smiled slightly to as he recalled with surprise, the ease in which his father accepted his news—even speaking encouraging words about Beau's decision regarding marriage.

As he mounted the front steps, a butler pulled open the great front door and Beau entered. The manor was quiet except for a faint whispering between two maids in the nearby hallway. He quickly made his way to his room where James awaited to help him ready himself for dinner.

****

Eve watched Beau from her chamber window as he walked confidently from the stables to the manor. Her heart caught as he neared and she faced anew his handsome looks and masculine form. He was so beautiful...Beau....how utterly fitting.

She closed her curtain and stepped back into the comfort of her room. It was nearly dinnertime, soon she would speak with him again, enjoy his charming ways, and perhaps even delight in a stolen kiss or two...or three. She exhaled as the warmth from her toes spread to her cheeks in anticipation of the evening. She smoothed her emerald green, satin gown over her stomach where flutters of unknown origin had seemed to take up permanent residence. How could a mere man make her feel such things?

She had never been the sort of lady to allow a gentleman to take liberties, not that she had let Lord Beaumont...Beau. But she had certainly come close—dangerously close to losing control. The emotions and feelings he stirred within her were as unknown to her as Lord Beaumont himself. Yet both were a welcome mystery, one that Eve was finding great delight in discovering.

The day had been laboriously long and dull. Even with Katherine's excitement and the packing and preparations, it just dragged on. But now, the sparks shooting through her veins, signified, the day had just become exciting.

She placed her spectacles upon her nose and inspected her coiffure once again before descending to the dining room. All was as it should be; she looked the very epitome of English decorum. Only her heart knew it was a façade. Deep inside, waves of anticipation washed over her, embers flared, and tremors flooded her normally serene disposition. Soon she would see him again.

Eve joined Katherine and Lady Sands in the parlor where Katherine was happily explaining her trip and the coming of her new little niece or nephew. Lady Sands looked lovely as always. Both women stopped chatting and turned to greet Eve.

"My, you look lovely tonight Eve." Katherine began. Her dark satin gown wrapped low around her petite shoulders, narrowing in at the waist and floating gracefully to the floor. "Your eyes are so alive tonight, my dear."

"Thank you, my lady. You too are lovely this evening." She replied.

Lady Sands turned to look at Eve and her mouth fell open. "Oh my, you certainly do look lovely, and so very...ready for dinner." She smiled more at Katherine than Eve as if they were sharing some private thought.

"Thank you, my lady. I was just admiring your gown; it is such a unique design." Lady Sands wore a midnight blue chiffon gown, with black swirls flowing through the material. With her dark hair and eyes, she was a vision to behold.

"My dear Eve, you and I seem to share a similar taste in fashion. My dear friend presented me with this gown earlier today. He said he saw the fabric and gave it to my modiste several weeks ago. It was quite a surprise, I must say."

"So may I assume your visit was enjoyable?" Eve asked.

"It is always good to see my husband's family. It reminds me of the many happy moments we all spent together, the holidays, the balls, the weddings, and the births."

Eve smiled and nodded as she began to imagine for the first time, enjoying some of the special moments Lady Sands had described.

"I understand I am to be your chaperone during these next weeks. I believe we shall have such fun with your handsome Lord Beaumont."

"I'm certain everything will be quite proper and perhaps a bit mundane." Katherine added. She looked at Eve as if to confirm her unspoken order.

"Oh I believe Lady Sands' glass half-full description of *courting* suits me a bit more than the *proper and mundane* you are suggesting." Eve smiled playfully.

"I believe I can speak plainly before Lady Sands when I say, be cautious. You have the look about you of a lady in love."

Eve was somewhat taken aback. "I assure you, I am merely a lady enjoying the company of a handsome and intelligent gentleman. That is the only look I have about me."

As if on cue, Donald and Beau entered the parlor to escort the ladies. The air nearly bubbled with an underlying current of expectancy. The moment he filled the room with his presence, their eyes met, held, and spoke to each other. It was as if they were alone, the sound of rushing water blurring the comments of the others, and the only melody Eve could hear was the music of his deep, inviting voice.

"Good evening, Miss Purity."

He watched her lips, as if in slow motion she mouthed the words, "Good evening." And in truth, the night was now complete. No dinner ever satisfied his hunger the way her presence satisfied the emptiness in his soul. She was perfection and more. He admired her lush figure, her gown hinting at the loveliness only he knew lay concealed beneath the silken folds. He fought the urge to groan, for never before had his commitment to remain a virgin until he wed seemed such an impossibility.

Just looking at her, he knew the love they could make would be unprecedented. The burning excitement he experienced simply by her nearness, was a clue to the passion they would share if he could only touch her—

Donald's amused voice broke into his thoughts causing him to remember there were indeed others present. "Shall we escort these lovely ladies to the dining room? I am simply famished."

Beau offered Eve his arm, and she gracefully set her hand upon it. She looked up and his heart jolted as he realized the intensity of feeling within the depth of her gaze. Could it be he was somehow now in heaven?

"I'll take these lovely ladies." Donald held an arm out for his wife and Lady Sands. "Two for me, only one for you."

Amused, Beau replied, "One is all I need."

The dinner was exceptional as always. The breads with warm honey and jams were served first, followed by vegetables basted in savory sauces and then meats spiced to perfection. As the five friends conversed, Eve reveled in a sensory bliss.

Every word he spoke was kind, smart, and full of his unique and witty charm. The candlelight set the room aglow with sparkling crystal, and the musical sound of tinkling silver upon china added to the ambience.

"As you know we will be traveling tomorrow, but what of your plans, Beau?" Donald asked.

"I believe I should like to visit Mr. Rockwell tomorrow. Perhaps Lady Sands and Miss Purity would like to accompany me."

Lady Sands looked at Eve. "Oh I should love to accompany you, Lord Beaumont. With the cooler weather, I feel much like being out and about."

"I too would enjoy an outing." Eve injected.

"I believe you ladies will enjoy it very much. Mrs. Rockwell has the most unique gardens. Even someone who knows little about flowers and plants can well appreciate the uniqueness Mrs. Rockwell displays in her growing and care of exotic herbs and such."

Eve was genuinely eager to meet this couple. Perhaps there was some way they could help her mother.

"I too had looked forward to visiting the Rockwells, perhaps when we return from Scotland." Donald mused.

"Most assuredly. I will take you at your earliest convenience." Beau replied.

The footmen began to place platters of

marzipan, tarts, and tiny cakes upon the table. Katherine surveyed the sweets with an expert eye for detail and chose one of each. Lady Sands chose two chocolate confections with whipped cream upon the tops, and Donald chose a marzipan orange.

Eve settled back in her chair. "I greatly enjoyed dinner; I am quite full and fear I cannot partake of dessert."

Beau smiled at her, "I too am quite full. Perhaps a walk in the garden would better suit us instead?" He looked at Donald, almost as if he dared him to refuse.

Donald tilted his head slightly, "I believe the night is quite pleasant. Perhaps Katherine and I will join you when we are finished."

"Very well then." Beau helped Eve up and escorted her outside.

The night was cool and clear, the velvet sky aglow with a million stars dusting the gardens with their silvery lights. The night could not improve. It was as if she walked in a glorious dream. This feeling had never before been hers to know. This must surely be the motivation for poets, musicians, and artists. And now she was privy to their secret muse.

Could it be love? Was it merely romance, perhaps a touch of desire? Or was it more than that, and if so, how could she know?

She left her thoughts and decided to allow her senses to indulge in Beau's nearness. He guided her slowly through the gardens, but instead of leading her to the fountains, they moved towards the east of the manor. Moonlight was plentiful and illuminated the gardens softly.

"Wherever are you taking me, my lord?"

"I may have a small surprise for you, Miss Purity." He spoke in a nonchalant manner, quite casually.

"I am not overly fond of surprises, my lord." Eve's attempt at playful banter held a grain of truth. For so long she had to take great care and plan her outings cautiously.

"Forgive me. I hoped if I surprised you, it might help to win me a place in your heart." He raised his eyebrows somewhat like an unaccomplished actor, and his dimple winked at her.

"I see. Well, I certainly wouldn't want to thwart your well thought out plan. But do tell, where are we going?"

"It is just a bit farther, you shall see it in a moment."

True to his word as they rounded the well-tended fruit trees, they came upon a large, white gazebo, set aglow with several lanterns. The gazebo had been a gift to Donald from Katherine when she learned she was expecting Glennora. They had often picnicked there and Katherine planned to hold a luncheon within in the weeks to come.

"Have you ever had the pleasure to see the gazebo before?" He asked.

"Yes, Katherine also told me she took great pains in having it built to the exact specifications as the one her family owns at their Dover estate."

"I did not realize you knew so many details about the structure." He turned and stepped closer.

His scent, the warmth of the night, and recent memories of his kisses intoxicated her anew. She looked up into his eyes; there she saw desire, and something more...

Gathering her nearly departed wits, she said, "The gazebo was a gift to Donald from Katherine to celebrate the baby he had given her."

"How thoughtful." Beau lowered his lips to hers and pulled her closer.

He felt her arms encircle his neck and her fingers play gently in the hair at his collar. He deepened his kiss, and she allowed his tongue entrance and met each thrust with her own. She was his, melting in his arms, and he vowed at that moment it would remain so forever.

Too soon... some unwanted voice of reason called to his consciousness. *Slow down.* He gently pulled away from the embrace.

"I fear I am in danger, Miss Purity."

"Danger?"

"Of losing my heart." He looked into her eyes and found them filled with emotion. "To you."

"But, we have only just become acquainted."

"That is indeed a truth, but Miss Purity, I assure you, when I find what I know I have been searching for, I am certain of it at once."

"And my lord, you are certain?"

"I am."

I am certain too. Eve wanted to reveal the secrets of her feelings for him; in fact, she had so many secrets to disclose. But if he were to learn of her deceptions, would he still feel as he did now?

Beau Beaumont was a man of great integrity. How would a man such as himself accept a woman who had run, lied, and hidden? Even if he understood her plight, would he still want a woman capable of such deceit?

"Come with me, I hear music playing." He took her by the hand and began to lead her to the gazebo. Just the tender feeling of his hand in hers caused the heat to spread throughout her body.

"Music, my lord?"

"Most certainly." He led her to the center of the gazebo, like a priceless diamond glittering in the night. But still, she heard no music.

"I believe I hear a waltz. Would you do me the honor?"

She stepped toward him, and he took her in his arms and began to dance with her in the lantern's glow. She floated with him across the floor melting again in his arms, and then he began to sing to her.

She didn't understand the words, as they glided together, but she reveled in his voice. A deep baritone, pouring out Italian words of love and passion. She knew at that moment, she was his.

They danced for some time, his husky voice fading to silence. Still he moved her to the rhythm that was theirs alone. He pulled her closer than was proper, and she clung to him—mesmerized by his presence. They danced amid the passion they felt for each other. Neither of them daring to stop for fear the moment would be lost. Eve knew if she danced a million dances throughout the rest of her life, none would compare to this one.

"Eve, we must return."

She sighed in his arms. "Yes, we must."

Still they clung to one another. "One more kiss?"

In answer, she tilted her head back. He met her unspoken request with all the passion they had stirred within each other. Their lips slanted perfectly together, tasting the sweet wine of their love, reveling in the essence of desire. She felt her heart soar and lost ability of any rational thought.

He savored her taste, memorizing every nuance of her fragrance—yes, vanilla, that which he had craved these last days. He found himself wanting her in ways he never knew existed and could barely wait to explore.

Using every ounce of strength, he lifted his head. He could hear her breathing, and wanted more than anything to cause her even more pleasure. *Soon...*

"Thank you for the dance." He smiled.

"Thank you. The music was lovely."

"Not as lovely as you are."

When they were back on the path, he stopped her again. "Eve, you are the most beautiful woman I have ever beheld. Every moment I am with you is more pleasurable than the last. Every word you speak intrigues me, calls me to know you more. Every minute I spend with you passes so quickly that I am left longing for more. I say without exaggeration, you have turned this once pragmatic man into a romantic dreamer."

His face softened as he spoke, and Eve believed his words to be sincere. She knew she must reveal her truth to him. As she gathered her courage, she prayed he might somehow understand why she had deceived him as she had.

"My lord, the words you speak to me are so kind and sincere, but truly how well do you know me?"

"I know you well enough to ascertain your goodness, your sincerity, your intelligence, your honesty."

"Yes, well, therein lies the problem." She cast her eyes downward, unworthy to look into those eyes of fire.

"I find no problem with you."

"My lord, Beau...I have secrets I have not shared with you. I wish you to know me, really know me, but these things I have kept to myself are difficult to reveal."

They came to a stone bench and sat together. He faced her and took her hands in his, "In time, perhaps you will come to trust me with your secrets. I am a patient man; I have no need to rush you before you are ready."

"Even so, so much about who I am has been hidden from you."

He gently plucked the spectacles from her nose. "Like wearing spectacles of which you have no need?"

She looked down—ashamed. "How did you know?"

"You tend to slide them to edge of your nose and

look over them when you converse with others."

Eve was afraid to meet his gaze, but she raised her head and looked into his eyes.

"Why would you want to hide those magnificent eyes of yours?"

Magnificent… his words warmed her… "I cannot tell you…yet."

"I can wait. But please, tell me this, have you hidden your true feelings about me? Are you simply stringing my heart along, having fun for a time until someone more to your liking is found?" His eyes danced with amusement, but his tone held a seed of seriousness.

"Surely a gentleman as skilled as you would recognize deceptions such as what you are describing." Eve nervously smoothed her gown, wondering if he was playing with her or truly serious.

"I have always thought myself astute enough to recognize insincerity, but now as my heart has been captured, I fear I may be blinded by that fact." He brought her hand to his heart for added emphasis.

His hand wrapped around hers was enough to send jolts of pleasure through her body, but the feeling of his firm chest, the heat of it, the pulsing of his heart, sent shivers to her core.

Eve struggled to regain her composure. She cleared her throat softly, "Perhaps, my lord, you can explain to me how a proper English gentleman such as yourself was given a French name and sings beautifully in Italian?"

"So we must turn our conversation from your interesting secrets back to my boring existence."

"My lord, there is nothing boring about you."

"My first nurse was Italian, and it was the first language I learned as a child. My father was careful to always have a governess for my brother and I, who could converse with us in our grandmother's tongue. He never wanted us to forget the influence of our mother's heritage." He leaned towards her to kiss her again.

Eve smiled and turned her head away. "And what of your name, Beau?"

"Kiss me first and then I'll tell you."

"Tell me first and *perhaps* I will kiss you." Her voice was soft and breathy.

He lowered his head until his lips were nearly upon hers and waited only a moment. 'Please," he whispered.

Their lips touched again, softly at first and then stronger, they held on to each other as if the garden was spinning off into the night and rode the wave of pleasure together. Finally, they pulled apart.

"I find it difficult to resist such a well-mannered gentleman."

"My mother did insist on her sons always being polite." He said a bit unsteadily.

"We shall have to add well-mannered to your lengthening list of charms." Struggling to regain some semblance of propriety, Eve continued, "Now, my lord, you must tell me how you acquired your French name."

"My mother chose the name. She simply liked it."

"Your mother chose well. I should have liked to have known her." Eve added warmly.

"My mother was…a unique woman."

Eve struggled to turn the conversation back to her identity. How would she even begin to reveal all she needed to share? She hoped he would be able to understand her reasons for deceiving him and perhaps have the grace to forgive her.

"My lord, Beau, I am not exactly as I appear to be—" she began.

"My dear Eve, I do not care if you are a chamber maid."

Eve straightened her back and gently withdrew her hand from his. "I am not a chamber maid...but I am not at liberty to yet share with you my full name and station in life."

Beau sat up straighter, "Do Donald and Katherine know of your *situation*?"

"Donald and Katherine are helping me. They know everything and have been more than gracious to me."

Beau took her face in his hands, "Eve, I trust Donald implicitly. If they are helping you, you can be assured, I too will do everything in my power to help you as well. You need not worry of divulging anything you are not yet comfortable with—I can wait. However, I will protect you and help you in every possible way."

Eve smiled shyly. "I thank you for your understanding, perhaps one day I will call upon you to help me..."

Chapter Thirteen

The streets of London were often fit for genteel people to walk about, mingle, and enjoy all the city had to offer. But in the wee hours of the morning, in the shadowed alleyways, murmurs could be heard, vermin scurried to and fro, and evil men hurried their evil deeds before the dawning of the early morning light.

It was at this time and place a man was sought and found. Gregory watched his footfalls carefully, not wanting to step in anything foul or splash disgusting muck upon his trousers. He moved through the alley—holding his breath out of fear and necessity.

The building he sought was crumbling and ominous. Several doors had no numbers, only peeling paint and sagging wood. He continued on— his frantic heartbeat reminding him to be cautious. Finally, he spied the number he was looking for, *Thirty-one.*

Gathering all the courage he could muster, he mounted one step and raised his hand to knock upon the grimy door. Before his hand touched the wood, the door opened.

Gregory inhaled as he beheld the shape in the doorway. It was taller than he was by at least two inches. Long, tangled hair stood out from its head, matted in places, and snarled much like the expression on its face.

"Wot do ye want?" growled the thing.

Gregory mopped a drop of sweat from the side of his face with his sleeve and wiped it on his trousers, the move helped to steady his already trembling hands.

He assumed his usual air of arrogance, although terrified. "I've come looking for Mr. Sorrows." He didn't dare extend his hand in greeting.

"I'm Sorrows, wot ye want?" The thing opened the portal a bit wider and motioned for Gregory to enter.

The room reeked of unknown filth and stale liquor. Gregory kept a fair distance between himself and the foul Sorrows—this meeting had all the markings of disaster. Sorrows turned and began to walk into the dark, rank room. Something twisted in Gregory's stomach as he heard a scraping sound. *Bloody Hell! What could it be?*

Sorrows quickly lit a lantern and set it atop a table. "Need a bit more privacy, do ye?" He motioned for Gregory to sit down.

Gregory, pressing his handkerchief over his mouth, swallowed once, and then cleared his throat; somehow, his voice still came out in gravelly whisper, "I've come to engage your services

"Have ye now?" The thing smiled and in the soft lantern's light, Gregory could determine the blackness of his eyes matched his teeth in a sickening way. Again, the stench in the room nearly overwhelmed him, and he longed to escape from the presence of this creature.

Gregory produced a miniature of Evelyn from his coat. For the briefest of moments, he waited for his conscience to object to the evil he was about to commit, yet it remained silent, and thus he carried on.

"Her name is Evelyn Purittson. She lived at Kentwood Manor until about six months ago, when she ran off." He fought to steady the quiver in his voice, "We do not believe she is hiding alone, and need to find her at once." Gregory revealed any information that might be helpful. Finishing, he pulled a heavy pouch from his pocket and set it upon the rickety table.

Sorrows picked up the pouch and then let it crash back down on the wood. "I'll take this now and another like it when I bring ye the chit."

Gregory would pay anything to have her in his clutches. "That will be acceptable." He stood to go.

"I believe I'll have me-self some fun with the chit before I bring her to ye."

Now, the fear that had accompanied him to this god-forsaken place vanished. "No, you shall deliver her to me unharmed, so that I may have my fun." Gregory rose to his full height and glowered at the creature.

"There may be a scrape or two, if she's a feisty one." Sorrows' eyes reflected evil in the lantern's light.

"Nothing more than a scrape or two then." Gregory, in control once again, turned and headed to the door, but the creature was quicker and more agile. It startled him, as Sorrows limped in a strange manner, with his left leg somewhat dragging against the dirty floor.

"Don't let me injury worry ye, I'll get her, and I'll get her soon."

"I'm counting on it, Mr. Sorrows. I am counting on it." With that he left instructions on how to contact him when the man had Evelyn, and then he hurried back through the maze of alleyways, back to the waiting hack, and as fast as the horses could run, back home.

****

Eve rose early to see Donald and Katherine on their way. She was happy to note Beau was already at breakfast when she entered the dining room.

"Good morning, Miss Purity." His deep voice did the loveliest things to her stomach.

"Good morning, my lord." She granted him a full smile, filled with a promise of so much more. Moving to the sideboard, she chose her breakfast from the tempting fare and sat across the table from him.

"Will you and Lady Sands be my companions today as I pay a visit to the Rockwells?" Beau asked.

"Why certainly!" Lady Sands entered the room just in time to answer Beau's question. She was dressed in red this morning and brought a refreshing brightness into their presence.

Katherine swept into the room next with Glennora in her arms. The lady's excitement founding a refuge on her flushed face. "Donald and I took our breakfast in our chamber this morning. We shall depart momentarily, after of course we say our goodbyes."

Eve rose and went to Katherine. She lifted the chubby baby from her arms and embraced Glennora tenderly. "I will miss you, little one." She planted a kiss upon her auburn curls and handed her back to her mother. "I wish you well as you journey. Give my love to Julia, and please tell her I will be calling on her when she is quite recovered from the birth." Eve embraced Katherine warmly.

"I shall send word when the babe is born." Katherine's smile conveyed her pride at the thought of becoming an aunt. She made her way to Lady Sands and Lord Beaumont and bid them farewell.

Donald stood in the doorway. "Shall we depart?" He nodded to the guests in the dining room and then escorted his lovely wife and daughter outside to the waiting coach.

Eve, Beau, and Lady Sands followed and stood beside the carriage as it rolled away. Eve hated herself for it, but as she waved her dear friends off, a tear escaped down her cheek.

"Miss Purity, they shall be back scarcely before we have the chance to miss them." Beau stretched out his hand to offer his handkerchief. For the briefest moment, their fingertips touched, and Eve felt what was coming to be a familiar longing for more. "My lord, it is but a tear of joy. The birth of a baby always seems to make me sentimental." She wiped away the tear and smiled up at him.

"As well it should. It is a miracle and a joyous one at that." He offered his arms to both ladies as they turned to make their way back inside.

They re-entered the dining room, and Eve returned Beau's handkerchief.

"When do you wish to depart for the Rockwell's home?"

"Whenever we are finished with breakfast, if that pleases Lady Sands—"

"Oh, my dears, anytime suits me just fine. I so love outings." Lady Sands sipped her tea joyfully.

Soon the trio was off. The grayness of the early morning was replaced by a brilliant blue sky and abundant sunshine. The temperature while warm was quite comfortable for travel.

Eve and Lady Sands sat on one side of the carriage, while Beau sat directly across from Eve. They chatted amiably and then fell into a comfortable silence. Lady Sands drifted off to sleep, and Eve relaxed back against the velvet cushions.

Beau discreetly watched her face as they traveled. She was working hard to disguise her eagerness in arriving at the Rockwell home, but he took notice of it and wondered why. His gaze traveled lazily beneath his lowered lashes, down her well-formed body—caressing the curves of her breasts and the narrowness of her waist. He relaxed in his seat and allowed himself to remember, only for a moment, the lush woman bathing in the fountain merely a few nights ago.

As his body began to react to his secret musings, he opened his eyes to find her stealing her own secret glance at him. He allowed her gaze to draw him in, looking intently into her eyes until his body seemed to smolder with melting fire. In her aquamarine orbs, he saw the same emotion reflected.

And there it was again, *the feeling*. The wonderful, insatiable craving he experienced whenever he was with her, whenever he was missing her and whenever he was dreaming of her. And then it hit him, *the feeling* had become a part of him, a need he could no longer endure. He knew at that moment he must have her, all of her, forever.

He must discover the mystery behind her secrets. He would move heaven and earth to relieve her of her burden and once she was free from it, he would marry her.

Beau smiled as his heart thrummed loudly in his chest. Although he had suspected his feelings for the beautiful miss, now that he was certain, he would take her as his own. And may God help anyone who dared stand in his way.

Eve reached inside her reticule and removed her fan. She slowly fanned her face, praying her emotions could not be read on her heated cheeks.

Oh, the things he did to her. She felt as if she were melting in her seat and wondered if he knew of the effect he was having on her. The secret places that longed for him in ways she didn't fully understand, yet, she was so very ready to discover the answers to the yearnings that assaulted her.

Finally, they arrived. Lady Sands sat up and smiled brightly, "What a wonderful ride, barely any ruts or holes."

Beau exited first and then turned to help the ladies out. As soon as Eve raised her head, she quickly drew in her breath.

There stretching out before her, in every direction, were the most amazing gardens she had ever seen. The first garden she noted surrounded the tiny white stucco cabin. It was at least twelve feet wide. Tall, colorful dahlias stood proudly against the walls, nearly reaching the roof. Shorter gladiolas, sunflowers, and other varieties, Eve had never seen, were next and of varying colors and shapes. The flowers continued in variety and height all the way down to the pale lavender and bright blue ground cover that made up its border.

If one looked to the left, a large rectangular garden with neat rows and stone pathways sat beneath the shade of several large trees. This garden looked to be filled with herbs, unusual plants, and small bushes, Eve did not recognize. She guessed this to be the medicinal garden; a quick look to the right seemed to confirm her thought.

To the right of the cabin, a large round garden, again with stone pathways held roses. Small wild growing blossoms, in pinks and whites, served as a hedge around the perimeter with sections of long-stemmed roses, tiny sweetheart roses, and large ornamental varieties filling in the circle in well planned sections. The center held a rough-hewn wooden bench and a simple fountain. The fragrance from the roses suddenly met Eve's nose, and she inhaled deeply, feeling like a flower fairy in flower fairy heaven.

"This is amazing!" Eve's face lit up.

"It truly is and that's why I wanted to bring you here." Beau turned to address Lady Sands and found her in the rose garden, walking the paths and inhaling deeply the combined fragrance of thousands of roses.

"Come ladies, I will introduce you to the artist and genius behind these lovely gardens."

Lady Sands and Eve smiled as they approached

the humble cabin. After only one knock, the door opened and a joyful greeting sung out across the trio.

"Ah, Lord Beaumont! Welcome." A rather short, rather stocky, smiling man stood before them. "And what have we here, not one, but two lovely ladies." He turned his head and yelled out, "Ginger, come at once, we have guests."

Beau made the introductions, and Eve could tell William Rockwell was a warm and wise little man. The four chatted excitedly for a moment and then were greeted by a petite, vibrant, fiery haired woman.

She quickly approached the group, "Lord Beaumont, what a lovely surprise!" A genuine joy spread across her face. "Please, introduce me to these beautiful ladies."

Again, Beau made the introductions. He had barely finished when Ginger exclaimed, "Come, you are just in time for tea. Please sit down, allow me to serve you some refreshment."

She motioned to a well-worn oak table near the fireplace. Beau stayed in the foyer with Mr. Rockwell—already deeply engrossed in conversation. As Eve followed the ladies into the dining area, she looked back at the gentlemen and for a moment, her eyes met Beau's. A small sizzle ran through her body, and she privately took delight in the sensation.

Turning, she joined Lady Sands at the table. The interior of the tiny cabin looked to be a combination gardening shed and art studio. Tiny bundles of herbs and flowers lined every rafter and filled every basket. They hung above the fireplace, between portraits and large pots overflowing with their bounty filled every corner. Their blended fragrance was both delicate and alluring.

Ginger carefully removed what looked like an often-used kettle from the fire and filled the bright yellow teapot that sat at the edge of the table. She then disappeared into a small room just to the left and quickly returned with a plate of scones and a tub of preserves. She spread the refreshments out for the ladies and began to pour their tea.

"What brings you fine ladies to our home today?" She spoke the Queen's English, with a unique accent.

Lady Sands answered first, "We are all staying with the Earl, visiting for a time. Lord Beaumont told us of your magnificent gardens, enticing us to join him here today."

"He certainly did not exaggerate in any way. I have traveled to Vauxhall and to Paris, and never have I seen anything that can remotely compare to what you have here." Eve added.

"Oh pish, William and I look upon these flowers as part of the family. We love them and enjoy their company." She smiled and Eve noticed grooves on each side of her wide mouth. Ginger looked like she smiled more often than not. Eve admired her bronze skin. She smiled to herself, knowing how five minutes in the sun would result in sunburn for Katherine, yet this redhead was so brown, her light blue eyes nearly glowed against the darkness of her skin.

"We are off to the glass house, Ginny," William called as he and Beau exited through the front door.

"Do tell us Mrs. Rockwell, how you have come to know so much about all these lovely flowers and interesting herbs," Eve implored.

Mrs. Rockwell set her scone upon her heavy dish of pottery, "When William and I met, I knew he had a love for herbs and healing. He came upon this passion quite naturally from his grandfather." Pausing, she sipped her tea and then smiled, "I too had a passion for things that grew; only mine were for flowers, and at that time, I liked only to paint them." She motioned to a beautiful painting above the mantle, a grouping of exotic flowers, orchids, lilies. And some so exotic Eve had never seen them before. "This was one of my paintings from the earlier days."

Waving her hand in humility she continued, "Anyway, after we were married, our first journey was to South America. It was there, I became interested in my husband's life's work."

"What was it that sparked your interest?" Lady Sands was staring intently at Mrs. Rockwell.

"We had been in the jungle for about three weeks. William had collected many different herbs and plants and had packed them carefully for our journey to our next destination, which was to be India." She picked up the yellow teapot and offered more tea to her guests. The ladies both refused, entranced with her story.

"As we were nearing the docks to set sail, a thin, dirty girl, quite young and quite upset called to us in her native tongue. I did not yet understand the language, but William turned and went to her immediately. After she sobbed out her sad tale, William explained to me we must hurry to her hut— her tiny son was quite ill and he hoped we might be able to help with some of the herbs we had collected."

Mrs. Rockwell's eyes glittered with tears as she went on, "When we arrived at the pathetic hut, we found a baby, lying upon a mat—he was limp and listless. William examined him and noted a large foul colored ulcer on the boy's leg. He immediately mixed his herbs with some milk, cooked it for a short time over the fire, and when it cooled, applied it to the boy's leg."

Her voice strengthened as she finished her tale, "Within seconds, the mixture began to work, fizzing away the infection. The ulcer turned pink, and the boy began to stir. William mixed up another concoction and gave it to the boy to drink. Upon taking several sips, the little child sat up. Color returned to his round sweet face, and he even began to make his usual baby sounds."

"How wonderful, how miraculous!" Eve exclaimed.

"Indeed." Lady Sands chimed in.

"It was at that moment, I became involved with these herbs. I saw first hand the good they could do when properly administered, and so I too have made the collecting and growing of them my life's work." She smiled as she took another scone.

"And what of the flowers?" Lady Sands asked, "Is that simply a hobby or has this fulfilled your love of art?"

"Well, as God would have it, sometimes William needs flowers for his formulas. I grow as many as I can to aid him with his remedies and concoctions. To enjoy their beauty and surround myself with them is simply a bonus."

"Mrs. Rockwell, you are an amazing woman." Eve began, "Please tell us about your travels."

****

After the ladies finished their chat and been given a tour of the flower gardens, they met up with the gentlemen and shared a delicious mid-day meal with the Rockwells. At last, it was time to depart, and although the trio had enjoyed themselves immensely, they were tired and ready to return to Beckinbrook.

"Please come to visit again, ladies." Mrs. Rockwell smiled warmly, "And you may even bring *him* along if you wish." She motioned playfully to Beau.

"Thank you for your kindness and your hospitality," Eve began, "this has been a day I shall never forget."

"My dear lass, it is our privilege to make your

acquaintance. Any friend of Lord Beaumont's is truly a friend to us." Mr. Rockwell's eyes reflected his sincerity. "Please remember us if ever you have need."

Eve would never forget them. She was hoping, against all odds, that Mr. Rockwell could help her mother. Her optimism didn't allow for doubts—only a need to find a way to bring them together. She would never allow this rare privilege to know this man of medicine to go to waste. He could hold the key to releasing her mother from the prison of her mind.

Beau, with the graciousness of a king, thanked the couple and then helped the ladies into the carriage. Ever so tall and gallant, he spread his goodness wherever he went. He seemed at ease as he joined them inside the carriage, a faint smile upon his magnificent lips. Eve's gaze focused on that mouth, that beautifully formed place God had given him to express his thoughts, his dreams, and his passions. Momentarily, all thoughts of her mother, healing, and the Rockwells departed her weary mind.

She closed her eyes, trying to collect her emotions. Perhaps tonight she would tell him her secrets. Perhaps he would help her bring Mr. Rockwell to Kentwood; perhaps they would once again share the magic of a kiss...

Chapter Fourteen

Dinner was a fine affair even though the master and mistress were not in attendance. Beau, Eve, and Lady Sands enjoyed delicious entrées, aromatic wines, and sumptuous desserts. When their bellies were quite full, they adjourned to the library.

With the heavy drapes pulled back, they enjoyed the stars that lit the darkening sky as the moon took center stage in all its glory. The evening's fair air washed over the content companions. Eve reveled in the sensations Beau silently willed upon her with his glances that dragged like honey over her body. Conversation had been interesting tonight, she learned even more about this intriguing man who was slowly invading her heart.

Eve was thankful for Lady Sands' presence. She had kept the conversation flowing when her mind wandered to the almost scandalous moments she had shared with the handsome lord. Lady Sands knew when to ask a question, or interject a comment, and the lighthearted conversation would proceed. Eve's desires fought against each other. She wanted to know the man who sat before her, know the circumstances which shaped his life, discover his dreams, hear his stories, and to learn more of the secret drive that caused him to be so great in strength and character.

She also wanted to taste his passions, again and again.

Eve suspected the feelings she had for Beau

were mutual. His gaze held hers a moment longer than what propriety dictated. She noticed his sapphire eyes on her lips, then flicker to her bodice. She delighted when his hand lingered upon her arm. She heard him exhale, knowing all too well the secret battle he fought within himself, this man who lived according to God's precepts.

Eve chose a spot on the settee, where she could enjoy the moon's warm glow. Lady Sands challenged Beau to a game of backgammon. They took up their places before the window out of which Eve looked, before she rolled the dice.

"I must warn you, Lord Beaumont, I am quite competitive when it comes to games." A wide smile and a wink were offered up in the way of a challenge.

"My dear Lady, I welcome the opportunity to be bested by you."

"Oh, you may say that now, but do not expect mercy from me when I have won your family estate and you must take up residence in my stables."

"I never gamble and would be a fool to do so with an expert *games woman* such as yourself."

Eve spoke up, "Is that true, my lord? That you never gamble."

"Quite true."

"You do not wish to risk that which you hold dear?" She looked into midnight blue eyes dancing with something mysterious and mischievous.

"Well, yes…there is that. But also, I could not in good conscience take money or property from a man who may not truly be able to stand its loss." Beau said.

Lady Sands rolled the dice and moved her piece.

"But if the man freely made the bet, why should you not take what you have won fairly?" Eve asked.

"Because, my dear lady, many men bet what they cannot afford to lose. It would be like taking bread off the table of such a man's family."

"I should have expected no less from you, my lord."

"But, make no mistake; you are correct in what you first stated." Beau rolled the dice.

"What did I first state?"

"I do not risk that which I hold dear." His tone was calm but his meaning obvious.

"I see." She watched him move his piece around the board sending one of Lady Sands' pieces to the center.

"And what if you are certain of victory, do you then wager?"

"If I were certain of victory, I would not need wager. Winning is reward in itself, especially when the prize is one long desired."

Oh. Why must he speak of desire? Eve brushed her sweaty palms across her gown, as nonchalantly as possible. Had the room suddenly grown warmer? Lady Sands bit her lip, trying not to smile, but Eve saw her clearly, and Beau seemed not to care about the discomfort his words has caused.

Charles, one of the younger footmen came into the room bearing an envelope upon a silver tray. "Miss Purity, this just arrived for you. I was asked to deliver it to you at once."

Eve picked up the letter and recognized the handwriting as Mary's. A slight tremor ran over her heart, and she offered up a silent prayer, *Oh Lord, please let my mother be well.*

She sat looking at the letter. Beau and Lady Sands had ceased their conversation, only the shaking of the dice could be heard and the moving of the pieces. Eve composed herself and then looked up at her companions.

"Please excuse me for a moment." Her trembling smile betrayed her calmness, and she hurried from the library.

She made her way to Elizabeth's sitting room and was grateful for the lantern burning within. She sat at the tiny escritoire and tore open the envelope. Taking a breath and gathering her courage, she read,

Dearest Evelyn,

I realize you must be concerned about your mother, rest assured, her condition has not changed. I am writing to advise you of some interesting developments here at Kentwood.

Gregory has fled home. There are men looking for him, they claim he owes them several thousand pounds. I do not know where he has run off to, but he took several trunks and left enough funds behind to run the estate until at least winter. He did not leave us word as to how we may contact him, only saying he would be sure to contact us before he returns home again. He does not know that some of the other servants and I know about the men who are looking for him.

I hope you are well my dear. I am caring for your mother as always and will continue to do so as long as you wish. Take caution, Evelyn. I do not know the depths to which these men seek him. They may also seek you to settle his debts. I will send word if I discover anything else regarding this matter.

Yours,

Mary

Eve exhaled in relief. Her mother was still holding on. She read the letter once more and then again to be certain she had not missed a thing, then carefully held the corner of the paper to the lantern and watched as its flame transformed it to ash. She dropped the burning letter into the fireplace along with the envelope and waited till the job was finished. Then straightening her skirts, she turned, and made her way back to the library.

Beau rose when she entered, and she took her

seat upon the settee again.

"Is all well, my dear?" Lady Sands asked.

"All is quite well, thank you." Her relief so intense, she could not hide a smile.

"Very good. Would you care to challenge the winner of our game to a match?" Beau asked.

"As I am not an avid player, I fear Lady Sands would have me living in her stables before long."

Standing, Lady Sands replied, "Nonsense. Your Lord Beaumont has already won. I am retiring for the evening, so your wager will be with him." Grinning wickedly she added, "We already know, he does not wager."

Beau stood as Lady Sands made her exit. "Thank you for a challenging game, I scarce remember having such fun."

She shook her head, "You are welcome, my lord. Take care with my dear charge tonight. I am trusting you both will retire soon."

"Yes, my lady. I shall try my luck against your worthy opponent and then it's off to bed."

"Very well. Good night dears," she called as she left the room.

Eve took Lady Sands' place as Beau arranged the pieces to begin playing.

"I truly enjoyed dinner tonight." Beau began.

"Cook has out done herself, most certainly."

"Yes, but I was referring to the company, I enjoy having dinner with you."

"Thank you." Eve felt her cheeks flame just a bit.

"How would you say our courting is progressing?" He asked.

"How would *you* say it is progressing?" She looked up and discovered her mistake at once. Emotions poured off of Beau, so much so she wasn't sure she even knew her name. And just what was her name? Was she Evelyn? Or was she Eve?

Was she the adoring daughter and caretaker of her dear mother? Or was she a young woman falling in love with a handsome gentleman? If he knew she was Evelyn, would he still feel the same?

"I think our courting is moving along splendidly. I am eager to speak with your father regarding our relationship."

Eve rolled her dice and made her move. "But there is still so much I must tell you."

"My heart has told me all I need to know. I would like to have dinner with you every night and picnics in the afternoon, and strolls along the garden paths late in the evening. Do you desire those things as well?"

Beneath her satin gown, her heart thudded wildly. Must he continually use the word *desire*? "I do desire those things...I just need some time to resolve a very important situation."

"Then let me help you." The dice sat idle upon the board. He reached out and gently grasped her hand. How could such a subtle movement evoke so many sensations?

Dropping his warm hand, Eve stood up and paced the room. Back and forth, she walked upon the lavish carpet.

"I can help you. I know I can."

Everything about him was upright, honest, and straightforward. Would he be willing to steal a sick woman from her bed and bring her here to Beckinbrook? Was she completely mad to even think about asking him such a thing?

"My lord, I cannot ask you to do something that might compromise your unwavering principles." She stopped pacing and looked at him. Had a shadow crossed his golden countenance?

He stood, crossed the room, and pulled her into his strong arms. His face just inches from hers—his warm breath caressed her cheek, "Why should helping you compromise my principles?"

Fear, desire, longing, and passion all seized her at once. His hands upon her arms sent shivers of delight over her body. Her knees felt weak and her head, suddenly light.

"Because it will..."

Before she could consider what to say next, he lowered his mouth and sought the depths of her lips. Eve melted in his arms. Her body relaxed against his strength, and she desired to remain there within the comforting protection of his embrace. She wanted to trust him—yet couldn't bear the thought of losing him. What would he think of her rouse?

After several heavenly moments, they both pulled away from the kiss.

Huskily, he whispered, "Let me help you."

"I want to."

Beau moved away from her. He motioned to the settee, "Please, sit down. Let's discuss this." He then moved into the hallway. Several moments later, he returned with a tray of tea.

"It's quite late for tea, is it not?"

"I have all night. I want you to talk to me, tell me what you can. I don't want to press you, I just want to help."

He poured them each a cup of tea and then positioned a chair across from Eve.

"Please tell me what needs to be done."

Eve made her decision—she couldn't move forward with their relationship if she kept her secrets. Even though he may not choose to help, he would never betray her trust. She carefully stirred her tea and then spoke without looking up.

"I need to bring someone here to Beckinbrook, someone who is quite ill."

"Very well. I shall send my carriage at once and we shall bring the person here."

"Beau...we cannot let anyone know we are

taking her, and the servants here can not find out."

He paused, for a moment before questioning, "May I ask why?"

She set her teacup down carefully and met his inquisitive gaze. "Someone is looking for me, someone who would very much like to hurt me. If he knows my…friend has been taken, he may find a clue as to where I am."

"You have no need to fear, I will keep you safe from this person. Why does he seek to do you harm?"

"He wants to punish me for embarrassing him and for refusing his advances."

"But my darling, there are laws to protect you from scoundrels such as you are describing. We can obtain the assistance of the magistrate. With Lady Sands as your chaperone and under the care of the Earl, you are quite safe and living within what propriety dictates."

Eve stood and began to pace about the room again. "I have no protection from the laws. In this instance the law is in *his* favor." The intensity and fear of the conversation became evident in an uncomfortable tightening at the base of her neck. She absently began to rub it.

Beau stood also, "Eve, are you married to this man?"

She quickly turned to face him, "Of course not."

"Then how is it that you are left unprotected by the law?" He crossed over to her, standing only inches away.

"He is my guardian…he is my brother."

Beau approached her, lifted his hand to her neck, and began to rub it. He worked the tightness from her neck and shoulders and finally exhaling, she turned to face him.

His silence caused her hopes to plummet. What must he think of her? A well bred, titled man, so strong in his convictions and committed to holding such high standards. As she lifted her gaze to join with his, instead of loathing, she saw acceptance.

"My lord?" A tear escaped and then another. An unexpected trembling shook her frame.

He pulled her into another embrace, "Why are you crying?"

"What must you think of me?" She hiccupped.

He pulled away but held her gaze, "I think you are an exquisite young lady who has been the victim of some unfortunate circumstances. I think in your attempt to keep yourself safe, you chose to rely on two very reliable souls and now again you have chosen wisely. You are allowing me to know you and to help you."

"But will helping me compromise the very essence of who you are?"

"Absolutely not." She felt his hands tighten slightly on her arms as he continued, "I want much more than to court you. I want you to be a part of my life always." *I want you to be my wife.* He didn't say it out loud, but Eve hoped he would soon.

"There is still much you do not know." She shook her head.

"Then tell me all there is. Please."

Eve slowly sank onto the settee. He sat beside her, offering his silent support. "Very well." She began, "My real name is Evelyn. Evelyn Purittson." She looked up at him and watched a smile spread across his chiseled face.

Chapter Fifteen

One thought tumbled into another as Beau began to process Eve's words. She relayed her story, beginning slowly, shyly, then gathering courage and speaking it out confidently.

With every word, a question was answered—yet several more arose. Here before him was the young lady his father had been searching for, the heiress to a substantial fortune. Muddled facts emerged from the fog of the night with clarity as he realized it was her mother she sought to bring to Beckinbrook.

Still she spoke as if a dammed up wall had finally tumbled down, flooding the air with her musical voice spilling her sad tale. Yes, unasked questions were being answered, but as Beau encouraged her to continue a panicked feeling began to uncoil in the very depths of his stomach. It was that name, that name that haunted him, that woke him from peaceful sleep, silver grey eyes swimming in tears. *It couldn't be the same Searsly—couldn't be.*

But even as he tried to deny the facts that were rising up to hold him captive in a wall of self-loathing, deep in his soul, he knew the truth. His deepest secret, his darkest memory had come back to seek its revenge at the most inopportune time. The bony fingers of the past had come to steal the promise of the future.

As Eve unburdened her heart, she observed the face of the man she had come to know so intimately. He nodded and asked questions but as she answered them, something in his countenance changed, the man of such strength of character and confidence bore a look of uncertainty.

As she went on with her story, he began to look exceedingly more uncomfortable. "My lord?" He seemed as if he was absent somehow, lost in his thoughts, a wide gulf now dividing the closeness they shared only moments before.

"Eve. Evelyn. My darling, I will help you." He spoke now as if it pained him. "I will bring your mother here as soon as it is safe. We shall see to it she receives the finest care a physician can provide."

Finally, her fervent wish had come true, she should be jumping joyfully, celebrating this opportunity to be with her mother again, in safety, but she could not. Eve felt the hollow shell of heartbreak instead. Perhaps he could not abide her deceptions, her lies. As a gentleman of highest regard, he would never reveal this to be the truth.

She did not speak; looking into the eyes once filled with liquid fire, now plagued by fear, sorrow, and hopelessness. What had she done? She had alienated him, pushed him away with her underhanded tactics. But she must hear it from his very lips, she could not endure the distance and silence so inconsistent to the man she had come to desire.

"What is it, Beau, what is troubling you?"

Searsly will never agree to a marriage between the two of us. If he gossips about the incident, it will produce a scandal of epic proportions. Your name will be ruined, and you deserve more, so very much more."Is there any chance of reconciliation between you and your stepbrother?"

To that her eyes widened, she sat up a bit straighter, "I certainly do not wish any such association. He is an evil man, and he will not stop until he has his revenge on me."

Lisa Hill

Beau already knew as much. "I will keep you safe, my dear." He moved to sit beside her, the full moon's glow bathing the library with romance and mystery, he was drawn to her side, a silent plea went out from her body, calling to him, and in return, his body answered, *I am here.*

But he didn't take her in his arms. He sat, stiffly—the aqua eyes he looked into begged for the familiar intimacy of his soul, but he knew now, he was no longer free to give it.

"When shall we go for my mother?" She asked.

"I shall arrange for my own carriage. I will take the precautions necessary to avoid detection from the servants, here and at Kentwood." He absently looked out the window into the darkness, letting it surround him and seep into his weary core. "I will do my best for you, Eve...er...Evelyn."

"You must call me Eve. I have grown accustomed to the name." She looked beseechingly and even sadly at Beau. "I believe I will retire to my chamber, I wish to begin working out the details to our plan at once."

The *feeling* he had questioned, craved, and even reveled in, he now pushed away. How much could he truly care for her if he dared risk his most secret sin becoming her ruination?

He rose and ran his hand through his hair. He looked around the cozy library, a place only moments ago filled with carefree conversation, sultry words, and the promise of love. The feelings evoked here would no longer be welcome to him. He mourned their loss for a moment, then smiled sadly at Eve as she made her exit.

Disgusted, his shoulders bore the weight of shame and regrets. He thought how a real man would be raging with anger at the thought of a blackguard like Searsly touching such a dainty rose, instead he found himself paralyzed with the irony of it all, ashamed and regretful. Finally, he too climbed the stairs to seek his rest.

Be assured your sin will find you out... he tried to ignore the roaring acid of his conscience. He thought he had laid it to rest firmly and finally in the past, but now its ugliness sought to devour him once again.

He numbly removed his clothes, letting them lay where they fell. He thrust his hands into the tepid water, and splashed the wet contents on his numb face. Stalking across the room, he fell upon the bed, while the memories he fought so long and hard once again played with his defeated emotions.

****

"Dance with her." His brother Paul smiled mischievously.

Looking across the crowded ballroom, aglow with candles and swirling pastel gowns, a girl sat near the shadowed corner. Beau noticed her demure little smile, her fingers tapping discreetly upon her pale blue gown, and her head bobbing to the left and to the right ever so subtly. Behind her, her brother Gregory stood—arms crossed like a sentinel guarding a treasure, yet in his eye, he carried the look of a hang-man—who for a high price, would sell his beloved sister to the devil himself.

Beau walked across the floor, ignoring the married and single ladies who swirled gracefully around him. He was ashamed by the secret looks that lingered a moment too long and the exhalations of breath as he strode through the throng.

"May I have this dance?" He bowed before her.

She rose slowly and whispered, "I'd be delighted."

Felicity joined Beau, and Gregory offered a perfunctory smile. How could lechery and warning be so succinctly conveyed in the twisting of one's lips? He pondered this momentarily, as he escorted the young lady to the dance floor.

They joined other couples who waltzed with perfection, gliding across the floor as if it were ice.

"How lovely to see you again, Lord Beaumont. It is good to have you back in Bath." She batted her eyelashes.

"I am very glad to be home, although I enjoyed my travels. What have you been keeping yourself busy with these last several months?"

"I just finished with my studies. I am helping Father run the household and spending afternoons calling on my friends." She smiled shyly, but Beau sensed something more behind her innocent expression.

"Your father is lucky to have such a fine young lady to rely upon. I'm afraid at our home; we are forced to endure nothing but masculine company and conversation. It is all quite dull, I assure you." He carefully guided her around and smiled into her silver grey eyes.

She was a lovely young miss. Ribbons and lace embellished her light brown hair and adorned her modest dancing gown. She danced well, as if she had practiced often, yet she wasn't guided by an inner drive. Her movements lacked passion.

Beau appreciated her calmness. He was not looking for a bride, and his reserve conveyed this to all who knew him. It would not do to dance with a young lady, only to have her imagine feelings that just were not there. Miss Felicity Searsly was of a practical nature, not one given over to romantic notions.

When the dance ended, she drew him away from where her brother stood guarding her empty chair, to a secluded corner of the room. "My lord, would you care to join me in Lady Sutherby's sitting room for lemonade. I understand she has a collection that may pique your interest."

"We must ask your brother to accompany us. I wish no harm to come to your reputation." He nodded across the room to Gregory.

"Oh dear, I hate to interrupt his plans, Gregory has his eye on a sweet young lady. He would be dreadfully angry if he missed his opportunity to dance with her. We will only be a moment or two."

"Then my dear, if you are certain your brother would not object, I would love to see this...collection is it?"

"Yes, I am certain you will find it alluring. Let me go ahead and be sure Lady Sutherby has the room lit, come as soon as you are able."

"I shall bring the lemonade." He smiled as she walked out of the ballroom.

Before he could fetch the drinks, Paul arrived smiling broadly. "What has you in such a state?" Beau asked.

"Miss White just gave me the nicest dance. I believe I shall ask for another." He winked.

"Don't break her heart, brother. She's an innocent girl who looks at you as if you carved out the seas with your own hands."

"I like that in an innocent girl." He moved his head from side to side, proud as if he had orchestrated just that task.

"Just be careful not to lead her to believe there is more to it than just a dance."

"Aww, you know how to ruin a man's fun."

"Well, I promised Miss Searsly I would look at a certain collection with her. I shall return momentarily." Beau plucked two glasses of cool lemonade from a footman's tray and made his way down a long, narrow corridor. The sounds of music and voices became faint whispers.

At the end of the corridor, he turned left. The sitting room would be the last door on the right. He wondered what sort of collection Lady Sutherby had acquired. The last time he had come to the castle, there had been a collection of rare butterflies from varying places around the world. She collected hats, spoons, bells, small mirrors, and even lady's pistols. Her eccentricities were well known and complimented by the ton.

He approached the door, and as he pushed it open with his foot, he realized, he must have arrived first. Miss Searsly was not there, and there was only a small lantern burning on a dark carved table across the room. He set the glasses down upon the mahogany side table and for a moment admired the unusual bamboo decoration on the piece. Lady Sutherby certainly had a penchant for acquiring unique items.

Beau moved deeper into the room, looking amidst the many objects d'art for another lantern. Turning around, he saw her standing in the far corner.

"Lord Beaumont?" She spoke as if there was some question as to who he might be.

"Miss Searsly, let me light another lamp, then we can enjoy the collection properly." He smiled and continued to look around the room.

He heard her skirts swishing as she approached him from behind. Something suddenly seemed amiss. Before she reached him, she softly closed the door, darkening the room considerably. An uncomfortable knot began to twist in his stomach as he turned back around. He almost fell backward at the sight that greeted his virgin eyes.

In only a moment, she had lowered her gown and her chemise. She stood still before him, bearing her small breasts. The previously innocent look in her eyes—replaced by something darker—primal. Beau tried not to look, but he couldn't resist as his eyes betrayed his intentions.

"Miss Searsly...please, this isn't proper." He

moved towards her—then stopped, not knowing if he dared get any closer.

"You may touch me if you like." She invited in a shaky whisper.

Pulled by an invisible magnet, he took another step closer, the image of her burning like a smoking brand into his brain, "Miss Searsly...please." He did not know if he begged for her to clothe herself, or for her to let her gown fall completely to the floor.

He reached her and stopped—his heart thudding wildly in his chest. Somehow, he found his voice, "Miss Searsly, let me help you." He grasped the sleeves of her gown and yanked them up upon her shoulders. "Your gown, it must have a broken clasp or a button." He looked toward the closed door, desperate for escape. "Let me send a lady's maid to assist you."

Felicity's face changed from a sultry peach, to an emblazoned scarlet. Her eyes began to form tears, which she struggled valiantly to contain. "My lord...you do not want me?" It was almost a whisper. Her gaze cast downward.

"Miss Searsly, you are a lovely young lady, but I have decided to keep myself pure until I marry." Did he really think she would understand as she stood there humiliated? Did he even understand himself, how he could resist such a tempting young thing, when all the other gentlemen of his standing would quickly sample the sweets she so innocently offered?

A choking sob escaped her mouth, and tears washed her cheeks, falling upon her pristine blue gown. Beau reached for his handkerchief, and she took it, letting one sleeve fall and exposing her breast again.

It was at that moment, the door to the sitting room opened, framing Gregory Searsly in the dim light. He saw the flickering lantern and his sister's dishabille on display.

Gregory stepped into the room, moved forward, and his fist struck out and landed with a smack upon Lord Beaumont's face. "You bastard!" he bellowed.

"No, please, Gregory..." Felicity tried to stop his attack but to no avail.

Another paltry punch was thrown; Beau easily blocked it and then held Gregory's hand tightly. "You are misunderstanding the situation."

"What do you take me for? I misunderstand nothing," enraged, he continued, "You will marry her, you filthy scoundrel!"

"Gregory, listen to me." Felicity had managed to right her gown; she stood before her brother and looked up into his eyes. "I tried to seduce him. He would not have me." Another tear rolled down her wet face. "I will not have a man who does not want me."

Gregory's breathing began to slow; he shook himself out of Beau's grasp. His beady eyes shone hatred. "Is that so? My sister isn't good enough for the likes of you?" Saliva pooled in the sides of his mouth like a rabid dog.

"I have nothing but the highest regard for your sister. She is a lovely young lady, but I would not take her virtue. It would be sinful, she could become with child. I am not that kind of scoundrel."

"Oh, I see, you are quite a man of honor, aren't you?" His face twisted in hatred.

Beau sought to calm him. "Any man would be fortunate to have a gentle miss such as your sister, but I have my convictions."

Felicity slid into a chair in the corner. "Gregory, please, just let him leave." She lifted her head, the stain of embarrassment lighting her cheeks. "We shall speak of this no more." She gestured with her hand, for Beau to leave.

"Good evening, Miss Searsly. I do heartily

apologize if I have given you the wrong impression." He bowed and looked for only a moment at Gregory. The moment was enough to know the hatred and vengeance that lived inside this small man's heart.

"Good evening Mr. Searsly." He nodded and left the room.

If only that had been the end between the three of them, but ten months later, while Beau diligently worked in his father's study, Gregory submitted his card for calling. The winter winds whistled heartily outside, whipping stray snowflakes about in a frigid frenzy. The fire warmed the room, and the only sound inside was that of Beau's pen marking upon his ledger.

"Someone here to see you, sir. A Mr. Gregory Searsly."

Gregory staggered through the open library door. "You!" He pointed a shaky finger at Beau.

"Mr. Searsly...can I be of some service?" Beau pulled out a chair for the well-imbibed man.

"I'm not sittin' in yur fancy chair, you rotten bastard. You killed her."

"Mr. Searsly, what are you talking about?"

Searsly dropped into the chair, his narrow shoulders shaking in great sobs. "She's gone and hung herself, my sister...because of you...you, all high and mighty, telling her she wasn't good enough."

Beau stood perfectly still in shock. "When?"

"We just now found her. I'd kill you, you bloody weasel, but my father is courting a woman with a fat purse, and the scandal would scare her off."

Beau re-seated himself. How could she take her own life, over something so minor, a man she barely knew? And why now, after all these months?

"I couldn't have known she would do such a thing." He ran his hand over his aching skull. "I am sorry for your loss."

"For weeks she moped about, not eating, crying all the time...she avoided her friends, kept to her chamber, and stopped coming down for meals."

Beau listened intently as Gregory sobbed.

"When Father or I tried to speak to her, we found her in bed, still in her nightclothes, no matter what time of day..."

Beau tried to offer a handkerchief—Gregory slapped his hand away.

"If only, if only..." she would mutter. Her eyes blank, her face taut with sadness."

"Why are you here? What can I do?" Beau asked.

"It's a bit late for doing, don't you think?" He snarled, his features growing angrier.

"I am sorry, truly sorry. I never meant to hurt her. It was just a dance, one dance, was all it was. I scarcely knew her."

"Scarcely, yet you managed to undress her before I could find you."

"She undressed herself. She invited me to follow her that night. I thought I would be observing a collection." He shook his head in grief and frustration, and then lowered his voice, "She told you herself, it was she who tried to seduce me."

"And man of honor that you are, you rejected her like she was a cheap tart."

Gregory rose and made his way to the doorway, "I'll find another way to even things up between the two of us. Someday, you will find something of value, and I will find great pleasure in taking it from you." His silver eyes glowed with vengeance and insanity.

It was that very night the nightmares began to plague him.

****

And now, as Beau lay tormented upon his bed and the walls of his chamber began to close in around him, he realized, Gregory had found his revenge without lifting a slimy finger.

And then he thought more about Gregory's lecherous reputation, his attraction to things perverse and shameful. And now Eve; so pure and beautiful, she embodied everything Gregory wasn't. He recalled the story Eve shared, the narrow escape from that evil creature's grasp, and anger began to coil low in his belly.

How dare he try to touch her? How dare he? Beau rose and began to pace the room. He would die before he allowed anyone to hurt her. He would let the past lie for now, instead focusing all of his thoughts and efforts on keeping her safe.

Perhaps he would never be good enough to enjoy the love of Evelyn Purittson, to hold her in his arms, to make her his own, but one thing he knew for certain, Gregory Searsly would never lay a filthy hand upon her again.

A tiny spark ignited deep in his soul, kindled by a silent yearning. He was never one to give up easily. The small flame began to grow. He sat up and saw her eyes, clear as the freshest water flowing in the afternoon sun; he smelled the faintest essence of vanilla, the shape her gown so gently hid, and her glorious hair flowing out behind her as she rode through the deep night.

She was a gift, and he would hold on to her— grasping for himself a measure of happiness, never letting go of this rare jewel. He would fight for her— the demons of the past, the worries of tomorrow, and he would strongly secure a future with her by his side.

Beau offered up a softly spoken prayer, "Help me, Lord." Then, resigned for battle, Beau closed his weary eyes.

****

On the other side of the sitting room's window, a dark form smiled in the night. Invisible, for the grime on his face and the blackness of his teeth hid his stooped form in the darkness. He'd watched the woman read and burn the letter, saw her angst and joy and knew without a doubt he had found the one he sought. Turning and slinking soundlessly into the woods, he seemed to disappear into the very night itself. The only evidence of his presence was an unseemly stench and a strange dragging mark on the path.

Chapter Sixteen

Eve practically bolted from her bed the next morning. A steadily growing, potent, excitement pulled her forward. *Soon her mother would be here!* And then she would begin to recover. Physicians, the best in the country—the very queen's if necessary—would be summoned, and her mother *would* be healed.

She slathered the herb mixture through her hair and dressed quickly. She nearly flew down the stairs, hoping to find Beau already having his breakfast. She forced herself to slow to something near a dignified pace, took a breath, and entered the dining room. It was empty except for a lone footman setting out tea and rolls. The morning fare's aroma was always a pleasant delight, but today, Eve had no patience to sit and enjoy the offering.

She grabbed a roll, shoved it in her mouth, and chewed quickly. No jams today-too much time would be wasted. She gulped her tea, only to find it *hot*. Tears sprang to her eyes, she quickly swallowed, and motioned for some water. At last, breakfast finished, she wondered what to do. Should she try to find him? Perhaps he was still asleep. Should she wake him?

When Donald and Katherine returned, they were not going to be happy to find another person using their home as a refuge. If they were to hear about Eve visiting Beau's room, it might be the last straw. She would just have to wait.

She decided a morning walk in the gardens would help her pass the time. She felt her blood racing through her veins—would today be the day? She needed to send word to Mary. Mary would need to pack her mother's belongings, her medications, her Bible. As details filled her anxious mind, she realized she was standing amid the trio of fountains. The lightly trickling water, always so inviting, began to relax her.

She sat for a moment on the bench she had shared with him. *Just trust him.* He would see to all the details. He had given his word, which Eve knew was better than gold. As she sat, she realized part of her anxiety had more to do with Beau's puzzling behavior than the worries of bringing her mother to Beckinbrook.

He had seemed so far away last night; his soul as distant from hers as the moon. She longed to bridge the gap but without knowing exactly what it was, she could not imagine what antidote might prove effective.

She went to the fountain where only nights ago she had swam with Prince. Absently she swished her hand back and forth in the cool water, hoping that for once in a very long while all might work out as it should.

As she stood there looking out toward the path strewn with roses, her breath caught. Beau stood in the morning light, like a regal bronze statue. His dark hair combed back, revealing his chiseled features handsomely. His eyes were alive and bright, beckoning her silently.

"My lord?" She smiled as she recognized the familiar air about him, the strength, the confidence, the simmering masculinity. Oh, he was so enticing, so captivating.

In two strides, he crossed and took her in his arms. She was a refreshing waterfall in the midst of miles of barren desert. Beau held her tightly, inhaling her fragrance, drinking it as if it were the finest brandy. His body tingled with awareness. *That feeling*, that glorious feeling evoked by her presence, her scent, her laughter...

He lowered his mouth to her waiting lips. Her eager response sent him reeling. She slid her hands up his back, pulling him closer. Her generous curves crushed against his chest. His heart began to beat fiercely—he drew her even closer. Their lips were on fire, their tongues, mingling like sensual dancers in a furnace of passion.

He softly stroked the side of her face, his hand drifted lower to her throat and lower still to the delicate skin beneath her collarbone. Her sighs of delight spurred him on.

His hand then went to her neck and massaged it slowly, before he moved it to her hair, and began to remove the pins, all the while devouring her lips as if she were a lavish banquet.

Eve's hair cascaded down around her shoulders and still he kissed her. She gasped for air, her face flushed, her lips moist, and her breasts torturing him. Eve was perfection. She pulled away from him, only for a moment, and looked into his eyes.

He felt their touch in the farthest recesses of his being. His desire screamed back to her in that molten gaze.

He felt her melt beneath him. Liquid ardor shone clearly in her aqua orbs. Her lips parted in an attempt to breathe, and he lowered his hungry mouth to hers again. He consumed her in that kiss, laying claim to Eve in the only way he could—for the moment.

Somehow, he guided her back to the bench they had shared in the past. Still he kissed her, his breath ragged as his mouth trailed down her neck.

"Eve... what you do to me."

"Beau, my lord, you have no idea what you have done to *me*."

His kisses intensified, and he knew he was losing control. If he didn't stop soon, or moments ago, it would be too late. He dragged himself up, off her trembling body.

Without speaking, he helped her sit upright again. Her hair flowed around her in heavy waves, dark and light mixed together. She was an angel with her uncommon beauty and sensuality. He could not live without her. "Eve, you take my breath away." He looked down for a moment.

"Good morning, my lord." She offered.

"I agree completely."

They laughed together for a moment. He took her hands in his, their softness more than he could bear and again he fought the urge to plunder those moist lips.

"Good morning, Miss Purittson. What a pleasant surprise to find you here so early."

"I couldn't sleep. After all I told you last night and the excitement over seeing my mother again, having her here where I can properly look after her, it was simply too much."

"Eve, about last night...I am sorry for my demeanor, the way I responded. It had nothing to do with what you told me, it just reminded me of an unpleasant event from my past." He looked intently at her and found her eyes warm and welcoming. "I just want you to know that I do not find fault with you in any way for anything you have done. I realize you did exactly what you should have done to remain safe; in fact, I commend you exceedingly in choosing to come here to Beckinbrook."

"I worried you were displeased with my deceit."

"You were only trying to protect yourself. I understand."

"I'm glad. You seemed so distant, almost fearful,

and I knew that just wasn't like you."

"No, normally it isn't like me."

"Tell me about it."

"I will tell you when the time is right. Right now, I want to get your mother here and be certain she is safe. Let us concentrate on that for now."

"You have already proven yourself trustworthy and strong in character. I have no worries. I trust you, my lord." She brought her hand up and gently stroked the side of his face. "You are my knight in shining armor, and you are about to help the woman I love most in the world."

"Good, now, there is something else I'd like to talk to you about." The feeling of her hand on his face was beginning to have an effect on him.

"Other than moving my mother?"

"Yes."

"What is it?"

This was not the way he intended to tell her, to ask her, it was all so unemotional. "Eve, please kiss me."

She moved closer to him laying her hands upon his chest. Before she could move her lips to his, his arms came around her pulling her closer and taking her mouth with his. The sensations that had only just settled resumed their frantic grasp over his body, swallowed him up once again.

He felt himself losing the battle of self-control. She now controlled him, every thought, every emotion, every feeling, every wish, and every dream. He no longer existed for himself, instead he existed to please her, fulfill her every need. His fingertips vibrated with a need to have her softness beneath their touch, yet he denied them in favor of his need to tell her his story.

Now was the time, he gently pulled from their kiss. "Eve, Evelyn, you have become so important to me. You have become everything to me. I cannot look to the right or to the left without seeing your face, your beautiful exquisite face. Your body calls to me and leads me around like a slave, and I like it."

"Beau…"

"Please… let me finish. I want to be with you all the time. When I go to dinner, my hunger is for you, when I conduct business, it is to impress you. I feel your soul. When I am not with you, it calls to me, and I long for it." Her eyes reflected his intensity back upon him. "When I speak with you, listen to you, I feel calm. I feel a purpose, I feel like protecting you with my very life. What I am trying to tell you, quite poorly I might add, is that I have fallen in love with you."

She exhaled. Tiny teardrops which had formed in the corners of her eyes now spilled forth. She leaned into his waiting embrace, held him, and cried.

"I love you too. I know that which you speak of, that wonderful feeling has captured my heart—you have captured my heart. I feel incomplete when I am apart from you. I had hoped and prayed you might return my feelings."

"My darling, I will return your feelings from now until forever."

"Kiss me, my lord, kiss me."

He kissed her, and their love blossomed within the passion they shared. They clung to each other desperately, yearning for physical release and emotional oneness.

Beau knew he could wait a little longer. Now that he realized she was the one, he knew the time was short until he would have her.

Again he broke the kiss, "Eve, I want to marry you. Please say you will be my wife."

"I will be your wife." She smiled and new tears streamed down her cheeks.

"I hope you will end my torment soon. I do not know how much longer I can remain a gentleman in your presence."

"I would like to marry you as soon as possible."

"Soon is the word I am working and praying for. I can barely keep my hands from you. I am trying to be a gentleman, to respect your virtue, but you tempt me beyond reason." He spoke sincerely and then smiled wickedly.

"Will you be content to be tempted only by me, once we are married?" She raised her eyebrows and then winked.

He laughed. "My darling, you tempt me to distraction of everything else. I am quite certain, no other shall ever captivate me for I am already hopelessly lost to you."

"Hopelessly? That sounds very dark and dismal."

"Indeed. That is what my life has been and what it will be if you are not by my side as my wife."

"I would never want you to endure a moment of hopelessness. Let me endeavor to take away the hopelessness of yesterday." She reached up to his face and stroked his freshly shaven jaw. Then as demurely as a cat in heat, she pulled his lips to hers and kissed him seductively.

Their kiss was slow, wet, and full of promise. He broke away shaking his head, "I can see I am headed for trouble."

"My lord, you are no longer headed for trouble, you are knee deep in it, and I for one am exceedingly grateful!"

Their laughter, their love, the beauty of the day, all surrounded them causing them to feel hopeful, invincible, and incredibly fortunate. They stood to go back to the house. Beau slid his arm around her waist, pulling her close. He ran his fingers lightly over her ribs, and then lowered them to sit just above her hip. They spoke softly and laughed as they made their way—gazing longingly into each other's eyes. As the trail ended, Beau noticed something unusual.

"Look," he pointed to what looked to be a man's boot print with a drag mark beside it, "I wonder what made that track?"

They stopped and turned around. The tracks moved away from the manor, along the same path they were using. Beau bent and examined them closely. Then he walked up a bit and mentally measured another set. He moved back and forth for several moments and finally looked to Eve.

"It is as if the person who came this way was dragging something to cover his left foot print."

"Why would someone want to cover their foot print?"

"I cannot guess."

"Perhaps they were dragging a parcel or tool of some sort."

"Perhaps." Beau was uncertain, but he was beginning to feel a slow measure of uneasiness uncoiling in the pit of his stomach.

"My darling, please promise me not to come out here alone, especially in the evening."

"But why? Surely it is just one of the gardeners."

Be that as it may, I would prefer, we bring your mother here, see to it she is safe, and then we shall unravel this little mystery—if indeed it is one."

"Now you sound like Donald."

"Forgive my desire to protect you, but you are my only hope of salvation from a lifetime of hopelessness, and I intend to see you fulfill that duty."

"Protecting your investment, are you?" She smiled playfully.

All humor left his face. His features grew serious; he answered her slowly, "With my life."

Chapter Seventeen

When they arrived back at the manor, they joined Lady Sands in the dining room. The unspoken words between the couple were evident on their flushed faces and in their shining eyes.

"Good morning, my dears." Lady Sands began, cheerful as always, her lemon yellow gown reflecting her effervescent optimism.

Beau and Eve returned the greeting. They sat across from the brightly dressed woman, lost in their dreams of the future.

"What is it?" she asked, "What has everyone so preoccupied so early this morning?" She looked expectantly to Beau then to Eve.

Eve smiled warmly at Beau. "Lord Beaumont has asked me to marry him, and I have accepted!"

"Oh!" Lady Sands jumped up and spilled her tea on the white linen tablecloth. She laughed and cried simultaneously. "What wonderful news!" Looking to a footman, she cried out, "Please bring us some champagne!"

In a blink, the table linen was changed and a footman arrived bearing a bottle of fine Champagne and three tall fluted glasses on his gleaming silver tray.

Lady Sands, taking a glass stood up. "To the bride and groom, may you share a matchless love and a joy-filled life together from this day on." She lifted her glass and clinked it against the happy couple's glasses.

They chatted and laughed a bit, Lady Sands declaring she knew it would happen all along. "The way he looked at you that first night, I knew he was smitten."

Eve sipped her champagne slowly. The bubbles made her giggle, and she tried to fight their effect by remembering the many important details they needed to address. Beau smiled and seemed at ease in the ladies presence, but Eve could detect the planning and calculating in his expression. Finally, after several questions about the wedding and a discussion as to notifying Donald and Katherine, Lady Sands excused herself, leaving Beau and Eve alone.

Beau turned back towards Eve. "I am awaiting word from my brother. When he replies, I will explain a plan I believe will be quite effective."

"What about my mother?" She sipped her champagne. "I must write to Mary and see that her things are packed, her medications, her Bible, her miniature of father..."

"Is it safe to send word to Mary at once?"

"Yes, the servants at Kentwood are still overwhelmingly loyal to me and my mother. No one there cares for Gregory."

"I'm quite certain. Gregory's deceitful attitude gives cause for distrust in those who know him—even on a superficial level. I believe you should send word to Mary, then. Tomorrow night at midnight, we shall pick them up. Have her ready your mother and her belongings."

Eve struggled between elation and disappointment. She had hoped to have her mother here today, but tomorrow would be fine, it would be wonderful, in fact. Yes, tomorrow night, she would hold her mother, read to her, and care for her. And she would talk to her, telling her of the great love in her life who arranged it all to come to pass.

****

Correspondence flew between estates during the early hours of the day. Eve sent word to Mary, who instantly replied. Beau received word from his brother, evidently putting his mind at ease, and he sent a missive to Donald and Elizabeth telling them of his proposal to Eve and her acceptance.

Eve paced the length of Katherine's drawing room. She looked up to find Beau's eyes fixed on her. A slow, sweet emotion uncoiled in the pit of her stomach. He looked so virile, invincible, and confident standing casually in the door's frame.

"My love, why are you fretting?"

She felt a warm sensation flow from her cheeks to her slippered toes. "I am excited to see my mother. I have a strong impression that once she is here in my care, she will improve."

He walked slowly across the room, the sunshine playing in his thick dark hair finding the streaks of gold and setting them to glimmering. "I have no doubt of that, my sweet." He looked down into her eyes, "When she recovers, will she grant me your hand in proper fashion?"

Eve swallowed in spite of herself. Is this how each day would pass from now on? Would she spend her life melting in his presence and longing for his lips? "I dare say, my lord, she would grant you anything you desire."

"Well, then, that would be your hand and the lovely arm it's attached to." He bent and pressed a light kiss upon her wrist. "And the shapely shoulder that connects it to your glorious chest," he bent and kissed her neck, "and that delicate neck, that leads to these lips," he took her lips and ravaged them. The heat he brought to her mouth was almost liquid, sending fire throughout her sensation heightened body.

She fell into his arms and together they

unleashed a passion that only grew stronger. Never satiated, they continued to seek it, to moan in ecstasy, to draw close to the most dangerous temptation of all, before finally withdrawing.

She fell upon the settee as he released her. She inhaled and sighed in complete bliss. Contented? Never. He had stoked a flame that felt as if it would never be quenched. She wondered if she could ever function rationally again.

He bent his long legs and sat beside her. "You leave me speechless."

Finally, after several moments of silence, Beau spoke again, "Although I have no doubt about the competency of your nursing skills, I wonder if you would allow me to call the Rockwells to pay a visit to your mother. Perhaps they have herbs that will aid in her recovery."

"Since I learned of their unique healing ability, I have wished for little else." *Except for you.* "Please, send word to them, I will be so very grateful and will compensate them for their kindness."

Beau then remembered the provisions her father had left her. In all the excitement about their newly declared love, their plan to marry, and many details involving bringing her mother here, he had forgotten to tell her.

He looked at her now, sitting in the streaming sunshine, her face at peace and recalled her frantic pacing of only moments before. He would wait to tell her. She had so much on her mind at present; he would protect her for a time from anymore stress-causing situations.

Later they shared the mid-day meal with Lady Sands. After luncheon, Beau left to ride out to Hartford Estate to speak to his brother and bring back his carriage. He promised to return for dinner and left Eve trembling as he softly kissed her good-bye.

Lady Sands took the opportunity to speak to Eve as a mother might with her daughter. She led her into the library and quietly closed the door. "So, it is a love match, is it not?"

Eve was still standing and at that, she slipped into a nearby chair. "I believe it is." She smiled the smile of a woman in love.

"When will you marry, my dear?" Lady Sands took a place across from Eve, a knowing expression in her eyes.

"Soon, I hope." Eve shifted and then added, "Lord Beaumont sent word to Donald and Katherine, and I must make arrangements with my family."

Lady Sands lowered her exuberant voice several octaves, "My dear Eve, as your mother is in Paris and the Countess with her family, I would be happy to answer any questions you might have regarding marriage...and the wedding night."

Eve felt her face heat up. She raised her gaze to meet Lady Sands'. Thank you, my lady, but I fear I do not know what I should dare to ask."

"I recognize your shyness but a woman who glows with love as you do, must certainly think now and again about the wedding night. Do you have an understanding as to what will take place?"

Eve had always enjoyed her scientific studies and generally knew how a male and female mated. She had seen her father's stallion sire several offspring and could imagine what went on between a man and a woman.

"I believe I know basically what I can expect." She remembered her heart pounding in anticipation and a craving need that nearly overwhelmed her whenever Beau kissed her.

Lady Sands spoke softly now, "My dear, there is so much more to it than the physical act itself. I know it is not quite proper for me to speak of such things, but I believe I can trust you and want you to be aware of what you may expect."

She sipped her tea and continued. "When a man makes love to his woman, there is something magical that happens. Your heart will no longer be yours alone. In giving your body to your husband, your heart will now be in his care, and my dear, this is something one cannot control. If you have a good husband, as I did, and as you will have, you will enjoy this intimacy above any you have ever shared." She reached out to Eve's hands folded primly on her lap and held one. "Although in the beginning, the newness of it all will overwhelm you both, but as you grow in your love and in experience together, your lovemaking will surpass your wildest dreams."

Lady Sands sat quietly for a moment as if she was re-living some magical moment of her own. "What I was never prepared for, was the intensity in which I felt the love of my beloved husband…there were times, afterward, when all I could do was hold on to him and cry."

Eve sat still, letting the words sink into her soul. She could hardly imagine such an emotional experience, yet, before she met Beau Beaumont, she could never imagine the power of desire. She looked up at Lady Sands to find her eyes shining with emotion.

"Thank you, my lady. Thank you for sharing something so personal with me and helping me know what to expect."

Eve realized she had been self-absorbed so much of late, she'd been lacking in social graces. Time to remedy her lapse. "Did you enjoy your visit with Lord Penchotte?"

Lady Sands raised her eyebrows in surprise, "Why my dear, would you really care to hear about it?" Her eyes sparked with mischief.

"Of course I wish to hear, tell me what brings you back to Beckinbrook smiling so deep in your soul it shines forth from your eyes?"

"My, you are clever..." Lady Sands sat straighter, a light blush crept slowly to her cheeks, before she smiled widely. "I do believe Lord Penchotte and I have developed a ...unique friendship." She looked dreamily off into the nothingness behind Eve.

"Is it a love match?" Eve returned her smile, seeking to share this special secret with her new friend.

Lady Sands moved her head from side to side, as if in denial, but her smile grew brighter and her eyes lit up significantly. "It may be...time will tell..."

"What is he like, your Lord Penchotte?"

"He is very tall and very handsome...his eyes are green, deep green...he is the fourth son of an Earl...he prefers to remain in the country, here in Bath...he makes me laugh...he tells entertaining stories...he is full of passion..." She looked into Eve's eyes. "He is a widower, no children were born to his late wife...he makes me happy." The faraway look in her eye confirmed her words.

The ladies chatted a while longer, and then Eve excused herself to take a short nap.

Chapter Eighteen

The pub was dimly lit. Two small windows caked with dirt blocked out the mid-day sun. Only one man sat in the mid-sized dining room.

He pulled out his watch fob and checked the time; screwed up his lips in disgust and exhaled—rendering his disappointment to all. Could he count on no one? Every blasted person he had hired had been successful only at failing. He was getting tired of waiting; soon he would take more drastic measures.

A pale-haired maid carefully approached the table. She set his glass of ale down, just beyond his stunted arm span, and backed away—slowly. He glanced at her and delighted when she shuddered at the intent he revealed.

Replacing his watch in his pocket, he jumped as he noticed the scraggly creature standing directly before him. He was even more repugnant in the light.

The grime infested thing before him smiled, revealing black teeth and holes where teeth once had been. "Are ye waitin' for Sorrows? Heh, heh."

Gregory sat up straighter, taken aback by the wicked thing. His clothes were little better than rags, and his face bore an expression that was both evil and amused. Again, he found himself repulsed by the evil one's wicked odor.

A wave of fear passed over Gregory, yet he drew upon his most lofty voice,

"You're late and I don't like to be kept waiting." He snarled at the filthy thing.

"I'd been doin' a bit o' yur dirty work for ye'. But if yur' too busy to hear what it is I've found, then I'd better be a' goin'."

Impatiently Gregory responded, "Have you found anything of consequence, then?"

"P'haps. P'haps not." He looked almost bored as he continued, "How much blunt have ye?"

"You've already been paid. Are you going to deliver or shall I have you disposed from my presence?" Gregory was in no mood to be played along.

"It's up to you, gov'ner. I know where yur' lady Ev'lyn is. How much is it wurth to ye?"

"Our agreement was another bag of gold when you brought her to me." Gregory's tone was laced with hatred.

"Tis true, tis. But that be b'fore I knew where she was. My job is now a bit more diff'cult, so I'll be needin' more gold." His mouth stretched into a full black smile.

Inside Gregory cringed at the thought of ever touching him, but he wanted the prize that was on the bidding block. He reached inside his coat pocket and withdrew a heavy pouch. He smiled to himself as he realized the money had once belonged to Evelyn's father. How appropriate it seemed to use it to get her back. He dropped it lightly upon the table, "Don't make me regret this. I want her here soon, very soon."

Greasy fingers quickly took and hid the pouch between filthy rags. "No, there'll be no regrets, no regrets a' tall, gov'ner. I'll have her to ye b'fore the week is done." He turned and as quietly as he appeared, he left. All that remained was an unusual dragging pattern upon the dirt floor.

Gregory's face conveyed no emotion as he stared

after the man. "You better."

****

Eve was ready for dinner. She'd stayed inside her chamber all afternoon, moving her furniture around, and bringing in two small cots. One would do for her and another for Mary. She dressed the small beds in comfortable quilts and fluffy pillows. She moved her older gowns out of the wardrobe, making space for her mother's clothes, and cleared the nightstand beside the bed from all save the lantern.

Standing back and surveying her efforts, a small thrill surged through her heart. Soon Beau would be back. Tonight they would enjoy each other's company…a walk in the gardens, a game of backgammon, simply looking at him across the dining room table. She truly did love him. He was unlike any man she had ever known. The power of the love she already felt for him nearly staggered her in its intensity. And he was a good man, a moral man, a man she could trust with her secrets.

God had always taken care of her, but for the first time in many years, she felt as if God had looked down from heaven and smiled broadly in her direction.

When she entered the dining room, Beau was already there. He came to her side and escorted her to her place. He smelled clean and spicy; his scent a welcome effect on her senses. She closed her eyes and inhaled slightly, allowing a combination of memories and yearnings to wash over her.

Tonight he had dressed more formally. His simple black and white evening attire, accentuated his quiet elegance even more so than his usual clothing. His sapphire eyes sparked mischievously, and his dark hair looked like chocolate silk with tiny strands of gold woven throughout.

She sat and admired him.

"I'm hungry." His gaze slid lazily over her as if it were a physical thing.

She wore white tonight. The satin dipped low between her breasts, and rose nearly to her shoulders. The gown was comprised of many unusual tucks and pleats.

"You're setting the room on fire in that gown." His face grew serious, "I can barely stand to sit here and resist you." The blazing heat in his expression said even more.

"My lord." She bowed her head, ignoring the burning of her skin under his perusal. "Lady Sands will not be joining us for dinner this evening. She is resting and asked to have a tray sent up."

"Then I shall not have to turn my gaze from you, even for a moment."

She took a sip of her water. "My lord, you flatter me so, I can barely eat my dinner."

"Shall I then feed you?"

Eve felt her face redden. "Perhaps we will have to forgo conversation?" she teased.

"I'll try to be more lord-like but only for tonight." He began to cut the tender beef on his plate. "My brother will be here early in the morning. He is eager to help with the rescue of your mother."

"Tell me about your brother," she adjusted her position, taking a more formal posture, "why is he so eager to help a woman he barely knows."

"My brother? My brother Paul is five years my junior. He is a very intelligent young man who has a passion for travel. He just returned from Italy, where he spent time visiting with my grandmother's family." Beau sipped his wine and then continued, "Why does he want to help a woman he doesn't know? Because he knows he is helping me and that is good enough for him."

"I don't know how I shall every repay him for this kindness."

"Consider it a wedding gift."

She smiled. "I had always wished for a brother of my own, but I was the only child." Eve nibbled on a roll, "When I learned I was to have a step-brother, my hopes were high, but shortly after meeting Gregory, I realized the error of my hopefulness."

"You may consider Paul your very own brother. And I can assure you, he is nothing like Gregory Searsly." As he spoke the name, his countenance changed to one of disgust. He quickly regained his composure. "Paul will be as loyal to you as I am." He smiled.

Dinner continued at a leisurely pace. They spoke of the Rockwells, of Donald and Katherine, of Beau's father and of their love. They finished dinner and strolled through the gardens, walking hand in hand beneath a profusion of twinkling lights. They danced in the gazebo and kissed passionately amid the roses. Finally, they returned to the manor.

"Goodnight, my love." Beau kissed her forehead lightly, squeezing her hand simultaneously.

The clock's chimes served as a reminder that time was passing quickly—soon they would be together.

"Goodnight, my lord." She began to climb the stairs to her room; playfully she turned her head and added, "Dream of me."

He stood on the marbled floor watching the gentle sway of her hips and enjoying the crinkling, swishing sound of her gown as she ascended to the second floor. Almost in a whisper he replied, "I always do."

He stood there as she disappeared from his sight, the scent of vanilla surrounding him.

He wondered if Lady Sands was well, she had taken to her chamber often of late. He wished to check on her but feared awakening her if she was resting. He exhaled. He decided to retire.

"My lord?" Charles, the young footman called to Beau.

"Yes…"

"This was delivered while you were dining." He extended the silver tray to Beau. Upon it, another letter with the eerie handwriting he had come to despise.

Beau picked it up. "Thank you." The footman quickly departed.

Beau carried the missive back to his chamber. He set it on his bureau, undressed, and then decided to open it.

"Revenge will soon be mine. Don't bother to look up or down, you will never see it until it is done."

Beau examined the paper, looking for some clue as to the identity of the sender. But it was a mere piece of velum, ordinary in every way, just as the others had been. The ink was unremarkable as was the seal.

He opened the bureau and retrieved the last letter he received when he visited Hartford.

"I am waiting for you…we shall once again be together."

The only logical conclusion he could draw, was that these were attempts to frighten him, originating from none other than Gregory Searsly.

He put the letters back inside his bureau. Beneath his clothing rested a small revolver. He lifted it from the drawer and felt its familiar weight in his hand—heavy, smooth, and sleek—a partner one could always depend on. It had served him well when he had transferred information from various sources to his commander. Perhaps it would serve him well again.

After some thought, Beau concluded the best way to stop Gregory from interfering with his marriage to Eve would be to take the offensive. He could find him and reason with him, using whatever means necessary. He would not sit back and wait for Gregory to come calling in some drunken stupor, spreading lies, and hurting the woman he loved. It was time to find Searsly, put a stop to all this nonsense, and move along with his plan. It was well past time.

He had no way to know Felicity would take her own life, he had not led her on, and he had carried enough guilt to last forever. Weary and angry, he decided as soon as he had Lady Searsly safely settled at Beckinbrook, he would find Gregory and put and end to his threats of revenge.

Chapter Nineteen

Today was the day. Eve dressed slowly, careful to don her entire disguise of herb paste and spectacles. She entered the dining room and noticed several extra servants milling about. She wondered if they were there at Beau's request.

Before her tea touched her lips, the mystery was solved, Donald had returned late last night. Percy in his most formal and haughty accent informed her in a rather matter-of-fact way, than flashed a knowing smile. He knew something was a foot, and he guessed it had something to do with a certain Lord staying at the manor.

Eve felt relief and trepidation at the news. Donald had always been her protector, and she had never challenged his authority, but as she turned her well-being over to Beau's capable hands, would Donald be angry?

Eve ate ham, rolls, and eggs and drank her tea while waiting for Donald, Beau, or Lady Sands to join her. Finally, as she set her empty teacup down, Lady Sands entered dressed in a royal blue silk day gown. Her hair was styled in a more elaborate manner than Eve had ever seen and tucked into the crown of curls that encircled her head was a perfect yellow rosebud.

"My lady, you are stunning this morning!"

"Oh my, I think not...you, my dear are stunning every morning." Lady Sands filled her plate generously and took a seat across from Eve.

"What is the occasion that warrants such a lovely coiffure?"

"No occasion is needed to look one's best. I just felt like a rose this morning."

Eve loved Lady Sands' uninhibited spirit and knew she must possess a bit of it within herself. Her late night swims and passionate kisses in the garden must be somewhat of an indication. She smiled inwardly as she thought of those things. It would please her greatly to grow into a woman such as Lady Sands.

"Donald has returned from Scotland. I understand he came in quite late last evening."

"I hope all is well with Lady Julia." Lady Sands' expression showed concern.

"I feel quite certain it must be, else he would never have left Katherine." Eve replied. "I hope he comes down soon, I am anxious to speak with him."

Percy stepped beside Eve. "Miss Purity, the Earl has already partaken and is holding a conference with Lord Beaumont in the library."

Eve stood; ready to rush Beau's side, then paused. "Very good, Percy."

Percy bobbed his head and disappeared into the hallway. "Please excuse me Lady Sands, I must speak to Donald about a matter of some importance."

Lady Sands waved her hand, "Go on, dear. I shall speak with you later. I have some lovely lace I would like to show you, I have been saving it all these years for a special occasion. Your wedding may constitute such an occasion." Lady Sands laughed heartily, and Eve made her departure.

Her heart raced as she made her way to the library door. She pressed her ear against the crack but could hear nothing. Just as she was deciding whether to knock or just barge in, the door opened revealing Donald and Beau—both wearing serious expressions and looking somewhat amused to find her there.

"Welcome home. What...a...lovely surprise," she stammered.

"Indeed." Donald ran his hand through his hair in a way that made him appear fatigued. "Come join us for a moment, will you?"

"Of course." The men stepped back into the library and she followed. Beau's eyes twinkled at her, and he smiled a small but potent smile that did things to her toes.

She nodded at him, the devil, and realized again, how little it took for him to have such a strong effect on her.

Donald sat behind his desk, and Beau and Eve sat upon the settee facing him.

Never one to let moss grow beneath him, Donald started right off, "My dear Evelyn, Beau tells me of your plan to bring your mother here, your undying love for one another and consequentially, your betrothal." He paused as if he were contemplating more, than shook his head and smiled, "I've only been gone two days!"

Eve opened her mouth and found only air passing through her lips. She closed her mouth, wondering if he would say more, or if it were now her turn to speak?

She garnered her courage, "Donald...I know it may seem a bit unusual, unorthodox even, but one event seemed to lead to another...and before we realized what was happening...we had fallen in love."

"That is why I left you in Lady Sands' charge, so no *events* would take place."

Beau spoke up, "Donald, surely you are teasing Miss Purittson, as you know nothing untoward *has* taken place." Beau's words were stern, yet his manner relaxed.

"You are correct, I was teasing," he replied, "and

I believe the pair of you will make an excellent match." He paused and shuffled some papers on his desk, "I am only concerned about your safety. Once you are married, you will be my concern only as a friend, but until then, I feel the responsibility of being your guardian."

"I appreciate all you have done, but truly, Gregory has no idea where I am. He is so dimwitted, it would probably take months for him to find me, and by then, Lord Beaumont and I will already be wed."

Donald stood up and began to pace. "Yes, that probably is the case, but until you are wed, I cannot let down my guard. You did well in confiding in Beaumont, he is one of the few men I would deem trustworthy."

The heat flowed over Eve at the mention of his name. "Yes."

"How did you win her, old chap?" Donald looked to Beau.

"I used all the charm I could muster, most of which I gleaned from watching you in your bachelor days."

"Ha!" Donald laughed. "Rubbish and Poppycock."

Beau smiled broadly and Eve joined in. "How is Lady Julia? Has she delivered the babe?"

"Lady Julia is well and the proud mother of a son, William Richard. He was born ten hours after we arrived in the midst of a thunderstorm. Katherine was by her side and is as proud as a peacock over the arrival of our new nephew."

Eve clapped her hands and smiled. "I must send a note of congratulations at once!

Did you tell her of our plans to marry?"

"Of course. Katherine is ecstatic. She will return home in several weeks, enough time to help you prepare for the wedding. She also asked me to offer our home for the Bridal breakfast."

"We may be married by then. I wish to marry this lovely lady as soon as possible. In fact, my father is helping me procure a special license as we speak."

This was news to Eve, but welcome news indeed. "What of tonight?"

"My brother is here, probably still asleep, but here nonetheless to help us. I didn't know Donald would return, but now that he is here, he has decided to stay here with you as we move your mother."

"But, I wish to come along." Eve began to worry, "If my mother awakens from her stupor and sees two men she doesn't know, it could cause her serious trauma."

"Her maid will be with us. If your mother awakens, she will recognize her and will be told she is coming to stay with you." He offered.

"Still, she may be overwhelmed, and her mental state is quite shaky at present. Please...allow me to come along, I can help, I can see to her comfort..."

"My darling, she will be fine. I will care for her as if she were you...I will not allow any harm to come to her. I don't want you to be seen. Gregory may have people watching the house. They will not recognize us but will most assuredly be looking for you." Beau lowered his voice and pleaded with her, "Please, stay here. Prepare a room for them, and I will deliver them safely tonight."

Eve's breath flew out with her sigh, "Very well. I have prepared a place in my room for them. I wish to have my mother as close as possible."

"Good, the servants do not enter your room. That will help keep our secret from becoming known." Donald added.

Eve rested back against the settee. "Thank you, both of you. I am certain she will improve when I can care for her."

"In addition to your loving ministrations, I have invited the Rockwell's to come by tomorrow evening. They understand the discretion needed regarding the situation and will come bringing many of their medicinal herbs."

"Oh Beau...thank you." Tears slid down her cheeks. Soon, very soon it would be over. Beau took her in his arms and held her. Her sobs shook them both, and then she melted into the comforting embrace he offered.

"When we marry, she will come live with us. Of course, by then, I believe she will need her *own* room."

The three friends laughed together. Eve excused herself and went to rest; she wanted to be alert for tonight.

Dinner passed uneventfully, yet to Eve, the mealtime atmosphere seemed thick with anticipation. Lady Sands, chirpy as always, brought an air of levity to the room. But even with her intentional efforts, Eve's attempts at conversation were strained. Beau was more reserved than usual and Donald was as always, pensive.

"Has there been a death?"

Three heads snapped up, all looking at Lady Sands.

"This is the most somber dinner I have eaten in many years, and we have so very much to celebrate." Lady Sands looked at the three of them. "Remember, we have the birth of William Richard," she paused looking directly at Beau, "and I believe someone here is betrothed..."

"Well...yes...certainly..." Beau began.

"Would someone care to share with me what has cast such pallor over dinner this evening?"

"Perhaps it is all the excitement; it has us all a bit overwhelmed." Eve smiled innocently. "And

Donald, getting in so late last night, he must surely be tired."

Donald looked at Eve skeptically from over his forkful of glazed beef. "Yes, I am a bit lagging from the trip."

"And what of our guest, Lord Beaumont's brother. When shall I meet him?" She asked.

"He too is resting. He has been helping me with some business matters and will join us all tomorrow." Beau replied.

"Harrumph. I have never seen young people need so much rest." Her suspicion, quite obvious in the way she raised her eyebrow.

After the last bite of dessert was consumed, Donald excused himself and retired to his chamber. Eve was quick to follow, feigning a headache. Beau was left with Lady Sands.

"Would you care for a backgammon match?" She asked.

"My Lady, please forgive me, but tonight I must retire early. Tomorrow morning I must see to some urgent matters my brother has brought to my attention. I would greatly appreciate a match with you tomorrow evening."

Lady Sands nodded her head, "Certainly, my lord." He bowed and made his departure. As Beau made his way up the stairs, he heard her utterance, not quite beneath her breath, "Something is definitely…up."

Chapter Twenty

A soft knock alerted Beau to Donald's arrival before he entered the spacious room, Beau now shared with Paul. Both brothers were ready—dressed completely in black. A nervous tension sizzled in the air.

"We are leaving now." Paul began.

"Good. Return quickly and safely. I will keep Eve safe and calm."

Beau stepped forward, "Thank you Donald."

Donald patted Beau's shoulder. "She means a great deal to Katherine and I too. If anything were to happen to her, my lady would have my head."

Beau nodded, a tight smile stretched across his face. "Let's be off."

The two men slipped down the servants stairs and out to the stables. Their coach stood ready, and already inside was a makeshift stretcher fashioned to carry Lady Searsly safely through her house and out into the carriage. Beau and Paul set off quietly, the dim moonlight their only companion.

****

Eve answered the knock as a loud clap of thunder seemed to shake the foundation of the manor. "Come inside."

Donald stepped into her room and glanced toward the extra beds she had set up. Eve quickly sat down and motioned for Donald to sit across from her. She was already dressed for bed, a long dark robe concealing her nightclothes.

182

"Would you like me to wait with you?" He began.

"I certainly appreciate it, but I think I am going to try to get a bit of sleep. When Beau returns with mother, I may need to help settle her in, and I want to be well rested so I may aid her properly."

Donald exhaled. "Capital idea, my dear. You may well be needed later tonight. Get some sleep, and I will return when they do and help settle everyone in."

Eve smiled nervously. "I shall see you in several hours then."

"Sleep well." And he was gone.

Eve pressed her ear against the door and heard his footfalls down the hall. She listened for the familiar click of his door opening and then the click of it closing again. When she was certain he was in his chamber, she threw off the dark robe, revealing a dark blue chambray shirt and black trousers she had coerced from John the stable boy.

She stuffed her hair up into an old bonnet she had dyed dark brown with her hair darkening herbs. After a quick glance to make sure everything was ready for her guests, she quietly exited the chamber and crept down the servant's stairs. She ran as quickly as she could to the stable, where John already had Victor saddled and ready to go.

"Must you always leave in the middle of the night, amidst a storm?" He asked.

"I'll be back before dawn. Remember John, no one must know."

"I'm worried about you, Miss. Please...this doesn't sit right with me." John's words were kind, but Eve could not delay. "But Miss Eve, where are you going? Please you can trust me, just in case you meet with danger."

Eve sighed in frustration, "I know the Beaumont brothers have just left in their carriage. I only intend to follow them in case they meet danger and need some help."

"Miss Eve, they can take care of themselves. Please let me accompany you, just this once."

Eve swung up into the saddle and began to leave the shelter of the barn. She called back over her shoulder, "No. I must do this. Thank you, John." Determined to do what she must, Eve pressed her horse forward into the darkness.

She rode hard, hoping to catch up with the carriage but soon she realized it was futile. Beau had left at least a half hour before she did. She traveled at the fastest pace Victor would allow but could not out run the large raindrops beginning to pelt her body. The intermittent piercing took her mind from the task at hand only momentarily. She stayed beside the road, continually moving forward yet hanging in the shadows and seeing no one.

Finally, she glimpsed a large wooded copse. Her home stood just beyond. She left the familiarity of the road and entered the dark thickening woods. Her sense of direction guided her forward, but the enveloping darkness made her way difficult. She slowed Victor to a trot and sought the scarce streams of moonlight that barely managed to light her path.

Above, thunder cracked and lightning split the sky. Eve continued on, the rain no longer a deluge under the dense canopy of trees. Although the leafy shelter provided a semi-dry atmosphere, dark fingers of fear began to curl around Eve. She looked back over her shoulder. She could find no cause for her feeling of unrest, yet her sight was very limited.

Almost making it through the woods, she halted Victor as the profile of her home rose before her in the distance. For a moment, she longed to gallop forward and join up with Beau but that unsettling feeling held her back. She inched forward, careful to guide Victor quietly.

Now at the edge of the woods, she waited in the

rain and shadows to quell her concerns about her mother's safety. She couldn't see the carriage and wondered if it were in the stable. If so, how would they get her mother out to meet it? It was quite a trek and the cool night combined with the soaking rain could cause her mother to catch a chill.

If she were with Beau and his brother, she could hold a blanket over her mother as the men carried her out to the stable. Perhaps she should ride out and see, perhaps at this very moment they were in need of some help and an extra set of hands. Her head pounded. What should she do?

Victor, sensing her nervousness, shifted back and forth. He began to snort and stomp, it was as if he were on the verge of bolting. Eve peered out into the night, the rain obscuring her view and she waited…

Suddenly, a hand smothered her lips. She couldn't breath. She tried to kick Victor, but someone jerked her off her mount. One hand still covered her mouth; the other clasped her hands tightly together behind her back.

She struggled and squirmed to escape, but his grip remained iron-like.

"Don't ye scream. If ye do, I'll shove this dirty rag in yur mouth. No one can hear ye over the storm anyway."

The voice wasn't Gregory's! Eve almost sighed in relief, although she remained silent, her captor still kept her mouth covered. She realized he was waiting for her acknowledgement and quickly nodded her head.

His hand slowly moved from her face, "That's a good gel. Now yur gonna git up on me horse and we're goin' for a little ride."

Her head instinctively moved from side to side. She shouted out over the storm, "Who are you? Why are you doing this?"

He roughly yanked her closer and whispered in her ear, "Lower yur voice, if ye know what's good for ye."

Eve shuddered, tears mixed with rain on her cheeks. "What do you want with me? Let me go, I am of no use to you."

His laughter came from a deep pit and surrounded her. "Oh me dear Evelyn, ye will be of great use to me."

She felt him pulling on her hands and then a rope encircled her wrists. He took no caution for her well-being; instead, he pulled the rope so tight her hands quickly became numb.

"Please, loosen it," she cried.

The man hesitated, then loosened the rope the smallest measure, and then moved to stand in front of Eve. A shriek ripped into the night as she stared at the most hideous looking man she had ever seen. In an instant, she was lying in the dirt, felled by sheer terror of the god-forsaken creature. The rain poured down upon her body, while she feigned a loss of consciousness.

****

Beau and Paul moved Eve's mother into the carriage without incident. Her trunks were loaded and her lady's maid sat beside her, carefully drying raindrops on the lady's pale cheeks.

The carriage departed with a jolt, and Beau sighed in relief. With this task completed, he could now concentrate on his impending marriage. Thoughts of Felicity still plagued him, but somehow he would fight to forget the shame and reach for his ray of happiness.

Laura traveled well; she slept peacefully as the carriage bounced now and again. With every tiny bump, Mary checked her mistress watching for any sign of discomfort.

"That was almost too easy." Paul began. "All

went as planned."

Beau nodded in the darkness, a sense of dread hovering around him. "I shall feel better once we are back at Beckinbrook."

They continued on, the quiet in the carriage broken only by the pelting rain and lessening cracks of thunder. At last, they arrived at the castle. They pulled the carriage up to the front drive. Most of the servants had been dismissed for the night, allowing Laura and her maid to settle in secretly.

Beau and Paul carried Laura up the stairs as she slept soundlessly on the stretcher. They made their way to Eve's room and halted just outside her door. From down the hall, Donald emerged and approached the group.

"She is sleeping. She wanted to be rested to help settle everyone in when you returned." He nodded to Mary and she curtsied before him.

Donald knocked softly on the door, but no answer came. He knocked again, with a bit more force and still there was no reply. He motioned to Mary, "Please go in and wake Eve, and we will wait to enter until she is covered.

Mary opened the door slowly and entered the chamber. Beau waited impatiently until Mary returned.

"Come, you may lay my mistress on this bed." She motioned to the largest in the center of the room. Mary pulled the covers back slowly.

Beau and Paul lowered their charge onto the bed and as Mary covered her lady, they looked around for Eve.

"I thought you said she was sleeping..." Beau looked Donald square in the face.

"She was headed to bed when you two left. I came to wait with her and she told me she would rather sleep a bit as to be refreshed when you arrived." Donald answered.

"Perhaps she has gone to the kitchen for refreshments." Paul offered.

"None of the beds have been slept in." Beau began to feel suffocated, a wave of panic rising up inside him.

"Perhaps she slept here on the chair." Donald motioned to the place she had been sitting. "Look, here is her robe."

"I'll go check the kitchen." Paul offered.

"I am going to return the carriage to the stables, come find me when she returns." His mouth was set in a grim line, he nearly ran from the room and then down the stairs. He drove over to the stable and rushed in.

John was pacing but abruptly stopped when Beau charged in. "Did she leave here tonight?"

The man's features were pale, his brows pulled together in a frown. "Aye, she followed you, wanted to be there in case you needed help."

Beau felt a sickening rage. He didn't speak but walked back to saddle Wind Keeper. In a moment, he was ready to depart. "Go tell the Earl immediately what you have told me. Also tell him I have gone to search for her and will not return until I find her."

John took off running for the manor. Beau began to ride out into the night. The storm had ended but probably had washed away any helpful tracks. *Why had Eve followed them? Why couldn't she just have stayed and waited for them to return?* When he found her, he couldn't be responsible for what he might say or do—he just prayed he found her safe.

Beau forged forth, his horse moving at his command. Driven by a raging need to protect the treasure he had only just found, he could not still the fear of terror gripping his heart.

His intuition told him, he would find her near

her ancestral home. He could think of nothing but Eve—her face before him. Her innocence, her sensual eyes revealing her thoughts, her needs, her desires... He remembered the fragrance of her, her hair, the gentle touch of her fingertips against his chest. Her full, moist lips—parting for him, speaking his name, laughing... He drew in a ragged breath; the memories tortured him.

He must find her. He would invade hell itself to bring back his beloved. *Oh Eve, why did you go?* He was nearing Kentwood Manor. He noticed a wooded area to his left, knowing it would lead him to Kentwood he stopped for a moment. *Would she have gone through the woods, to stay concealed?*

He knew when it came to her mother she would have no fear. That was the way she loved—with complete abandon. No thoughts for herself, only for the one her heart had chosen. He was about to enter the woods when he saw a horse emerge. It looked like Donald's horse, he approached it, and the animal did not flee. It resembled the horse Eve had ridden the first time he had followed her to Kentwood. Examining the saddle, his fear was confirmed, the saddle bore the crest of Beckinbrook.

He tethered the horse to his own and entered the darkness where Eve had been only hours ago. Here the trees had shielded the rain from falling and with the early morning sun's ascent, Beau could see where her horse had recently traveled.

He followed the tracks, yelling out her name as he moved. He was able to stay on the trail until he came to the edge of the wooded area. Here the tracks stopped. Another horse had ridden up; it looked like there had been an accident. Many large footprints in the mud, an impression as if someone had fallen. *Oh Lord, what had happened?*

Beau forced himself to remain focused. Perhaps she had fallen; maybe another rider had rescued her, taken her to his home to care for her. He knew other scenarios existed but he would not think on them.

He saw that the other rider had turned west, the way from which he had come. He followed the tracks for a while and then they disappeared. Still Beau rode towards the west looking for a sign—any sign of her. He would find her, he would bring her home, and he would marry her.

Chapter Twenty-One

Hours later, sweltering in the mid-day sun, Beau admitted temporary defeat. He could find no trace of her, no clue to her direction, or who may have taken her. He decided to return to Beckinbrook, speak with Donald, and re-double his efforts.

Wind Keeper as well as Eve's horse needed rest, so Beau stopped at a fast moving stream to allow the horses some time and refreshment. He dismounted and splashed the cool water on his face. His mind was racing. Without speaking to Donald, he knew the next logical step would be to find Gregory.

He mounted his horse and urged him back toward Beckinbrook. Gregory's threat now ringing in his ears, *"Someday you will find something of value, and I will find great pleasure in taking it from you."*

The day was bright and painfully cheerful, but as Beckinbrook came into sight, Beau saw only her face. *I am coming.* If there were a way to transfer his thoughts to her, he now wished he could. As he rode hard to the stable, he prayed for her safety.

Before Beau crossed the threshold, Donald was there. "How have you fared?"

"I found her horse, but not one bloody clue to determine where she is now. It looked as if she fell off her horse, there were other tracks, but I could not find Eve or the other horse's rider." A few moments later, Beau leaned against the wall in the grand foyer. The house was quiet as if in mourning for the light that had vanished so suddenly.

"Come, sit down, eat something," Donald motioned to the dining room, "We will find her." They walked slowly to the dining room; Donald spoke to a waiting servant and then joined Beau at the table.

"I should have stayed with her...I should have known she would try something crazy like following you."

"There is no time now for regrets. Every moment that she is away, her danger deepens..." before he could complete his thought a tray laden with meats, vegetables, cheeses, and breads was set before him.

"Eat now and let me tell you what I've been doing."

Beau took a roll and started to pick at it.

"I have three of my former comrades combing the area for Eve. These men have assisted me in various espionage endeavors and have proven themselves to be competent and loyal."

"Kiran?" Beau asked.

"He is in charge of the operation."

"He'd better not fail."

"Kiran never fails."

"Gregory is an evil and depraved man. He will hurt her in malicious ways for his own pleasure and enjoy revenge against me all the while."

"Why would Gregory take revenge against you? Are you even acquainted with him?"

Beau was about to answer, not certain how much to reveal when Percy, the head butler appeared, "A Mr. and Mrs. William Rockwell here to see you, Lord Beaumont."

Beau had forgotten he had invited them— forgotten Laura laid upstairs in need of medical treatment. All his energy had been focused on finding Eve.

Donald stood, "Show them in here, and set extra

places for them."

Beau stood and watched Percy escort the Rockwell's into the dining room. Ginger, well tanned and full of color, carried two large baskets filled with bunches of herbs and extracts in glass bottles. William also carried a large satchel that released a pungent odor as he neared the table. Beau introduced them to Donald.

The Rockwells looked at Beau curiously. He had been soaked, muddied, and now dried over these last hours. He knew what picture he presented, his beard shadowed his usually clean face, and his hair was tangled and wind blown.

"Have we come at an inconvenient time, my lord?" Ginger spoke first.

"No. I am glad you are both here. We have a bit of a situation but having you here will alleviate at least one of my concerns." Beau replied.

William and Ginger looked at each other. "How can we be of assistance?" William asked.

Beau lowered his voice, "The patient, Eve's mother, is upstairs resting. I wish you to evaluate her condition and give her any medication you deem appropriate to aid in her recovery."

William stood, "We wish to see her at once."

Ginger stood too, waiting to be escorted to the room.

"As I mentioned, this need be kept quite confidential." Beau stressed. The Rockwell's nodded; they knew the deep importance of the matter. "I apologize for my unusual appearance, and also for my absence, as I must soon leave to attend to an urgent matter."

"My lord, please, see to your matter and we shall care for your patient. Be assured I will look after her as if she were my own sister." William offered.

"My sincere thanks. Let me show you to the room and then I shall depart." Beau escorted the

Rockwell's, with Donald bringing up the rear, to Eve's room. Mary sat brushing Laura's hair but stood at once to greet the visitors.

"Miss Mary, please allow me to introduce Mr. and Mrs. Rockwell. They are here at Miss Purittson's request to help care for her mother."

Mary curtsied low. Ginger held out her tanned hand in greeting, "It is obvious you take great care with your patient."

"She has been in my care a number of years. I would guard her life with my very own."

Ginger motioned Mary to the sitting area, "Come, tell me about your dear patient."

Mary quickly sat. She cast a glance to her charge to find Mr. Rockwell holding Laura's hand and listening to her breathing.

"I bathe her every other day. I give her sips of tea and broth when she is absent in mind, but every so often she emerges and eats quite heartily."

"What does she speak of when she is lucid?" Ginger asked.

Beau watched the Rockwell's with a silent awe. He knew calling for them was exactly what was needed. Deep in his heart, he felt Lady Searsly would greatly benefit from their presence and their medicinal knowledge.

"She asks for her daughter. She expresses concern for her safety. Sometimes she asks for Dr. Ford."

"Who is Dr. Ford?"

"Dr. Ford had always been the Purittson's family doctor. He was a distant cousin to the late Lord Purittson." Mary paused as if trying to remember every detail, "When Lord Searsly took ill, Gregory dismissed Dr. Ford and instead retained Dr. Colton. It is Dr. Colton who treats her now."

"Who is Gregory?" Ginger wondered aloud.

"Gregory is Lady Searsly's stepson." Mary

looked again over at Laura, where Mr. Rockwell shook the vial of medication Dr. Colton had supplied.

Beau now approached William, observing him as he uncorked the small bottle.

William lightly sniffed the dark liquid, and his brows rose several inches. Interrupting the ladies he asked, "Where did you get this?"

Mary answered at once. "Please take care, Mr. Rockwell, the medicine is precious. Dr. Colton makes this for my lady."

Beau watched as William withdrew a small china bowl from his satchel. He took a small vial of yellow liquid and with an unusual measuring device, portioned an exact amount and dropped it into the bowl. He then poured one drop of Laura's precious medicine into the bowl and immediately the liquid turned white and began to smoke.

William began to shake his head. "What is it?" Beau asked. Something warned him the news would not be good.

"This is *not* medicine for any ailment." Holding up Laura's bottle, he announced to all who were present, "This liquid is made from a rare herb that causes hallucinations and many illogical symptoms for those who partake of it. It is not ever meant for medication, in fact, in some countries, it is used to kill large animals humanely."

Mary cried out, "This is the same medicine Gregory gave to his own father." She put her hand over her mouth as a flood of tears washed over her face. She began to sob, "To think I spooned that into her trusting mouth!"

Ginger moved to her side. "You had no way of knowing," she patted Mary's head and offered a handkerchief.

A flame of rage grew inside of Beau. Never had he felt so much hatred toward another person. *Gregory was poisoning Laura! He had even poisoned his own father!*

Turning to William he asked, "Can you help her? Can you heal her from the effects she has already suffered?"

William did not answer immediately. He rummaged in his bag again and then went to Ginger's basket. "I believe I can help her." He mixed two powdered herbs together and then added the leaves of a third. He removed a small lantern and asked for some water.

Mary quickly stood and poured a glass of water for William who mixed it with the herbs and began to cook it in a glass bowl over the lantern's small flame. When it bubbled, he removed it and set it on a stone tile. "When this cools, give the patient a spoonful twice a day." He looked at Ginger, "You may see an improvement in just a few days." Ginger smiled and nodded slowly. She moved to her husband's side and began to re-pack the various herbs.

Beau tried to control his rage and turned to William, "How can we ever thank you?"

"My friend, your faith in me and my wife has meant the world to us. No thanks are necessary. My work is to heal and if our patient recovers, then that is enough for me."

Beau's voice was low, filled with weariness, "Still, I must express my deep appreciation."

William stood. "Perhaps I will leave Ginger here for a day or so. She will know what our patient needs and can mix some herbs herself."

Ginger smiled pleasantly and nodded. "I would be happy to help."

Finally, Donald, who had been silent the entire time, spoke, "Mrs. Rockwell, it would indeed be a pleasure to have you stay as our guest."

Donald motioned for Beau to join him in the hall. "What do you make of this?"

"He is poisoning his parents and now he probably has Eve. Perhaps he will poison her as well."

"We will remain hopeful for the best." Donald offered.

Beau rubbed his face; the fatigue of the last several hours combined with his anguish over Eve was taking a toll. "Where is Lady Sands? I have not seen her about, even with all this commotion."

"She has taken ill. I sent a breakfast tray up to her this morning; still it remains untouched outside her chamber door."

"Perhaps the Rockwells can check on her. They may be able to help."

"Go and rest." Donald commanded. "You are always so concerned for others."

"I cannot lie down. Not when I don't know what horrors she might be suffering. How can I rest while she endures God knows what?"

Donald reached for Beau's shoulders and turned him briskly, "You too will soon need the services of the good Rockwells if you do not rest. How can you think clearly if your mind is muddled from exhaustion? I have my men looking for her." Donald released his grip and then gently added, "I will look for her while you rest."

Beau's eyes stung with unshed tears of worry. He knew Donald was right. He needed to think clearly. This was a time for careful planning, along with action; he would be unfit for either without some sleep. "Yes. You are correct, I should rest a while." He dragged his hand through his hair.

"Go. I will wake you when I return. Perhaps I will have some news then."

****

Eve lifted her head from the cold, hard, dirt floor. Disoriented, shivering, and encased in darkness, she tried to make sense of what had happened, but the events she recalled were so bizarre, they seemed to be some kind of dream or nightmare.

Slowly the memories of terror returned to her mind. As she struggled to stand up, a furry creature ran across her hand. A scream lay trapped in her throat. She didn't want anyone to know she was awake…yet.

She pushed her hands against the floor, feeling pain in her wrists. She remembered the rope that had cut into her skin and touched the spots to find them sore and bleeding. *At least my hands are free now.*

Once on her feet, she inched around her prison. It had to be a cell somewhere deep beneath the ground. The musty smell, the cool air, and the unrelenting darkness all confirmed her suspicions. With her arms outstretched before her, she moved around feeling walls of stone on three sides and iron bars on one.

She tested each bar, pulling on it, careful not to make a sound, and found the bars quite intact. Cut bars indicated where a door might be, and she circled the cell again to be certain. She retreated to the stonewall opposite the door, where a small cot stood.

She sat carefully. She ran her fingers over ever corner of the straw stuffed mattress, trying to find anything that might serve as a weapon. She found only foul smelling, limp straw.

Her heart pounded fiercely inside her chest, the sound nearly deafening her. She wanted to cry out for help, but something told her to be still and patient. She conceded to her better judgment and reviewed all that had happened.

In flashes she remembered—the hand over her face, falling from the horse, the rope biting into her flesh, and then the face. She shuddered as she relived the very moment she saw the terrifying face of the creature who grabbed her...then all went dark.

Now she was imprisoned somewhere...why? Before a moment passed, a raw fear slid over her trembling body as she realized the one who was behind it all.

He must have planned the whole charade. He wasn't hiding away from Kentwood Manor—he was probably holding watch. He knew Mary would contact her, and he knew she would come.

Had Beau been successful? Had he secreted her mother away? Perhaps Gregory had sent his monster to her while he himself took Laura. Tears slipped from her eyes, she quickly wiped them away.

At the thought of Beau, her heart lurched. *Oh my darling...* She wished she hadn't been so foolish, had she jeopardized her chance to be with him? Would she ever be free again?

A loud *creeaak* interrupted her worries. Somewhere a door opened. She sat stone still, listening for footfalls.

The sound that met her ears sickened her. Something was not right—someone was dragging something. She shivered as the sound came closer. She moved to the door and glimpsed a faint glow of light. It grew slightly as it approached. Someone rounded the last corner and her gaze spotted her captor.

The tangled hair of black coarse wire hung wild about him. His mouth was open, a grin of victory upon his face, evil in his eyes. She held her breath, and backed away from the door.

He didn't open the door of bars, but just stood there, leering at her. "I see yur awake now. I brought ye some vittles."

Eve remained still; the putrid odor permeating the air caused her stomach to roil. She gagged. "Just put them on the floor."

"Are ye sure now, Missy? The rats will git it b'fore ye will."

"I'm sure." She wished she had a handkerchief to press to her nose.

She watched as he set a rough stone cup down just inside her cell, and then opening his waistcoat, he withdrew something wrapped in cloth and set it beside the drink.

Eve stayed where she was and watched as several rats ran to the offering.

"G'ahead. I'll not bother ye. I'm ta keep ye fed until he comes for ye."

It was too late; a large rat pulled the small roll from its fabric covering and scurried to the far corner of her cell. The others followed and Eve listened to them devouring her meal.

"Too bad you didn't eat, ye'll be hungry now. But ye'll eat the next one I bring ye, nicely or with some help from me."

"What concern is it of yours what I eat?" Her defiant voice concealed her complete terror.

"I'll not git me gold if yur not well, and rest assur'd Missy, I'll git me my gold."

"How much is he paying you?" An idea began to take shape in her mind.

"Enough." His gruff voice revealed a trace of uncertainty.

She forced her voice to sound confident, "I'll pay you more, double, in fact."

He paused for a moment. She wondered what evil he contemplated. Then he spoke, his words measured. "How much have ye got with ye?

"I haven't any with me now, but I can arrange to have all you require brought to you." His face broke once again into an evil smile. He shook his head slowly and began to laugh. The sound low and cruel, and then it increased to loud and full of hatred.

"I'll not take any chances with ye and yur rich nobleman. I have someone who'll pay for ye—eagerly." He looked directly into her eyes.

Eve gathered her last shreds of courage, "But can you trust him to pay?" She swallowed, hoping God would put the words in her mouth to change his mind. "I am a lady of my word. All I want is my freedom. You will be a rich man if you bargain with me."

"I cannot trust 'im, in that ye are right, but I have no need to trust 'im. If he doesn't pay, I'll kill 'im."

Of course you will, she thought. "Please, consider what I have said."

"I'll leave this candle for ye." He set the offering down beside the bars. "I've not a mind to hurt ye, missy," and then evidently thinking more he added, "Just don't ye cross me."

He turned and began to make his way out, the stench of him lingering, the scraping sound fading, along with her hope.

Chapter Twenty-Two

Beau lay upon his bed, weary, and worried. Although, he knew he should try to sleep, he would not find respite while she was away. He moved from the bed, splashed his face with water from the stand, and headed to the stables.

Donald and Paul were already there. John, the stable boy had saddled their mounts. They stood straight and alert, ready to mount and ride off. The air was thick with humidity and concern, a grim determination settled about the men.

"I thought we agreed you would rest awhile." Donald began.

"I'm going with you." Beau moved to motion to John, but he was already leading one of Donald's stallions from the stable.

"I don't believe this is the wisest course of action. How good can you be? You haven't slept all night." Donald said.

Beau approached his friend; he was in no mood to be ordered about. He lowered his voice. "I'm going." He could feel the anger rising up, anger that really wasn't directed toward Donald, yet, it was there, and Beau's patience had peaked several hours earlier.

"We depart at once." Paul smiled.

"We all stand out like nobleman in workhouses." Donald motioned to John, "Bring us worn hats and the shirts hanging in the side room."

The three men stripped off their shirts,

waistcoats, and jackets. They quickly donned the servants' clothing and hats.

"Let's depart." Beau said. "I've no intention of lolling about all morning."

Donald picked up a handful of dirt and rubbed it over his face. Beau and Paul quickly did the same. Finally, Beau mounted his steed, "We're off."

Paul and Donald followed and the trio silently headed north. The blazing sun gave no mercy to the hunters as they continued to ride.

"This way." Donald motioned to his right. It was the first time he had spoken since they had left the stable. Beau followed, for he knew Donald was meeting his man. *Would they find her? Would she be unharmed?* Thoughts of Gregory Searsly touching his beloved caused his heart to race. He hoped he would have the chance to wrap his hands about the man's throat, for what he had done.

Paul interrupted his thoughts, "We will find her."

Beau looked over to his brother. "I'm not going back without her. She is my life."

Paul met his eyes for a moment, offered a slight smile, and remained silent.

It wasn't long before they arrived in a small country town. Dust rose from the road and welcomed them with its powdery coating. Only a few men entered and exited the shops and inns. Beau guessed most of the town's inhabitants were in the fields or tending their farms.

Donald dismounted and walked his horse slowly as if to evade suspicion. The other men followed his example and also dismounted.

In a matter of minutes, they came to the end of the road that led through town.

Donald motioned slightly with his head, and Beau and Paul followed him out behind a large barn.

A dark man of Indian descent met them. His

hair and eyes were of the deepest ebony, while his coffee colored skin gleamed in the mid-day sun. He sat regally upon his dove grey mount, eyes slanted, confidence and humility oozing from every pore.

"Kiran, it is good to see you." Donald began.

"It is good, indeed." The man replied, his accent nearly indiscernible.

Beau could sense the man had news. He didn't have to wait to find relief.

"I have news of your Lord Searsly."

Donald's expression betrayed nothing. He was as impassive as if he were casually conversing over dinner.

"What have you discovered?" Beau asked.

Kiran looked to Donald for approval. Donald nodded his head once. "There is another small village one hour west of here, Stockford. Are you familiar with it?"

Beau nodded.

"The Lord Searsly you seek has been staying at the Westings Pub for the last several days." Kiran glanced behind him, and then looked into Beau's eyes. "He has been utterly rude and arrogant, lying to rest any doubt of him being the Searsly you are seeking."

"Have you seen him yourself?" Beau asked.

"Yes. A slight man, with pale, watery eyes and thinning light brown hair. He tries to grope the young serving wenches and demands the owner to cater to his whims."

"Let's depart." Beau began to turn his horse.

"Wait. One moment." Donald extracted a heavy pouch from his saddlebag. He handed it over to the dark man.

Kiran raised his hand in refusal. "It honors me to help you, my lord. You may call on me again if you have need."

Donald slipped the pouch back and fastened his

bag. "You have my sincere gratitude, I consider myself indebted to you."

"Never. We are indebted to each other." Kiran sat proudly. "I must depart. Go find him. Godspeed to you."

The three men watched as Kiran rode off toward the lush countryside, his back straight, his manner purposeful.

"On to Stockford." Beau called.

"I believe we should wait until nightfall. We shall overtake Searsly and have her back with certainty."

Beau drew his horse to a stop. "I'm going now. If you wish to return to Beckinbrook, then so be it. I'm going for Eve."

Donald stopped his horse beside Beau. "She isn't with him. I know how these things evolve. Night will be better. We shall have the element of surprise on our side, and Searsly will have no chance of escape."

Beau could feel his heart pounding wildly. He wanted to rescue her now—he couldn't bear the thought of her at Searsly's mercy. But Donald could be correct. If they returned in the evening, he would never see them coming.

"Fine. We travel at nightfall." Beau led the way back to Beckinbrook, barely controlled fury his companion.

****

Eve sat on the cot, her eyes scanning the small circle of light the candle provided. The rats had stayed away, satisfied for now with the bread they had stolen. She didn't care. She felt no hunger, only longing.

Fear tried to wash over her, but she valiantly fought it off. She must face this ordeal regardless of her emotions; she vowed she would face it bravely. Her eyes narrowed as she tried to contrive a plan to escape.

Picking up the candle, she walked the perimeter of her prison—looking again for anything she could use for protection.

Just beyond the bars, she saw a dark shadow of an object. She moved the candle closer but still could not see it clearly. Carefully, she set the light down and reached out to grab whatever it was.

Straining as far as she could, her fingertips barely grazed it. Again, she tried, stretching herself to the farthest limit, still coming up the tiniest bit short. She went back to her cot, examined it, looking for anything she could use in her quest.

Inspiration struck—she removed her leather shoe. It was not the delicate shoe of a lady but the serviceable shoe of a servant. She moved back to the gate, again, carefully setting the light aside and scooped the object closer. A slight *clanking* rang out, and Eve prayed no one could hear it.

Reaching out, she closed her fingers around the object, pulled it inside the cell, and looked it over in the light.

It appeared to be the remains of a rusty manacle. A rough, edge of metal protruded jaggedly from one side. The other side, smooth and unbroken had not suffered the same effects of time. Smiling in the candlelight, Eve moved to the decaying mattress and tore a strip of the soiled fabric. She quickly wrapped the manacle in the rag, and fastened it carefully to her chemise. It poked her a bit, but she could endure that slight discomfort. After all, she now had *a weapon*.

Barely having a moment to celebrate her good fortune, she heard the eerie scraping of *his* withered foot. Slowly she sat down and tried to hide the hope that bloomed within her spirit. Closing her eyes, she exhaled and sought out the most important disguise she had ever hoped to use, one of total dejection and fear.

The dragging continued until finally he stood at the gate. "No need to look so glum, missy. I'll be takin' ye from 'ere in a short while."

Raising her head, she drew back by instinct. He loomed larger than most men, and his presence called to mind all that was evil, sinful, and bad.

"Have you considered my offer?" A hopeful tone emerged from her parched throat.

"Nay. I've made me deal. Sorry missy."

Eve nodded and felt the comfort of the manacle beneath her clothing. "Very well." *She would not hesitate to use it.*

Once again, he opened his waistcoat and withdrew something wrapped in cloth. "Come, eat. Ye'll need yur strength when ye meet the gov'ner."

Eve hated to agree but she knew he was right. She would need her strength. She stood and tested her newfound bravery. Slowly she raised her eyes to meet the black ones leering at her openly. She walked forward, took the parcel he offered, and opened it—revealing a piece of roast mutton.

"Thank you."

He made no reply, just turned and headed back to where he had come, the scraping and dragging fading into the distance.

****

Eve swallowed the last of the mutton and wiped her face on the cloth wrap. She straightened her clothing, and checked to make certain her weapon remained hidden. There was nothing more she could do until her captor returned.

Dark sapphire eyes spoke love to her soul. A heady feeling washed over her, reminding her of the man who loved her, who waited for her. Did he look for her now? Did he long for her as she desperately longed for him? Her body remembered the sensations his kisses had wrought and she shivered in remembered desire. A tear escaped as she sat

207

bathed in tender memories of Beau. Quickly wiping it away she thought, *I'll come back to you...* all the while praying he would somehow hear this song of her heart.

After only an hour or so, she heard the familiar scraping. She waited, swallowed her dread, and called forth her courage. Now was the time for bravery. Now was the time to take advantage of every opportunity for escape.

She kept her head down—praying silently. The jingling of a key in the lock, told her indeed the time was now.

He did not step into the cell, but instead motioned for her to come out. Eve nodded her head and walked through the open bars.

"Don't ye bother screamin', thars non 'ere to 'ear ye."

"I'm not going to scream."

"Good. And don't ye run ahead, 'cause I'll catch ye and may burn ye a bit with me hot wax."

"I'm not going to run." Eve hoped her compliance would convince him to leave her hands free.

He stayed behind her and guided her through the dark, twisting passage. At times, it was so narrow she brushed both shoulders against the damp stone.

He touched her shoulder lightly from time to time, never really hurting her but keeping her in line with his intimidating presence. They began to climb crumbling stone stairs.

The air began to feel warmer—they must be nearing the top. Eve's heart raced as she willed her feet to stay slow. She did not want to alert him to suspicion.

"I'm gonna hold yur hands together like this," he grabbed both hands and squeezed them tightly behind her back. "The door's 'ere." He kicked and the door opened.

Eve's eyes were not accustomed to the dim light of the room. Although early evening, it was still too bright after her imprisonment in near darkness. Standing still, she waited to see what he would do next.

As her eyes slowly became adjusted, she took in her new surroundings. She stood in a small cobblestone building. The floor was roughly made of creek stone, as was the fireplace. An old, shabby table sat in the middle of the small space, with an even shabbier chair pulled nearby.

He relaxed his grip on her hands. She was thankful, but did not try to step away—she needed to stay close. His foul stench caused her stomach to contract, but outwardly, she strived for a calm appearance.

Surprisingly, he released her hands completely and moved around to stand before her. In the twilight of the evening, he was more hideous than ever.

Grease and grime covered every inch of his exposed skin. His clothes were little more than ancient rags, and his hair was a tangled mass of snarls. He moved carefully, dragging that leg behind him, yet Eve knew he would be a worthy opponent in a struggle.

She lowered her eyes and waited for him to speak. "I'll be bringin' ye to yur master now." He reached inside the waistband of his trousers and slowly removed a large pistol. He waved it in the direction of the door, "after you, missy."

Eve stepped outside and realized her prison had been beneath the ruins of a castle. The old structure must have been regal in its time, but now crumbling walls stood hauntingly. Weeds and small brush etched up around it, as if to hide its shame.

From beneath lowered lids, she looked out in every direction but found no clue as to her whereabouts. Raising her head, she saw a carriage with a driver and two matched bays.

"Git in."

Eve carefully entered the carriage, mindful of the cold metal pressed against her ribs. Her captor grunted a command to the driver and then slid in beside her. She held her breath and then resolved to breathe through her mouth. The carriage began its journey with a jolt. Eve kept her face turned away; looking out the window as the crumbling castle faded into the darkening night, and wondered what awaited her at the next stop.

****

Beau and his fellow riders had returned and washed at the stable after their fruitless search. They left their mounts and instructions for John, before entering the manor's library to plan for the coming night. Nothing would stop Beau from finding Eve. His determination drove him forward, while he focused on her rescue and Searsly's demise. Donald and Paul took nourishment and rested, while Beau refused, letting his hunger reach a dangerous height.

Now, hours later, they met again at the stable. John had three horses saddled and ready All three were dressed in black, their faces serious, strained and determined.

The moon hung full and low in the darkness. Stars formed trails in a myriad of directions, and as Beau looked up, he prayed they would lead him to Eve.

He longed to have her back in his arms again, to inhale her sweet fragrance, and take her beneath him, showing her all the love he'd been holding inside his heart. His longing fueled his anger. He could barely wait to have Gregory Searsly in his grasp.

Donald's terse command interrupted his

thoughts. "Let's depart."

He led the way, beyond the safety of Beckinbrook Manor. Beau and Paul followed closely. Pistols in their waistbands, knives strapped to their calves. They traveled in perfect symmetry, westward where the woman he loved would hopefully be found...waiting for him.

Chapter Twenty-Three

Laura's eyes fluttered open. Taking in her surroundings, she determined with complete assurance she had no idea where she was. The flickering candle on the bedside table provided just enough light to reveal the fact that she was not at home.

Sitting up, she listened carefully. She could hear the gentle snoring of another person.

"Excuse me, miss?"

The snoring stopped. A small, round form rose from her bed and stared at her.

"I say, excuse me, miss?" Laura tried again.

Suddenly the woman ran to her, "Oh, my lady!" Tears streamed down Mary's face, pure joy dancing in her still sleepy eyes.

"Mary." Laura recognized her. "Mary, where are we?"

"My lady, we are at Beckinbrook, visiting Evelyn," she replied.

"Why is Evelyn at Beckinbrook?" Laura sat straighter then swinging her legs over the side of the bed said, "I can't seem to remember anything."

"My lady, please...stay there for a moment. Let me explain a bit to you." She told Laura an extraordinary tale about being ill.

"Well, I feel fine now. I can't believe I have been ill so long, why it seems like only yesterday..."

"My lady?" Mary patted her hand gently.

"My darling Evelyn...Gregory tried to hurt her,

to ruin her innocence...I was going to send him away..." She turned to Mary, "Did I?"

"You became ill. Evelyn came here to stay with the Earl and Countess; she did not leave word as to where she was."

"Is my daughter...well?" Laura asked, suddenly fearful of the reply.

Laura watched as Mary seemed to stall for her answer. Before she could ask her about her indecisiveness, a red haired woman bustled into the chamber.

"Lady Searsly...how do you feel?" She asked.

"I feel quite well, except for my legs, they seem to be a bit weak." The woman approached her bed.

"Let us get you up for a moment; we shall support your arms. It would be good for you to walk around." Mary came around and supported Laura's right arm, while the other woman held up her left.

Slowly the women guided her around the room. Laura took to walking as if no time had passed since her last stroll through a garden. She waved the women away and carefully took several steps of her own.

"I am no physician, but I do declare myself quite healed. Is there anything I might eat now, I am a bit hungry."

Mary could barely contain her excitement. "I'll go fetch ye a nice snack, my lady."

"Thank you, Mary." Then turning to the other woman, "And who might you be, dear?"

"I am Ginger Rockwell. I am an acquaintance of your daughter's and her betrothed."

"My daughter is betrothed?" Laura sat, hope glittering in her eyes.

"Yes. Your lovely daughter is betrothed to an associate of my husband's. The gentleman's name is Lord Beaumont, the son of the Duke of Merdine. Lord Beaumont arranged for us to meet and care for you."

"I have never met a female physician."

"I am not a physician. I am a herbalist. My husband and I collect herbs from all over the world. My husband is a chemist, and he has found many uses for the combined mixtures of many of these plants. We were able to help you with one of his more recent discoveries."

"Tell me, dear lady about the gentleman my daughter is betrothed to, please."

"Lord Beaumont is a kind and well-distinguished gentleman. He has been a great encouragement to my husband and myself. With his generous investments, he has helped to provide needed medicine for many who desperately need it, yet, never would have had access to such relief."

"Does he love my daughter?" She asked.

"Oh Lady Searsly, he does not speak of the secrets of his heart to me, but I see the way he gazes at her when she is unaware. His manner and his regard are nothing if not gentle. He seems to treasure her company, the words she speaks, the very ground her feet trod upon..."

Laura nodded her head, smiling faintly.

"And do you believe she loves him?"

"I do."

"And Gregory has approved the match?"

"I am not certain, my lady. Perhaps your maid will know."

"Where is my Evelyn now? I wish to see her at once."

Before Ginger could reply, Mary entered carrying a large tray filled with scones, fruit, cheese and weak tea. She set the tray on the nightstand and began to fill a plate for Laura.

Laura began to nibble on the fare given to her—only to stop.

"Why will no one answer me directly regarding

my Evelyn?"

The two women looked at each other, but said nothing.

Laura forced herself to remain calm. She would give them a bit more time.

Ginger spoke first, "Evelyn is missing just now." Laura didn't blink, raising her eyebrows, she willed her to continue. "Lord Beaumont and his brother went to Kentwood last night to bring you here so my husband and I could care for you...your daughter was to stay here and wait with the Earl."

Mary took over, "Our Evelyn followed behind the gentleman for she had been terribly worried over your health these last few months. She has not yet returned to Beckinbrook."

Laura began to stand on her wobbly legs, "We must call the magistrate! My goodness, Mary, how could you keep something so serious from me, please send for the magistrate at once!"

"My lady, we did not want to worry ye. Ye have been ill for so long." Mary cried again, "I am so sorry, you know I love her as if she were me own." She moved to sit beside Laura.

"The gentlemen have gone looking for her, the Beaumont brothers, and the Earl. I have complete assurance they will bring her back soon." Ginger added.

She turned to Mary, "Never the less, you will do as I have requested, send for the magistrate, immediately."

****

Only the sound of the horses' hooves crunching against the road disrupted the almost silent night. The town was mostly deserted. A fine carriage sat at the entrance of town, no driver in sight. A few staggering men moved slowly down the main street, oblivious to the determined force that cautiously approached.

In shadowy recesses at the end of the street sat a small poorly maintained establishment. The slanting sign proclaimed it, *Westings Pub*. Beau took the lead and motioned for the others to follow him around back.

A weathered stable sat to the rear of the pub, inside a lone lantern burned. A large wooded copse nestled the stable. "I will see if he is in there and return in a moment." Beau dismounted and headed to the pub. He noted a sleeping stable-hand and three horses at the stable. As he neared the rear of the pub, his gaze took in windows coated with filth. He looked inside, but could not see the patrons clearly. To the left he noticed a servant's entrance and quickly ducked inside. A steep and narrow staircase was his only option, so he quietly picked his way to the upper level.

He found himself in a large foyer with three doors, one in every direction and a long hall with a fourth door at its end. He saw another staircase, intended for the use of the customers, and from the sounds drifting up, he knew it would lead down to the main dining area.

He moved from door to door, pressing his ear against the chipped paint, hoping to find a clue as to Gregory's whereabouts.

There was no sound behind the first door to his left. He moved to the next and heard the smoky laughter of a woman who was definitely not Eve. He listened for a moment longer and heard a man. He spoke with a thick Irish accent, and Beau knew it wasn't Gregory. The third room was also silent, which left just the door at the end of the hall.

His heart raced in anticipation. As he neared the door, he heard voices. He cleared his mind of all concern and listened carefully.

"We had an agreement, Mr. Sorrows."

"Yea. It's now time to make a new agreement." A

stranger responded.

"I have already paid you plenty for your shoddy service. I still do not have that which I am searching for." Beau knew it was Gregory. All at once, the memories he had tried desperately to bury assaulted him again.

"I 'ave what ye search fer. Er nobleman will pay double what ye're offren'. Since I've done all the work, I should make a bit o' profit, think ye not?"

"Listen to me, you filthy creature, I have already paid you quite generously. You'll deliver the wench to me, or I'll cut your worthless throat where you stand."

"If ye were man e'nough to cut me, ye'd have been man e'nough to get 'er yourself. Nay, ye'll not cut me, and ye'll not git yur hands on the chit."

Rage boiled to nearly exploding within Beau. His breath came hard, and his fists clenched at his side. It took every ounce of strength he had not to break down the door—he must not endanger her by rash actions...but he longed to grab Gregory Searsly and pound his fist into him relentlessly. He heard footsteps, and the doorknob began to turn.

Beau backed into the foyer. There was nowhere to hide. He quickly moved to the servant's stairs and backed up—allowing the darkness to conceal him.

He watched as Gregory's door opened and the dirtiest thing he had ever beheld slowly walked down the hall. Beau stood transfixed as he listened to the unusual dragging sound. A hideous stench accompanied the man and as he neared him, Beau saw how he dragged his left leg.

The strange footprints in the garden.

He had been at Beckinbrook...he had been watching Eve! Knowing the stranger had her, he watched as he began to descend the stairs into the common room of the pub. He was about to follow, when Gregory's door burst open with a crash, and

Gregory came storming out into the foyer.

The kidnapper turned and began to make his way back up the stairs. He drew a pistol from beneath his waistcoat and pointed it at Gregory's heart.

Gregory slid a long blade from its case and held it up.

"Yur no match fer me, Gov'ner." He pulled the trigger back and Beau heard the telltale click.

Gregory snarled like a provoked dog, "Bring me the girl—NOW."

"Pay me accordin'ly, and ye'll have yur spry missy."

Gregory slowly reached into his waistcoat and retrieved a heavy purse. The kidnapper's eyes followed the money with unbridled lust. He un-cocked his pistol and lowered it to his side. Then reaching out to take the purse, Gregory slapped his hand away with the knife.

"Not until I see the girl."

Something burned in the kidnapper's black eyes. His face reddened, and he spoke in a guttural tone, "Yu'll be sorry fer that."

Sorrows turned back to the stairs and made his way down, cursing.

Beau watched the relief flood over Gregory's normally pallid face and heard him take several deep breaths. He re-sheathed his blade and leaned against the wall...waiting for Eve to be brought before him, like a lamb to a rabid wolf.

He watched the coward retreat down the hall, back into his room.

Beau quietly headed back down the stairs, out beyond the stables, then broke into a run. He found Donald and Paul where he had left them and quickly explained all that had happened.

"I'll go after the kidnapper," Donald offered. Beau quickly described the godless thing.

"Paul, come with me. He is going to bring Eve back to that pub soon, and when he does, it would not surprise me if he kills Gregory."

Their plan quickly made, Donald rode off with a detailed description of Sorrows. Paul entered the pub and stayed in the main room, drinking whiskey, and feigning interest in the card games being offered. Beau crept back up the servants' stairs and waited for the creature to bring back the woman he loved.

****

The carriage door opened and *he* motioned for the driver to leave. Blue watery eyes glanced at Eve, then exited the carriage and climbed back into the driving seat.

"Time to go, missy." He smiled that black smile and bile rose in her throat.

Eve slid across the seat, knowing this was now the time to use her weapon. She complied easily enough, and soon she was out in the cool night air. She inhaled deeply, thankful to be out of close confines with Sorrows and his stench.

She looked around the small country town and recognized her surroundings to be Stockford. She hadn't been here since she was a young girl in ribbons, yet the town hadn't changed much in all those years.

"Keep yur mouth quiet, or yu'll be very sorry."

She would obey him, for now. The street was deserted, and she doubted anyone would be around to hear her scream.

He moved behind her and grabbed her arms, pushing her forward. *Now is the time.* "Please—leave my hands—my arms are aching, I am so very tired—just tell me where and I will go...please..."

He took pity and released her hands. He then told her to stop. She did as he said. He watched as she took a moment to stretch her arms and then twisted from side to side. She then stopped and bowed her head, waiting for his next command.

"Go on down a bit more."

They kept to the shadows and Eve made sure she moved slowly—she wanted to continue to give the impression she was too tired to do anything but obey. The hour was late, and the shops were all closed. Eve slowed a bit more, "May I stop and stretch again?"

"Only fer a moment, missy."

Eve twisted again and felt the manacle fall to her waist. She lifted her hands up high and stretched to the moon, and then as she lowered her hands, she quickly reached under her shirt and grabbed the rusty bar of steel.

She turned as quickly as she could, drew back her arm, and threw all her weight and frustration—every hope, every wish, and every last bit of life into hitting him in the face.

The metal made contact to the side of his head with a loud "clank". His face bore no expression as he fell fast to the dusty ground.

In shock she stood over his body, black unblinking eyes stared up at her. *Oh my Lord, I've killed him.* She closed her eyes and prayed, "Forgive me, Lord." Turning to flee, an iron grip reached up and closed around her ankle.

Eve screamed into the night. He held her with such strength she could not move. Still struggling to get free, she was unprepared for a second assailant.Gregory grabbed her arm, yanking her so hard, her teeth crashed together. Gregory would never let her go, he would probably kill her before he was finished. Eve quieted her racing heart—she needed to think. She still had the manacle in her other hand. Feigning acquiesce for a moment, she relaxed and then hit Gregory directly on the bridge of his nose with the rusty iron.

He dropped her arm at once, and held his nose, blood spraying out over his clothes, Eve, and the dirt-encrusted man lying in the street.

Eve stamped down hard Sorrows arm. He let out a howl and withdrew his hand—and Eve finally found her escape. She ran down the middle of the deserted street, screaming. With a thud, she hit an immovable object. She looked up into the deepest blue eyes she had ever seen. Strong arms held her as she trembled and sobbed.

"My darling, you are safe now." The velvet voice from her dreams sounded like music.

She reveled in his protective embrace. He held her tightly and stroked her hair—she melted into his body. Her heart pounded fiercely, and she let out a cry of joy.

"Oh Beau...thank God!"

Chapter Twenty-Four

She sighed in relief. It was finally over. Looking back down the street, she saw Donald and Paul making quick work of binding Sorrows and Gregory's hands behind their backs. Donald left both men in Paul's able care and crossed over to where Beau and Eve were standing.

"Are you harmed?" Donald asked.

"No, I'm fine...wonderful in fact." She spoke through her tears and gasps.

"I won't lecture you right now about the folly of sneaking out last night. I believe you have well learned your lesson, and I also believe you will soon no longer be my concern," He looked up at Beau. "Paul and I are taking these scoundrels to the magistrate and then we shall return to Beckinbrook."

"Donald, Beau, thank you for everything."

Donald answered, "No thanks required. I watched the way you pulverized those two sorry sops, and realized I could have stayed back at the manor in my bed." He marched back to the prisoners, and he and Paul proceeded to tighten their bonds.

"You have been here all along?" She asked.

"We arrived only moments ago. I found Gregory and overheard him bargaining with your kidnapper. Paul and I followed him out of the inn as quickly as possible. It was then we came upon you, although when we approached, it seemed as if you had matters well in hand." He smiled at her.

Eve looked at her hands and realized she still clung to the manacle. "The Lord was with me. He allowed me to find this wonderful weapon, and He allowed you to find me." She smiled brightly at him.

"Sorrows didn't hurt you, then?" His face creased with worry.

"Actually, he treated me fairly. It was *I* who may have hurt *him.*"

"Retribution for some past unpunished offense, I believe." He smiled again, "I am glad to see I have no worry of your welfare, it seems as if you are well equipped to protect yourself."

"No, my lord, I will always have need of you to keep me safe. As you can well see, when left to my own devices, I have a tendency to muck things up."

Beau chuckled softly. "I will always be here to keep you safe. I pledge you my heart and protection upon my very life."

He lowered his mouth and took hers in an instant. She opened eagerly to his seeking tongue, feeling the effects deep down to her serviceable leather shoes. He pulled her closer, and for a moment, she felt the evidence of his arousal. Desire uncoiled deep in her belly and gave way to the most delicious sensations she had ever experienced. Heat enveloped them as they clung to each other celebrating their bliss at finding each other again. Her soul had finally found its match and reveled in the delight of finally being home.

He thrust his hands through the silk of her hair, scattering her pins upon the deserted road. She pulled him closer—wishing to finally claim this union they had so longingly awaited.

Beau pulled away for a moment as a drifting cloud revealed the moon's soft glow. It was at that moment, Paul marched by with the prisoners. Gregory turned and saw Eve in Beau's arms and stopped.

Paul prodded him, "Keep going."

Gregory took a step and then recognition washed over him. "You! You killed my sister!" A mirthless evil cackle split the night following his accusation. "I'll tell all who'll listen...how the high and mighty Lord Beaumont used and tossed aside my innocent sister!"

Beau looked to Eve, the love shining in her eyes only moments before, remained. She *still* loved him. Her faith in him sent courage coursing through his veins, "I never killed your sister, you know that. I could not be held responsible for her feelings...she told you what happened that night and you refused to believe it."

Eve pulled his arm, "Come, my darling, we'll not listen to such prattle."

"What's the matter, stepsister? Don't you want to hear how I found your beloved in Lady Sutherby's sitting room with my sister half undressed?"

Eve looked up into Beau's eyes. "I have no worry of my lord's character. I'll not stand here listening to you accuse Lord Beaumont. You're nothing but a lying pig, Gregory."

Paul jerked Gregory forward, and the little man had the gall to chuckle all the way down the street. Every now and again, a decipherable word could be understood. "Scandal. Ruined. Reputation."

Beau, arm firmly fixed around Eve's shoulders led her in the opposite direction from the captives. He would wait until they rode out before taking her to his steed.

"Tell me what he speaks of." She asked.

Beau continued on in silence. He had no desire to offend this sweet innocent. Again, her persistence interrupted his musings.

"Please, tell me what has transpired between the two of you."

"Must we speak of this now? I have only just found you again. Let us enjoy our moment of happiness before it is quickly snatched away."

Eve stopped and looked up into his eyes. "No one shall snatch away our happiness." Beau's gaze darted back toward the disappearing figures. "Look at me."

He obeyed her command. "I love you, Beau. Nothing shall change that. Now I must insist you tell me what Gregory is talking about. I had never heard of anyone killing his sister."

"You insist, do you?" He responded almost mischievously.

"I am waiting, my lord." She crossed her arms and began to tap her right foot impatiently.

"You will most assuredly be the death of me, my darling." He drew her to the stoop of a closed book seller. He motioned for her to sit, and then joined her, his arm once again across her shoulders. Beau then drew her close to him.

"I didn't kill anyone." He began.

"I certainly never thought you did."

"But he blames me for her death..." Beau went on to tell about the fateful night, about Felicity's advances, and her subsequent depression.

"But all of that, although quite unfortunate, is not your fault."

"No, but still, there may have been something I could have done to prevent the tragedy...what was I thinking, accompanying a young lady into a sitting room without a chaperone? Perhaps I should have paid more attention to the subtle messages in her eyes...perhaps I should have never danced with her..."

"Perhaps, perhaps, perhaps...indeed!" Eve's eyes caught fire as her face flushed with heat, "I have spent many nights playing this very game. When Gregory attacked me I thought I must have sent some lustful message his way, my gown was too tight, I stood too close when I spoke to him...on and on I went, trying to take responsibility for an act I had no influence over. Gregory's own deplorable actions were the only cause of my problem with him and I dare say the same is true of his sister."

Beau sat still for a moment. "Yes, that is in fact the truth; however, because of my actions a young lady is dead."

"But you did nothing wrong." She looked at him, impassioned.

"Yet I feel as if I have."

Eve sat silent then, thinking of her retort. "Should you have ravaged the young lady? Been forced into a marriage by Gregory with a woman you did not love? Would you that were the outcome?"

"Of course not...for if I had been forced to marry her, I would not be free to marry you."

"And are you free, my lord?"

He ran his strong hand through his thick, dark hair. "I guess I am not quite as free as I once thought."

"Why would you say such a thing?" she asked.

"Because when we formally announce our betrothal, Gregory will spew his twisted version of what happened between Felicity and me, and you will join me as a victim of scandal."

"As long as I am joined to you, I will happily be a victim of scandal." She smiled.

"And if we are blessed with children, must they also pay the consequence of their father's misfortune?"

"Our children will be proud of their father. He is a man of great character and unwavering integrity."

He laughed. "Oh Eve...your confidence in me is commendable. You make me feel like the luckiest man in the world, yet if you are joined to me, all I can offer you is a lifetime of whispers behind your back and snubs by those you once felt were friends."

"You can offer me love."

"You are so very easy to love." His voice had dropped an octave.

"Then love me."

His resolve finally snapped. With her tenderness, she had gently coaxed him into revealing his deepest secret. Her logic and understanding had persuaded him to express the fear that held him entrapped for years. And in finding out the darkness in his soul, she still declared she wanted him.

He pulled her onto his lap and lowered his mouth to hers. She was ready—her mouth—molten like liquid velvet. Their tongues mated and danced while their bodies burned with the intense heat of kindled passion. Sensations, desires, yearnings, melded together. There were no more thoughts to think or words to speak; only the power of their love.

Beau allowed his common sense to overcome his desire. He would ravage her here on Main Street if he didn't get some control. He pulled his mouth from hers and with a gravelly whisper mumbled, "I need to take you back to the horse."

He lifted her in his arms as if she were a child and carried her behind the row of shops. As they began to make their way back, they passed a tiny stable. Fatigue had begun to take its toll, and Beau did not relish riding back to Beckinbrook quite so soon. He set her down carefully, his need overpowering his intellect.

An unlit lantern hung beside the door. Beau quickly lit it and pulled her inside the small shelter.

Fresh hay had been laid out; it smelled woodsy, yet clean. "Will you stay with me here, until morning?" He asked, setting the lantern on an empty trough.

She moved into his waiting arms. She slipped her slender arms around him burying her head in

227

his chest.

"Eve...Let me love you."

He kissed her again, and for a long moment, the only sound they could hear was the beating of their hearts and their impassioned gasps for air.

Entwined, together they drifted off to sleep. Although his body ached from utter exhaustion, his heart was yet unfulfilled. He yearned for her— yearned with such intensity it left him numb for all else. In dreams, he found his climbing desire, and embraced it as if it was real...

He lifted her hair from her shoulder and began to nibble on her neck, pushing her shirt collar lower and lower. She moaned softly in response, all the while holding on to him as if for dear life. He dragged his lips away from the soft, silky column and looking into her eyes he whispered, "May I?" His hands fingering the buttons of the shirt she had borrowed.

Slowly she nodded. His fingers unbuttoned the top button. Eve shivered. He opened the next button, his gaze never leaving Eve's. The third button gave way easily. He stopped and slowly pulled her shirt away from her body.

Her breasts strained against the nearly transparent fabric of her shift. He exhaled as she revealed her wonder to his hungry gaze. "You are exquisite...the most beautiful woman I have every seen, or dreamed of..." Her nipples hardened in response.

He reached out and cupped the fullness of her breast. He gently touched her in every possible way, bringing himself and hopefully her closer and closer to some unnamed ecstasy. Finally, he lowered her shift.

The fullness he craved lay before him like a feast before a starving man. Hungrily he kissed her, deeply, telling her without words of his intense need.

All the while, his fingers tangled in her hair, caressed her breasts, and encircled her hardened nipples.

He groaned and then lowered his mouth, suckling her, softly at first, then more firmly. Eve cried out. Without removing his mouth, he swept her up in his arms and carried her to the large pile of hay. Gently he set her down and then raised his mouth to find her lips again.

"Take off your shirt." She whispered.

He quickly unbuttoned it and threw it aside. "Oh." Eve's mouth barely made a sound.

He sat beside her and removed her shirt, then pushed her shift all the way down to her waist. She trembled at his touch. He just stared at her, her hair wild around her, framing her luminous eyes and feminine form. She was the loveliest vision his tired mind could ever conjure.

He joined her atop the hay—kissing her lips, feeling the heady torture of her full breasts against his naked chest, smelling her scent, a scent of innocent longing.

They strained to get closer to each other, knowing the only way to find relief would be in the act of making love.

He wanted her more than the air he gasped, more than food, more than his principles. His mind was completed addled by their growing passion, and he feared and hoped to find his release within the body he worshipped.

His eyes opened for a moment, and he realized he'd been dreaming. Eve was everything he had ever wanted, and she was more than that by far. Slowly, in great despair, his sense began to return to him. When her eyes opened, drooping with fatigue, he forced himself to speak.

"My darling, I want to make love to you, more than I could ever express, but we cannot."

Eve sat up slowly, her cheeks a tantalizing pink—he wondered if she had dreamt of making love also.

"We must wait until we are wed." He spoke as if telling of the death of a loved one. "I hope it will be very soon."

"Yes…you are right, of course." She whispered before moving closer to him, and he held her tightly in his arms. "It will be soon, if it is up to me."

"I have had my father arrange a special license. It can be next week if that suits you, my dear."

Suddenly Eve pulled away. "Were you and Paul successful at getting mother moved?"

Beau was eager to tell her about the rescue. "Yes. Your mother and Mary are safe inside your chamber at Beckinbrook. The Rockwells paid her a visit and expect her to begin to recover soon."

Eve jumped up and clapped her hands together. "Truly?"

Beau's heart lurched to see her so happy. "Yes, they had an herbal medicine to help your mother recover from the damage of the poison." After he spoke it, he cursed himself silently.

"The poison?" Her eyes were wide and then aflame with anger.

"Your stepbrother was giving her a slow-working poison. Apparently he had used the same concoction on his own father."

Deflated, she slumped against Beau. He took her in his arms and held her there. He stroked her hair as he relayed the information William and Ginger had informed him of only yesterday.

"Then in spite of this new horror, William believes mother will quite recover?"

"Yes, my darling."

"Then we shall await her recovery before we marry. I should like my mother to be there, with me, as she should be."

"Of course."

He held her close, then feeling a familiar tightening in his trousers prayed silently for her quick and complete recovery.

Chapter Twenty-Five

They rode out of Stockford as the sun began its lazy ascent. The birds chirped joyfully, serenading their trip back to Beckinbrook. Soon they were leaving their horses at the stable. Beau took her hand to escort her into the manor.

"I must look a mess," she tried to smooth her hair back, but could feel it bouncing out in all directions. Her pins had been left on the main street in Stockford and even if she had them, there certainly hadn't been a comb or brush to use anyway.

"Definitely not." Beau's gaze raked her slowly with undisguised hunger.

Eve conducted her own perusal of her beloved's appearance. He was as unkempt as she, yet he looked dangerous, handsome, and filled with wicked desires. His dark hair was tousled and wind-blown; his face concealed by a two day-old beard that made the blue in his eyes shine more fiercely. Dressed all in black, he was sleek, dark, and mysterious—his masculinity unparalleled. The awareness of his physical attributes caused a pool of desire to gather in some mysterious place deep within center.

"I am quite a fright, am I?" He asked.

"No, my lord." She paused, "You are everything a man aught to be."

He stopped walking and looked at her, then quickly claimed her lips, softly yet intensely, telling her he approved of her comment, telling her he approved of everything she was. She wondered if he could possible know the effect he had upon her.

"Oh my." She smiled.

"I cannot wait until our wedding." He smiled and winked, his dimple hidden behind his beard. They continued walking toward the house.

Before they reached the steps, the door flew open, and a small, frail form dashed out and fairly skipped down the stairs.

Eve stopped dead. "Mother?" "MOTHER!" She ran to her and held her; crying and laughing all at once.

"My darling, you are well. I was so worried." Her voice was strong, as it had been before her illness.

"Oh, Mother, *you* are quite well." Eve pulled back from her tight embrace to look at her once more. She was much thinner than before, and she somehow seemed delicate as if made of porcelain, but her cheeks were pink; and a bright fire burned in her light blue eyes.

"Mother, I am fine, in fact, I am wonderful..." then looking up into Beau's sapphire lights, "I am better than I have ever been before."

Finally, Laura turned to look at Beau. She took him in, raised her eyebrow, and smiled warmly at him. "You must be Lord Beaumont."

"My Lady," he bowed, "Please call me Beau."

"I understand I have you to thank for helping me to get well..." Her eyes filled with tears, "I might never have seen my Evelyn again had it not been for your Mr. Rockwell."

He stepped forward and took the small woman in his arms. "It was the least I could do. I am so glad you are feeling more yourself." Beau looked directly into Eve's eyes over the top of Laura's head and mouthed, "Next week."

****

It was difficult to discern whether Eve was more

excited over her wedding preparations or the recovery of her mother. The next day she floated throughout the manor, smiling, laughing, and shedding tears of joy. Lady Sands had risen later than usual, but she too joined in with the excitement and as if things could not improve more, two days later Katherine returned home from Scotland.

It was only the clouds in Beau's eyes that gave her pause. She knew he was eager to marry, yet, there was a grim sadness he sought to hide as she stared into those passion-filled sapphire orbs. She knew the origin of the sorrow he carried and wished desperately she could somehow free him from the chains that held him responsible where no blame should have been cast.

Her mind tumbled the matter over as she awaited her final fitting of the day.

Eve's chamber was full as she stood before a full-length glass in her little sitting room, as her mother's favorite modiste tucked and pinned her here and there. When at last Eve emerged, the pleasant chattering of the women waiting quickly stopped; silence filled the air.

No longer darkened, her hair, shone as fresh spun gold, streaks of palest blonde framing her face. Her honey complexion was flushed to a rosy pink that exactly matched the color of the silk in her gown.

And the gown was breathtaking. A barely pink silk seemed to float just above her skin, pink lace and tear drop crystals adorned the snug bodice which narrowly tapered to accentuate her waist. The skirt cascaded fully out in all directions, more crystals graced the hemline, and tiny lace rosettes were sewn in scattered lengths over its fullness. Matching pink gloves and slippers were equally lavish and fit Eve perfectly.

"Oh…" Laura gasped. "If your father could see

you, he would be so proud..." A tear slipped out. Laura quickly wiped at it and smiled brightly, "Evelyn you will surely be the most beautiful bride England has ever known."

"I couldn't agree more." Katherine added, tears in her eyes also. She held Glennora who also seemed fascinated with the gown.

Lady Sands gestured as if to say something but only seemed able to sob. She patted her stomach as if it pained her. "I don't know what has come over me...I am so emotional of late...seeing you so eager to wed reminds me of my own dear husband. Lately, I find myself missing him so."

Eve walked over to her and handed her a handkerchief. "Lady Sands, we understand." She patted her arm. "I am so thankful to count you among my dearest friends. No excuses are needed, you may cry whenever you like."

The others present mumbled their agreement.

"Well," began Katherine, standing, "Only four more days until the event. All preparations are well under way and now we can see the gown fits gloriously." She smiled at Eve."

"And Lord Beaumont is ready?" Laura asked, fully knowing the answer.

Eve smiled, secret memories carrying her away for a moment. She knew for certain Beau was beyond ready. She demurely answered, 'I believe so."

Katherine and Lady Sands laughed heartily at that. "He was ready to wed her after the first time he saw her." Katherine added, in a lower tone, "He sought Donald out the very next day practically holding his feet to the fire for information."

Eve closed her eyes in joyfulness. He loved her, he wanted her, he had waited for her, and now he was marrying her. All of her dreams had come true.

****

Beau and Donald brought their glasses together

with a cheerful clink. Bright sunshine illuminated the men as they sat relaxed, at last, in the comfortable library.

"Congratulations, old boy."

Beau grinned and sipped his brandy. It was awfully early for the libation, but they did have much to celebrate.

"Four more days until you take her off my hands..." Donald raised his glass again.

Four more days until she is mine. Beau closed his eyes and swallowed, letting the warm liquid glide down his throat. He reveled in hopes for the future until the image of pale grey eyes assaulted him again. He looked at Donald, draining the remaining brandy quickly.

"What is it?" Beau shook his head slowly, "A bit of unpleasantness from the past taunts me in my happiness."

"Is there anything I can do to help the past remain where it belongs?" Donald stood.

"I can handle all that needs done. I am going to Hartford to see my father."

Beau nodded to Donald, offering up a congenial smile and quickly left the manor.

****

Able to ignore her concern for Beau no more, Eve sought the familiar comfort of her mother. How wonderful to know she could once again go to her and share her troubles. When she was a child, her mother always had a soft answer or a bit of unconventional wisdom to solve the problem of the day. Eve wished today could be like that again.

She entered her chamber and was relieved to see it empty save for the one she was looking for. "Hello mother," she began cheerfully.

"What troubles you, dear?" Laura looked up from her chair, her embroidery hoop laid to the side.

Eve smiled in response, "You could always tell

when I had a problem, I guess things have not changed overly much."

"What could plague you at this time? Gregory is locked up and can no longer hurt you. You are about to marry a very handsome man who loves you, and we are together again as it should be."

"Yes, all that is true...but Beau is struggling with the guilt from an unfortunate episode with, of all people, Gregory's sister, Felicity. I realize Felicity died before you married Martin, but did he ever speak of what happened?"

Laura turned to face Eve more fully. She listened with rapt attention as Eve told the tale of the night Felicity tried to seduce Beau. She told how Felicity had lured Beau into Lady Sutherby's sitting room, how she undressed and was promptly caught by Gregory. She then told how Felicity hung herself in her great despair due to Beau's innocent rejection.

Laura's eyes lit with unrestrained emotion. "My darling, Gregory has certainly done well in seeking to harm your Lord Beaumont. Martin shared with me the events leading up to Felicity's untimely demise and rest assured they had nothing to do with Lord Beaumont."

Laura quickly relayed all Gregory's father had told her. Eve could barely believe the story her mother told, knowing obscure facts and details that would finally free Beau from the guilt he'd carried for years. Laura even remembered Dr. Ford's involvement. He would be able to confirm everything.

Before the sound of Laura's voice had finished reverberating in the cozy chamber, Eve was on her feet. "I must tell Beau the truth. He will finally be free!"

"Go my darling...Godspeed." Laura smiled to herself.

Eve dashed from the chamber and sought out

her beloved. Carefully she knocked on his chamber door. James answered and told her Beau had dressed for an outing but did not know where he had gone.

Eve sought Donald in the library. She rapped quickly and pushed open the heavy door. "Donald?"

He sat at his desk, papers strewn here and there, an absent expression on his face. "Good morning, Eve."

"Good morning." Eve did not want to waste time on formalities, "Do you know where I can find Beau?"

"He left about an hour ago. He was heading to Hartford to visit his father." Donald carefully set his pen down and rose, "Why do you seem so eager?"

"I must speak with him, it is a pressing matter." Eve wasn't certain how much she should divulge to Donald. She did not want to betray Beau's trust.

"He said he would return for dinner, can it wait until then?"

"No it cannot." Eve looked out of the window towards the stables, "I will have to ride to Hartford at once."

Donald crossed the room and stood before her, "*You will* take an escort. I will not have a repeat of the other night."

Eve rolled her eyes. "John will accompany me."

Donald began to shake his head, "Take Victor and be careful."

****

Beau left Beckinbrook directly after his toast with Donald in the library. He needed to pick up the special license and then there was the matter of revealing to his father that he now knew the whereabouts of a certain Evelyn Purittson.

When Beau entered Hartford Estate, his mood heightened considerably. Soon he would be bringing his bride here to live, to love, to begin her own family. Once more, there would be balls, dinner parties, and all manner of social engagements over which he and his lovely bride would preside.

He couldn't help whistling a happy tune as he entered his father's study. He found him going over household accounts with their dear, old butler, Carlton.

His father stood at once and embraced him, "Here he is, Carlton, eager for the altar." He smiled widely. "Can't wait for those grandchildren to start arriving…"

Beau laughed. "First let's make it to the church, shall we?"

"Congratulations, my lord." Carlton bowed deeply; familiar lines etched his happy face.

"Give us a moment, please." His father motioned for Carlton to depart and quickly he was gone."

"Have you the special license, Father?"

His father moved behind his desk, opened the top drawer, and removed a single piece of paper. "Here you are, my son."

For a flicker of an instant, guilt gripped his heart, the familiar vision of sad, grey eyes pleading for his love.

He shook his head as if to rid the thoughts. Enough. Gregory was in prison—he could make no trouble. It wasn't his fault Felicity jumped to such outrageous conclusions. He had never led her to believe he was interested in anything more than friendship.

Beau folded the license and carefully tucked it inside his jacket. He patted it twice for good measure.

"Another letter arrived just moments ago." His father looked beneath the stacks of papers on his desk and found it.

Beau recognized the handwriting at once. He crossed the room, sat down before the south window and opened the seal.

"*Come to see me at once, or you will both be sorry. I'm not finished with you yet.*"

GS

He actually signed it this time. Beau exhaled and looked up at his father's expectant countenance.

"What is it, my son?"

"There is something I must take care of." Beau stood to his feet.

"Let me assist you."

"Thank you, but no. This has been long in coming, and it is something I must attend to at once, before I can wed Eve."

Chapter Twenty-Six

Beau tied his horse at the post in front of the magistrate's office. When he first rode into the small town, he shuddered at what might have happened to Eve had he not been there. His head throbbed with anger, while his stomach twisted from worries of what Gregory's new plan might include.

His patience was at an all time low, and he hoped he would have enough self-control to allow Gregory to retain his pitiful life. The pounding in his head spread throughout his body at the thought of that slimy creature Gregory had hired to kidnap Eve. His gentle rose, subjected to such horror.

Pulling open the door, he was greeted by the hulking grey haired magistrate. "Good day, my lord."

The room was small and neat. Worn oak floors were swept clean, a well polished mahogany desk and two chairs adorned the office. On one wall hung a painting of a lush countryside, below it a plaque honoring the man behind the desk.

"Good day..." Beau found his name on the plaque near his desk, "Mr. Robertson."

Mr. Robertson nodded his head in a show of respect. "How may I be of service, my lord?" He motioned to a chair before his worn desk.

Beau sat down. "I'm here to visit one of the prisoners. Lord Searsly."

Mr. Robertson shifted some papers on his desk. He looked quizzically at Beau from beneath his bushy eyebrows. "May I ask why?"

241

Because he is trying to ruin my future and I've had enough. "I have some business to finish with him before he is taken to Newgate."

"I'll not open the cell. You can speak to him between the bars."

"That will do." Beau wondered if he could reach him through those bars.

Mr. Robertson rose, took a lantern, and motioned for Beau to follow. He led him down a single flight of stairs and then through a narrow corridor.

The prison was cool and quiet. The only sounds were those of their boots on the hard earth. At last, they came to several cells. Beau looked into each one they passed, all were empty. Finally, he saw Gregory.

Mr. Robertson handed Beau the lamp and turned to go back up. "Ten minutes only, my lord."

Beau nodded and watched as Mr. Robertson returned the way they had come.

He set the lantern down, rose to his full height, and approached the cell.

Gregory's face was streaked with dried blood, his clothes ripped and dirty. In the midst of his pathetic surroundings, he still managed a haughty air. "I knew you'd come...you owe me."

"I came because you actually had the courage to sign your letter. I was beginning to think it all a prank from some lad in napkins. But when I saw the effeminate handwriting, I knew they all had to be from you."

The sound of a chuckle could be heard from the next cell, and as Beau peered into the darkness, he saw the creature who had taken Eve from her horse, an evil grin on his skeletal face.

Gregory turned back toward the filth-covered man. "Keep quiet or I'll break your other leg."

The other prisoner laughed harder—a sound of

sheer evil. Beau felt something prickle the hairs at the back of his neck. Shaking off the feeling, he looked back at Gregory.

"I should kill you right now for what you tried to do to her."

"I'll help ye, gov'ner." The other prisoner offered.

Ignoring the prisoner, Gregory ground out to Beau, "You killed my sister and before I hang, everyone will know it. I will ruin your beloved's good name and reveal to the ton, the kind of *gentleman* you really are." As if to punctuate his tirade, he spit on the floor.

The knot in Beau's belly twisted. He did not want Eve to suffer for his previous actions. He thought carefully of his retort, but before he could speak again, Gregory cut into his thoughts.

"That is unless...."

Beau would not take his bait. He picked up the lantern. "I'm leaving. Soon England will be free from your presence, and Eve and I will go on with our lives. No one will care about your crazy ranting. I certainly don't."

"Than why did you come?" Gregory paused, "Could it be you are worried? The great Lord Winston Beaumont shaking in his Hessians? And, *my lord*, you have good cause. You see, there are other gentlemen, some might call them acquaintances, some may call them friends, who would be happy to avenge me after my death by telling the story of your mistreatment to my sister. Yes, you see, there are many men who have lost money and property due to your profits who would not mind seeing such a high one fall." Gregory smiled now. "They only need one word from me and it will begin."

Beau watched Gregory gloat over his imagined victory. He realized he was grasping at anything. He decided at that moment, he would not give him anymore of his time. Whatever consequences came, he would face them and would do so honestly. The hatred in his heart only moments ago turned to pity for the man who had only days left to live.

The other prisoner began to laugh again. "Yer a fool. Ye tried to git me to do yer bidding without payin me proper and now ye try to con this here nobleman. Yer a pitiful fool." He then spoke to Beau, "As I'll be meetin' me maker soon, I'd ask yer furgiveness gov'ner. I wish I'd done differently."

Beau hid his surprise and nodded his head.

Gregory nearly leaped to the bars that separated the cells and kicked the man in his good leg. He crumpled to the ground at once, shrieking in pain.

Beau walked back the way he had come. "May the Lord have mercy on your souls." He said it to both men, but as he climbed the stairs to the magistrate's office, he guessed Gregory would need it more so than the other prisoner.

"My lord?" The magistrate rose and took the lantern. "I heard a cry..."

"Lord Searsly attacked the other prisoner."

"I'd better go have a look." Raising the lantern and heading back down the stairs he called to Beau, "Good day."

Beau stepped out into the mid-summer afternoon and stood for a moment letting the sun's warmth wash over his body. It was done—truly finished. He would always carry the guilt for the death of Miss Felicity, but he would move on and face whatever demons might come.

He mounted his horse and looked down the small street towards *Westings Pub*. After taking a last look, he turned his horse to head back home. Back to his future, back to the life he'd only half lived until now. A peace fell over him and he breathed a sigh of relief.

"MY LORD, MY LORD!" The magistrate came

running out into the street. Beau turned back. Mr. Robertson's face was stricken.

"What is it?" Beau's heart began to pound harder.

With deep panting breaths and flushed face, he motioned Beau to come back inside his office. Beau immediately tied his horse, followed the man, and stepped inside.

"Mr. Robertson, what is wrong?" Beau felt something sick uncurl in his stomach.

Mr. Robertson sat at his desk and took a swig of something in a metal flask. "I went down to check on the one called Sorrows and found Lord Searsly quite dead."

"What?" Beau shot to his feet. "I left him quite alive, I assure you."

Mr. Robertson nodded his head. "I know, I know. He told me you did. He confessed to strangling him through the bars."

"The other prisoner? The one called Sorrows?"

"Yes. He confessed." The magistrate took another swig. "He wanted me to tell you. He wanted me to tell you Lord Searsly was dead and would not be able to summon his acquaintances."

Beau cradled his hands in his head. At last, he raised his gaze to meet Mr. Robertson's. "I'm sorry."

Mr. Robertson seemed to be recovering from the shock. "It's all just as well. He was to hang next week."

Beau stood up. "I must go now."

"Good day, my lord."

Beau inhaled and then exhaled. Dare he hope? "Good day."

Chapter Twenty-Seven

Eve and John rode with great excitement to Hartford. Eve could hardly wait to reveal the truth to Beau; finally, he would be free from the guilt that had so long kept him a prisoner.

"It's just beyond the curve." He motioned to Eve.

As they rounded the wooded bend, she saw the great manor fill the horizon. The classic home, formal, well tended, and very regal caused her heart to leap for a moment. Soon she would live here with Beau. She would be mistress of this graceful home, and would no doubt find many years of happiness behind the stately walls.

They slowed their pace and rounded to the stables, leaving their horses.

Walking seemed a snail's pace after their exuberant ride, and Eve felt as if her feet were dragging with each step. She smiled at John, "Come, let's hurry. Lord Beaumont will be eager to hear my news."

They finally arrived at the front door, and it was opened immediately by a friendly looking butler.

"Good day." He greeted them. "Do come in." He smiled pleasantly.

"We are here to see Lord Beau Beaumont." Eve began.

"Which lord do you seek, miss?"

"Lord Winston." Just saying his name caused her skin to tingle.

"I am sorry, miss. He is not here at the

moment."

"We have a matter of some urgency to discuss with him, may we wait for him?"

"Of course. Please follow me..." he led them into a small drawing room decorated in shades of blue. "I shall ring for tea." The butler disappeared while Eve and John looked around the room, admiring the well-appointed furniture, luxurious rug, and family portraits scattered throughout.

Minutes later the butler returned. "Your tea." He set the service down upon a cherry table and turned to leave.

"Excuse me, sir..." Eve began, "When do you expect Lord Beaumont to return?"

"I am not certain, Miss. He has gone on an errand."

Could he have returned to Beckinbrook? Surely, they would have passed each other.

"My dear sir, do you have any clue as to where he may have gone. The matter we must speak with him about is of utmost importance."

The butler thought for a moment. "May I ask your name, miss?"

"I am Evelyn Purittson, Lord Beaumont's betrothed."

The old butlers face split into a smile. "My lady..." he bowed. "Congratulations. We will be honored to have you as mistress of Hartford. I am Carlton, the head butler...I will see to your every comfort."

"You are too good," she said. "My only need is to find Lord Beaumont." Her voice was coming out much louder than she had planned, her words tumbling forth in exuberance.

The kindly butler looked down at Eve smiling. "My lady, the master received a letter just before he departed. Perhaps it holds some clue as to his whereabouts...although I do not know if he would object to us reading his correspondence…" His words trailed off.

"Is the letter here?"

"Actually it is. As the young master was leaving, it fell from his pocket. I picked it up and returned it to his desk. I am certain it is still there."

Eve smiled at John, then back at the butler. No servant would ever look at their master's correspondence…but the lady of the house might. "Carlton, I believe your master will not mind if I were to see the letter. Will you bring it at once?" Eve tried her most authoritative tone.

Carlton paused. And then, he made his decision. "Of course, my lady."

A scant time later, Carlton re-entered the room. The letter upon a silver tray. "My lady." He bowed and left.

Eve carefully opened the letter,

"Come to see me at once, or you will both be sorry. I'm not finished with you yet."

GS

"He's gone to Stockton…to put himself at Gregory's mercy…quick, we must depart at once." She began to pull John toward the door.

"Wait…we are not going anywhere. My lord made me promise to bring you to Hartford and return after our visit. We are not disobeying his order."

"Donald has no authority over me anymore. I am betrothed to Lord Beaumont, and he would want me to come at once."

"No he wouldn't." A deep voice standing just outside the door called. As Eve looked up, she saw from where the voice had come. The quiet confidence, the raw masculinity, the wry smile. Her man had spoken.

"Beau!" She ran to him, and he embraced her. It was completely improper and utterly delicious.

"To what do I owe the honor of your visit?" He smiled wickedly, "Missing me, perhaps?"

She had forgotten how his presence filled a room, negating all the non-essentials until it was as if only he and see were in the room. *she*

Eve looked at John who quickly excused himself. "I must check on the horses."

"I have missed you...so very much." She noticed the burning look in his eyes and slid her arms around his neck. He sighed.

"If you don't behave, I'll have you compromised before John gets to the stables."

Eve remembered her mission. "Where have you been, my love?" As she waited for his answer, she saw the letter on the floor. The letter that had caused her blood to run cold.

"I had an errand to run, tis all." He replied.

She withdrew from him and began to tap her foot. Tap. Tap. Tap.

Beau shook his head. "What is it darling? Why are you angry with me?"

Tap. Tap. Tap.

"Eve?"

"You went to see him, didn't you?" She looked into his eyes searching for sincerity."

"How did you know?" His face bore surprise.

Eve stopped tapping and picked up the letter. "Carlton was quite willing to help me find you; I believe he has an affinity for me."

Beau laughed. "You believe, do you?"

Tap. Tap. Tap.

Beau laughed again. "You are in quite a state."

"Be serious for a moment. Is this not madness to visit the man who has done such evil just because he summoned you? What did he want? Money? A chance to add to your guilt? Why did you go? Why?"

He took her in his arms—she tried to wiggle free, but he held her close and whispered in her ear,

"I love you, darling." She was still then. "Come, let's sit, and I will tell you a tale you may not believe."

They sat on the small sofa and Beau revealed the letters, the visit with Gregory, and Sorrows' act of guilt.

"You see my love, it is finally over. There will be no scandal. We shall wed and be happy until we are old and wrinkled. I have not been this happy since I saw a fair maiden bathing in Donald's fountain.

You saw my body...unclothed? I thought you just saw me after I dressed."

"Well I did both. And although I turned away in respect, I wasn't exactly quick about it." He smiled like an unrepentant rake, that dimple winking at her, "I fell in love with you that night. Never had my weary eyes beheld a more fetching vision, and it was then you cast your magical spell over my heart.

"When I went for a walk that night and came upon you bathing, you quite took my breath away. You were everything I had been looking for in a woman. I went to Donald the next morning, but he hid your identity from me...I guess he was trying to keep you safe in his own way..." He poured a cup of tea and sipped it.

He kissed her gently. Her arms slid around his neck and pulled him closer, he deepened the kiss sending sensual tingling throughout her body. She melted into his arms, the fears, the anger, and sorrow all turned into a quenchless passion. Tears trickled down her cheeks, the room grew warmer, all sound but that of his gentle breathing faded away. Oh, how she loved him.

It was as if the world had fallen away leaving only them to taste the first fruits of love. Their kiss continued pulling each of them into a glorious haze from which neither cared to emerge.

"Ahem...ahem..."

Eve looked up at a very handsome older version

of Beau. She immediately sat up primly.

Beau turned from her and stared up at his father. Then smiling like a cat with a sparrow in his mouth, he said, "Father, allow me to introduce you to my betrothed, Miss Evelyn Purittson."

Chapter Twenty-Eight

"My dear...welcome to our family." Beau's father pulled her into his arms and offered a fatherly embrace.

"My Lord." She curtsied when he released her.

"No more of that, daughter. Come let us sit and talk awhile...I would like to become more acquainted with the mother of my future grandchildren." He smiled warmly, and Eve saw again an older version of her beloved.

The elder Lord Beaumont rang for champagne.

Eve recounted all that had happened in her family over these several years since her father's death.

Finally, Beau spoke up, "I should be escorting Miss Purittson back to Beckinbrook. They are expecting us for dinner."

"First, let us toast this most happy occasion." Beau's father poured three glasses of champagne, handed them out, and then raised his glass high, "To my son, a man worthy of honor and my undying pride, and to his betrothed, Evelyn, a woman whose beauty and intelligence are matchless, whose kindness and love will be the comfort to my son and their many, many, children. Salute." They all laughed brightly, each realizing the culmination of their dreams.

After their toast, Beau seemed eager to return to Beckinbrook. Eve was eager to tell him the truth he so desperately needed to hear; yet as his father walked them out to the stables, she knew the time was not yet.

John had already returned, leaving Beau and Eve to ride alone. When at last they departed, Eve could hardly wait to tell him her news.

"My beautiful lord..." she began. "I must share with you some urgent news. Let us stop a moment before we ride any further."

"Beautiful Lord, eh? I quite like the sound of that." They had just left Hartford grounds but the Beaumont's still owned several acres. To their left stood a small cabin sometimes used for hunting outings. "Let us stop there," he pointed.

They rode up and dismounted. Beau tied the horses to a nearby tree and checked the tiny cabin. It was empty and they went inside.

Before she could speak, he had surrounded her with his strong arms, pulling her toward him, kissing her neck, and sending familiar longings deep into her soul. Her head thrown back, she moaned with pleasure and felt his knowing fingers massage her low on her back.

"Eve...Eve...we should never have stopped, I fear for your virtue like never before."

She smiled and began to extricate herself from his passionate embrace. Her body trembled in protest, but she knew she must speak with him at once.

"Come, my love, I truly have something of great importance to share with you." She motioned to an old sofa covered with a well-worn yellow and green quilt.

"Although I am intrigued, I much prefer you breathless and in my arms." He followed her to the sofa and sat down next to her.

She looked up into his eyes and found him watching her with some amusement. Unsure as to how to begin, she took his large hand in hers. At once sensations began to unfurl within her. Taking hold of herself, she focused on the task at hand. She must think clearly, this would not be easy for him to hear.

"Beau, as you well know, the Rockwells have helped my mother recover quite thoroughly..." She pushed back a tendril that had escaped her coiffure. "My mother's memory is very clear after only several doses of the herbal mixture they have given her."

Beau responded, "My darling, I know this has been your most fervent wish, and I am so thankful to see it come to pass."

"Yes, well, there is quite a bit more to it," she exhaled, "in fact, it greatly concerns you."

"Tell me then, my love."

"I asked my mother if she was aware of the terrible tragedy of Felicity's death." The amusement in Beau's eyes went flat. He raised his brows and waited, "as my mother had been courted by Gregory's father, Lord Martin Searsly, for some time before they wed, I wondered if he had told her anything of Felicity." Beau sat still, expressionless. Eve rushed on, "I had only first heard of Felicity from you. Gregory and his father never spoke of her to me."

"However, Martin had indeed spoken of her to my mother. He was a kind gentleman, different in every way from his son." Eve paused—Beau hadn't moved an inch. "Beau, Felicity did not die by hanging. She died in childbirth."

Beau suddenly shot to his feet. He walked quickly across the old wooden beams that comprised the floor in the room, pausing, then returning back to the sofa.

He raked a hand roughly through his dark hair, "But, I never even touched her. I told you, I rejected her advances and then Gregory showed up, and I took my leave."

"I know. Martin told my mother that Felicity was determined to find a wealthy and titled gentleman to wed. When her attentions failed with you, she sought out the favors of a Lord Farnsworth. Unfortunately he was not as pure in heart as you are, and he quickly took of that which she offered."

Beau sat as in amazement as she continued on. "After she discovered she was with child, they were to marry, but Lord Farnsworth was called to France to help settle a family matter. He never returned." She now picked up his hand and began to smooth her fingers over his tanned skin. "When returning to England, his ship capsized and he was lost."

"Felicity was indeed in a state, for her condition was no longer concealable. She stayed a prisoner in her chamber, away from society, by her own choosing until her time came." Eve squeezed his hand; his face was void of all emotion. "When Martin finally called for a doctor, it was too late. The babe was too large, both the son and the mother perished in childbirth." Eve's voice was softer now, "Martin and Gregory kept Felicity's secret to avoid a scandalous tale marring her passing."

Beau sat there—stunned. Finally he spoke, "Then why would Gregory come to my home and accuse me of such a thing?"

"My mother believes he was going to blackmail you. He had been wracking up gambling debts for years and needed a sure way to pay his markers should they be called in."

"For so long, I've been plagued by her death, the nightmares, the letters..."

"I'm sorry, my love. It is over now."

He smiled, although, a touch of sadness remained and then she saw it fade away. "It is all over. Only a future filled with love lies ahead now."

"You, my darling, are like an angel sent from God." He moved toward her.

"And you are the fulfillment of all my dreams, Beautiful Lord."

The emotion of their naked hearts hung heavy in the air, all had been resolved, there was nothing left to keep them apart. Fully they could give themselves to each other.

"You trusted me, although I could share so little, you helped me, and you saved my mother from certain death. When I watch you enter a room, I find myself in awe of your presence, your beauty and your strength."

"Eve, I have been waiting for you for so long, saving myself for my precious wife. Having you is the answer to all of my prayers, prayers spoken and only wished for."

He sat looking deeply into her eyes. His eyes were alive with fire, their sapphire depths glowing deep with undisguised passion.

"Kiss me."

"Eve, I cannot. I cannot touch you again until our wedding. The very last of my resolve has vanished. I fear if I touch you, I will lose all control. We are so close, I wish to begin our lives together in purity with God's blessing.

She sighed, but secretly relished his words. Only four more days, and they would be together forever.

****

Four days later...

Rich jewel tones shone through the stained glass windows, making the sedate chapel feel alive and warm. The morning was cool, but with every passing moment, the temperature in the church raised another notch. He stood at the altar dressed in a dark morning suit waiting for his life to begin. The door opened just then and she was there.

She glowed like an oil painting displayed in perfect light. Hues of rose and honey caressed her face; her skin radiant, like silk before a candle. She floated towards him, her aqua eyes shining.

She carried a bouquet overflowing with pale pink roses, scenting the aisle gently. She moved beside him, and his heart melted. No longer did he own even a tiny part, for it was all hers now. She was the sweetest gift and in giving all to her, he found his greatest joy.

He heard music playing in his mind. The scent of vanilla awoke the rest of his senses. Although she stood a short distance away, he felt her touch somehow.

Soon he slipped a large oval sapphire encircled with diamonds on her slender finger. She looked into his eyes with an intensity that warned him of the power of her love.

Beau's uncle, the vicar, asked questions and made pronouncements. At last, the directive came, "You may kiss your bride."

He meant only to brush gently against her lips, but there was no stopping now that she was his. His eager tongue found hers and he pulled her closer. She gave no resistance, instead struggled to move closer into the warmth of his embrace. Moments of ecstasy quickly passed, and Beau slowly backed away. "I love you." He said.

The Wedding Breakfast was lavish, overflowing with many exotic fruits, sweet confections, and gourmet delicacies. The fragrance alone set the tone for sensory perfection. Katherine had decorated the manor with pink and white lace garlands, pulled together with small clusters of fresh flowers. White candles in gleaming silver candlesticks were grouped together on every flat surface with lush bouquets in crystal vases. Footman held champagne and fruited wine on their polished trays, ladies and gentlemen moved throughout the rooms, an air of anticipation swirling everywhere.

The Bride and Groom sat close together in the

dining room oblivious of all save each other. Eve leaned closer to her husband, her fork filled with a cream laden morsel, "Open your mouth, darling."

He willingly complied as she slipped the fork between his open lips. He closed his eyes in delight, then grabbed her and kissed her hotly, sharing the sweetness with her.

Friends and relations offered their congratulations, and although charming and polite, the young couple could barely wait for the last guest to depart.

Eve and Beau spent much of the afternoon looking into each other's eyes, waiting for their wedding night.

"May I have a word with my new daughter and son?"

Beau and Eve followed Beau's father into the library where he immediately closed the door. He looked at Eve for a moment and then motioned to the settee. "Please, make yourself comfortable." They sat together, while he moved before them taking a sealed envelope from his formal coat pocket.

"Eve, before I had the great delight of knowing you, I knew your father." He handed her the envelope. "He hired me to be his attorney, to draw up a special will in case he passed before you married."

Eve turned the envelope over in her hand. It bore her name in her father's unique hand. A tear trickled down her face.

"Knowing the law as he did and desiring your mother to re-marry if he should pass, he wanted to see to your welfare so you would not be forced into a marriage for convenience or be forced to seek employment." He took another envelope from his pocket and held it as he continued. "He left some funds to me, to invest for you; however you saw fit and instructed me to give you the profits or the entire amount, should you ever desire to have it."

Now he moved closer and picked up her hand. "But by the time I learned of your father's passing, your mother was already re-married and widowed again. She was ill and you were gone."

Eve was stunned. She could not speak, only waited for him to continue.

"I tried to find you; even hired a bow street runner to search for you, but you cleverly evaded my best efforts. It wasn't until four days ago I learned of your whereabouts, when my son introduced us at Hartford."

"This letter you hold is from your father. I thought it might make a fitting wedding gift." He paused and handed her the other envelope, "This is a statement of your investments. Although I could not find you, I invested your money as I thought best and this is now your profit."

She looked at Beau through tear-filled eyes. "Go ahead, read it." He smiled warmly and she tore open the yellowed envelope.

Dearest Evelyn,

You have been a delight and joy to me since your first cry entered our home. I have enjoyed every moment spent watching you play, learn, and grow into a gracious and wise young lady.

I have no doubt your decisions will bring you happiness, but in the event of my early passing, I want to be certain to provide for you, regardless of circumstances. Lord Beaumont is holding a portion of my fortune to invest as you see fit. He is trustworthy and wise, and will serve you well should you need his assistance. My pride in your intelligence is well placed, and I have no concern for the soundness of your investment decisions.

Instead, let me write again of the love I carry in my heart for you, my pride in you, precious daughter, and my desire to see you well cared for. Let your heart guide you in marriage, remember your mother and I together were able to conquer all. I wish you that, my dear, and I wish you many children, who like you, will bring sweet happiness to their parents.

I love you, my daughter and will see you again in heaven someday.

Yours Always,

Father

Eve clasped the letter to her bosom and laughed, tears streaming down her cheeks. Beau wiped them away with his handkerchief, then drew her into his arms and held her there.

When she finally regained composure, she opened the other envelope and gasped in surprise. The money her father had left her was considerable indeed, and her new father-in-law had more than tripled it in five years time.

She thrust the statement into Beau's hands and exclaimed, "We are wealthy beyond belief."

He looked at the statement then into her eyes and smiled warmly at her, "Indeed we are, indeed we are."

Chapter Twenty-Nine

Just before the dinner hour, the last guest retired. Beau escorted Eve into one of his carriages, her bag already sent ahead to Hartford. His father and Paul decided to accept Donald and Katherine's invitation to stay at Beckinbrook to give the young couple some privacy.

Beau forced himself to patiently bid their friends and family members, old and new, good-bye. He helped Eve into the well-appointed carriage and sat as close to her as possible. It was almost painful for him to look at her, her profile a rendering of perfection.

He wasted no time in gathering her into his embrace. With a quick maneuver, he pulled her onto his lap, and as she turned to gasp in surprise, he captured her open lips and began his slow and delightfully torturous seduction.

His kiss grew more passionate, deepening, his lips pushing harder on hers. She matched his intensity with a fierce desire of her own, causing him to pull her closer and groaned in anticipation. The carriage moved along, rhythmically bumping and jostling them together—the pulsing rhythm combined with the frantic beating of their hearts was a toxic passionate combination. Soaring together, they were lost in sweet abandon.

He could wait no longer. His mouth found her neck and kissed her boldly, gently nipping and traveling lower moment by moment. Finally, he lowered her gown, releasing her full breasts to his hungry eyes. Beau stilled his moments—her breasts were even more alluring than he remembered. He allowed his eyes to devour the sensual sight and watched as her pink nipples hardened in response to his lustful gaze.

"You are so beautiful," he murmured, then lowered his lips to one and then the other as he began to taste her satiny skin. He reveled in his feast and held her tightly.

Eve was lost, floating through a place of ecstasy and desire. The heat he bestowed spread like fire over her skin. Somewhere deep within, she burst in ecstasy—for it was almost too much to bear. Gently, his hot mouth kissed and licked her breasts leaving her completely and utterly at his mercy. She enjoyed the love he so generously bathed her in, but she needed to give back her passion in return. Sitting up, she found herself struggling for a breath. At first hesitant, then eagerly she began to kiss his neck as he had done hers.

He raised his head, and she loosened his cravat, then finding a shirt button, she opened it. She opened the next one, and the next, and finally pulled his shirt apart. She turned fully into his arms and pressed her bare breasts against the fur of his broad chest and kissed him. Together they gasped for air, clinging wildly to one another.

"Darling," he whispered in her ear, "We are almost there."

Her swollen lips parted a denial, and her eyes opened to see the truth of the matter—Hartford was just ahead. She sighed in regret, then in anticipation of what was to come.

He pulled up her gown and straightened it as best he could. He then buttoned and tucked in his shirt, while Eve helped him straighten his cravat. Finally, they were almost as they were before, and yet completely changed by their encounter. The carriage came to a slow stop, and the side door opened.

"Welcome to Hartford, Madam." A white-gloved hand reached up to help her down.

Eve turned to look up at Beau. "Home."

The servants lined up to meet their new mistress. Beau painfully introduced her to each one for he was eager to take her to their chamber. But for each one, Eve bestowed a kind word and gracious smile. As they chatted with the cook, they arranged for dinner in their room.

Eve walked through Hartford much in awe. The home was spotless, well cared for, and elegant in its furnishings and décor. As Beau showed her each room, he encouraged her to change whatever tickled her fancy. "This is now our home, and I would have you customize it to our tastes and needs."

"Are you certain your father and Paul won't object? "

"No, my love. Since I came into adulthood, my father has always declared that my wife would be the mistress of Hartford. You have carte blanc to do what you deem best."

"As you wish, my Lord."

At last, they climbed the stairs to their chamber. Beau opened the door revealing a luxurious suite filled with priceless antiques, fine silk bedding, and sumptuous carpets.

"Oh..." Eve gasped. The room's colors were shades of mauve, cream, and chocolate brown. A room fit for a King and his Queen.

A small sitting room to the right looked like a lovely place to chat with Beau and one day sit with her baby. Beyond the sitting room, a feminine dressing room was lavishly decorated in shades of pinks. Silks and velvets covered all the furniture, and the small dressing table held an ornate mirror with jars of various scents, lotions, and salts.

"Everything is perfect." She looked up at him. "Thank you."

"Katherine insisted on helping me, it was she who advised me on your likes and dislikes."

Beau kissed her lightly on the lips. "Come to bed, my love. I have been waiting to have you for an eternity." His words hung heavily in the air, her limbs suddenly weakened, for she would soon be his wife in every way.

"Give me a moment." She answered breathlessly and then entered her dressing room.

Beau left her and made his way to his dressing area on the opposite side of the room. He quickly undressed and donned a navy blue silk robe. He waited for her by the foot of the bed, and started when she appeared.

She stood in the entrance to their bedroom wearing a sheer, aqua gown. It was completely unadorned and utterly transparent. His eyes drank in her beauty—he could not take a step toward her, for she was beyond his wildest imaginings. Her hair down flowed freely about her shoulders and toward her waist. Her skin glowed like melting honey and begged to be touched.

"My lord?"

"Eve..." he couldn't speak—his arousing passions no longer could be denied. He walked slowly to her and took her into his arms, caressing her skin ever so lightly. She was so delicate, so fine; he would take great care in loving her.

She pulled away from their kiss and looked up at him, "I love you."

He kissed her again and then brushed the thin straps of her gown from her shoulders—it fell soundlessly to the floor, and she stepped out of it. She was left clothed only in lustrous, golden hair, surrounding her like a shimmering light. He wasted no time but picked her up and carried her to the bed. Gently laying her down, he loosened the sash to his robe and shrugged it off.

Eve took in his appearance with a gasp. He was unlike any statue she had ever beheld, this man of flesh and blood. His hair was thick and dark, contrasting with the brightness in his eyes. His face, so finely chiseled was masculine and strong. The white of his dazzling smile complimented the rich color of his skin, and his shoulders stretched wide revealing toned muscles and soft furring across his chest. His arms and legs were strong and well formed, and his manhood proclaimed him ready to love her. Every inch of his beautiful form was perfection, *and he was hers.*

Her gaze returned to his and told him of her need. He lowered himself beside her and began to trail kisses down the length of her body. She moaned in pleasure, and he slowly touched her trembling skin, watching her reactions and finding the places most sensual to her liking.

Eve sank into the silk covering, the coolness contrasting powerfully with the heat of her inflamed body and the fiery touch of Beau's hands.

His palms circled her breasts slowly, carefully, examining them with his lips. Eve felt lost in his caresses and gave her body freely to him. He moved his lips to her waiting ones and kissed her deeply. One hand, now, carefully stroking her most private part. She could barely breathe for the pleasure he caused, as he carefully slipped a finger inside her woman's folds.

Her body was on fire, slick with desire, and clenched his finger tightly. He continued kissing her and moved slowly to cover her with his own form. "I love you," he whispered huskily. He continued to touch her softly, slowly, then more firmly. She could no longer think, for feeling was now everything. She let herself go into his worthy hands, releasing all her inhibitions, her fears—for she was his, and he was hers. Soaring uncontrollably, she kissed him deeply, tasting his passionate nectar, gently nipping his lips, telling him without a word, of her desire. She felt herself giving way to the passion he so easily wrought from her body and gave into the new and welcome sensations flowing over her body as it trembled and responded of its own accord.

Pleasure surged through her, weakening her, strengthening her, filling her with a hunger, a need. Could any love be sweeter than that which he had given?

She opened her eyes to find his gaze boring into her soul. His need was raw, strong, and she wanted to please him, to share with him the wonder of love.

Hesitantly, she lowered her hand to the pulsing member between his legs. She touched him as he had touched her. He was hard, and strong, yet silky and tender. She touched him with awe and gentleness. Her hand slid along his manhood gently, slowly, then faster and with more firmness. Beau closed his eyes. He kissed her mouth, the intensity building. Finally, he pushed her hand away. "Let me make love to you."

Carefully, he lay upon her body. He moved between her legs.

"Just kiss me." She said. And he did. He kissed her softly at first, then more firmly with desperate abandon. All the while, she felt him at her opening and longed to welcome him inside her yearning body.

He began to move into her. Slowly at first, then he retreated. At last, her body's craving was answered. Again, he moved forward, a little further now and again pulled back. Her hips lifted from the bed and matched his rhythm, together they moved closer and closer to ecstasy. Eve moved her hands over his body, feeling the bunching of every muscle, the dampness of his impassioned skin, the strength of his desire...

Finally, he found her virtue, and pressed forward, making her his completely. She stopped for a moment feeling a tiny surge of pain and then continued climbing with him to the unknown heights of complete satiation. They moved as one, knowing the rightness of it all, the splendor, the beauty...he tasted her lips and drank in her love, she pulled him deeper inside of herself, telling him without hesitation ...*I'm yours*...

At last, they found their release—flying together, they held on to each other and reveled in their love, their passion, and their fulfillment.

Later, they lay entangled in each other's arms. "I love you Evelyn Beaumont. You are mistress over my heart."

Eve was so caught in the emotion of his love, she could barely reply. Tears fell freely from her eyes, rendering her naked before him.

Beau looked deeply at her, "What is it? Have I hurt you? Have I disappointed you in some way?"

Sniffling, she smiled, "No my lord, it's quite the opposite." All at once, she remembered the secret talk she shared with Lady Sands.

"I love you, Eve, my only love for now and forever. You are beyond worthy of my wait..."

Turning and looking straight into his eyes, she replied, "And I love you, my Beautiful Lord."

Chapter Thirty

Six months later...

Lady Penchotte, formerly Lady Sands, surprised them all with news of her new marriage and her delicate condition. Six months later, a well-rounded baby made her debut, and was called by her proud papa, the very handsome Lord Penchotte, Sofia.

Evelyn and Katherine were two of her first callers. Lady Penchotte glowed with happiness as she escorted the ladies into her sitting room.

"Lady Penchotte, she is exquisite!" Katherine exclaimed as she held the tiny bundle close to her chest and kissed the top of her head lightly.

Lady Penchotte smiled in response, her expression hinting of a mysterious happiness. "You must call me Rosalind. We have been through so very much together."

The ladies smiled and chatted easily together.

Eve sat beside Rosalind and patted her own rounded belly...only three more months and she too would discover the joy of motherhood.

"She is a blessing I thought I would never enjoy..." Rosalind began. "I am so thankful to have conceived a child at such an age." She smiled broadly.

A young maid came and set a tray of tea down. Lady Penchotte began to pour, while Katherine held closely to little Sofia.

Smiling and winking she lowered her voice to a

whisper, "Donald and I are expecting again!"

Eve and Rosalind hugged each other and then congratulated Katherine.

"How soon, dear?" she asked.

"Seven months, I believe."

"Oh Katherine…" Eve's eyes filled and overflowed. "Our children will grow up together."

Epilogue

Three years later…

"My darling, come with me." Beau stood before Eve, holding her light wrap in one hand and extending the other to help her arise.

"What time is it?" She asked groggily.

"It's quite early. But you must come now, it's urgent."

She tossed back the sheet and stood up, her body moist with the heat of the night. She slipped her wrap around her shoulders and lifted her damp hair from her neck.

"Where are you taking me, Beautiful Lord?"

"I have a surprise for you."

"Does this have something to do with your desk in the library? Last time we shared that surprise, my backside was quite sore for a week." She smiled wickedly.

"No." He shook his head and smiled. "Now be quiet or you'll wake the baby." They tiptoed passed the nursery where their two and a half year-old son, Daniel, slept, and their four-month-old daughter, Laura, rested peacefully.

Beau moved quickly through the manor, and Eve struggled to keep up. The heat of the night seemed to stick to her, and she longed for the coolness of autumn that would soon come.

He led her out the back door to the gardens. The velvety sky boasted her glittering stars brilliantly, and Eve heard an unfamiliar sound of water trickling.

She stopped and looked at Beau. "Do you hear that?"

He ignored her, tugging her deeper into the garden.

Finally, she noticed several lanterns up ahead. As she followed him, the flickering light revealed a large fountain. She looked up at him as he smiled broadly.

"You had a fountain installed?"

"I did."

"But why?" She smiled, for she knew the answer before he spoke it.

"Because several years ago, I came upon a vision of loveliness bathing in a fountain and since then, my life has been better than any dream come true."

She smiled and slowly opened her wrap. He moved toward her, but she stepped back.

Beau waited, enjoying just watching her... but then she let the wrap fall to the ground, turned and made her way to the fountain.

Images of that night long ago rekindled in his mind and for a moment, he savored them. But then the reality of *this* night overtook his thoughts. Eve had grown more beautiful with the passing of time and the role of motherhood. Tonight he would partake in her beauty, as he had ached to do in what seemed a lifetime before. He watched her slip into the water, bending her head back as her full breasts came into view...

His mouth went dry, he slipped off his robe, and moved to join her in the healing water.

A word from the author...

My name is Lisa Hill, I am a new author with The Wild Rose Press. I am a huge fan of Historical Romance, although every now and then you might find my nose behind a Susan Elizabeth Phillips or Janet Evanovich novel.

I live in a 101-year-old Victorian home in the Historical District of Elmira, NY, am married and have three brilliant children.

This first novel, *Loving Purity*, is a Regency Romance that is both sweet and sensual. I hope you have enjoyed the story of Eve and Beau's love. It was fun to write and I look forward to hearing from you!

~Lisa

Contact me at
www.lisa-hill.com
lisa@lisa-hill.com

Thank you for purchasing
this Wild Rose Press publication.
For other wonderful stories of romance,
please visit our on-line bookstore at
www.thewildrosepress.com

For questions or more information
contact us at
info@thewildrosepress.com

The Wild Rose Press
www.TheWildRosePress.com

Other Historical Roses to enjoy
from The Wild Rose Press

from *Vintage Rose (historical 1900s):*
DON'T CALL ME DARLIN' by Fleeta Cunningham: In Texas, 1957, Carole the librarian faces censorship. Will the County Judge who's dating her protect or accuse her?
SOURDOUGH RED by Pinkie Paranya: At the end of the Klondike gold rush, Jen and her younger brother search for her twin, lost and threatened in Alaskan wilderness.

from *Cactus Rose (historical Western):*
OUTLAW IN PETTICOATS by Paty Jager. Maeve had her heart crushed; it won't happen again. Zeke has wanted Maeve since he first set eyes on her...
SECRETS IN THE SHADOWS by Sheridon Smythe. Lovely widow Lacy had taken in two young children—and the rambunctious little angels wasted no time getting her into trouble with Shadow City's new sheriff...

from *American Rose (historical U.S.A.):*
EXPEDITION OF LOVE by Jo Barrett. An up-and-coming scientist in the world of paleontology collides heart first with an unconventional suffragette who has no desire to marry. Can they resolve their differences?
WHERE THE HEART IS by Sheridon Smythe. Orphan Natalie Polk steps into the shoes of the errant orphanage house mother. The new owner not only accepts her as capable of running the home but falls in love with her, with obstacles galore. How can they have a future?

from *English Tea Rose (non-American):*
HIGHLAND MOONLIGHT by Teresa Reasor. Seduced by the warrior to whom she is betrothed, Lady Mary flees to sanctuary. But she is forced to wed him, to save him from the executioner. Was her dream as elusive as Highland Moonlight?
THE RESURRECTION OF LADY SOMERSET by Nicola Beaumont. An age-old mystery, a risky assignment, a marriage devised to suppress a secret... Lark has been hidden most of her life. With the death of her mentor comes the command to marry the new Lord Somerset. Without this marriage, the estate falls to his wastrel brother. Can either suitor satisfy the lady?

Breinigsville, PA USA
03 February 2010
231888BV00003B/1/P